LEAPE

Leape Years

By

Tony Sullivan

JANUS PUBLISHING COMPANY
London, England

First published in Great Britain 2009
by Janus Publishing Company Ltd,
105-107 Gloucester Place,
London W1U 6BY

www.januspublishing.co.uk

British Library Cataloguing-in-Publication Data
A catalogue record for this book is available from the British Library

ISBN 978-1-85756-689-5

Cover Design: Edwin Page

Printed and bound in Great Britain

CHAPTER ONE

I was a latecomer, maybe shouldn't have been there at all, and they were all piled on top of me. 'Never forget that we are your elders,' Jessie said. 'Do as we say, or you'll get belted.' She was the youngest of the elders; above her came Frank, and then Maggie. But Frank was really above everyone, even that occasional visitor – my dad.

'Our Frank's the real boss in this family,' Jessie said.

'He's the blue-eyed boy,' Maggie agreed, with a small smile.

Even as a babe in arms I was aware of the look he gave me as he passed through the kitchen, passed through the bower of Mother's smiles on his way to Scouts or the cycling club – a look that mingled repugnance with scepticism. Later, he came to accept me forbearingly, but it did not prevent me from feeling like an intruder and that inevitably became my role in life: an intruder – a usurper. I made a decent living out of it eventually.

It was Mother I wanted, but I could never get close enough; the others were always in the way and she never saw me at my best, never discovered what a wondrous creature I really was. On the contrary, I was a continual disappointment. This was apparent as early as The Spuds – I remember it in capital letters. 'Go and fetch me five pound of potatoes and don't lose the change.' She would never have called them 'spuds', a term only used by common people. I took the American-leather shopping bag and left the house, through the backyard and along the back-entry, roaring down to the shops in my Supermarine Spitfire; got the spuds and banked on a turn for home, zooming past shops, pubs and churches, weaving through traffic, tramcars and bicycles, pausing to admire a carthorse from the railway goods yard pulling a great wagon, its hooves clashing against the stone setts of the roadway. Flying back along the entry I grew anxious lest Jordan should come after me, flatten me and naller the change. His nasty flapping wellingtons ('Doan you call me names! I'll fucken marmalise you, y'cunt!'), his thick rubber wellingtons thudding after me. Jordan the ogre, squatting in his back-entry lair, fondling a heap of testicles torn from the loins of small boys.

I reached home safely and handed Mother the change, which she counted (I had been known to keep back the odd halfpenny). But when she examined the spuds, she found two or three that were slimy bad. In a mountain of potatoes, she would be sure to find a couple that were bad; life had formed her that way. She made her tragic face, her complaint against fate: 'Oh, look at this!' A thin embittered woman with heavy dark eyebrows in a bony Irish face, her dark hair drawn back into a bun at the nape of the neck. 'Oh, this is too bad!'

She wasn't speaking to me but calling on some unseen presence to witness her plight. Our Blessed Lord, probably; He watched over us. But then she bent her black brows on me: 'Why did you not watch when he was serving you? I can't trust you to do anything right. By Heavens, if it had been Frank, he wouldn't have got away with it! Well ...' She fastened the handle of the bag into my hand. 'You'll just have to take them back. Tell the man he's got to change them.'

'Ahr, ey, Mam! Please, Mam!'

But whenever I wailed like that, she would incline her head, her face impassive. She rarely told me to shut up, she would just incline her head as though she had not heard clearly and was waiting for me to repeat the cowardly wail. If I did so, she might fetch me a stinging crack across the face.

'Off you pop. Don't be long. I don't want to see one bad potato when you bring them back, mind.'

I was numb with misery. All my life I've hated returning anything to a shop; I would rather throw it away and buy new. I dragged back along the entry almost wishing Jordan would fall on me and hammer me soft for calling him names; then I would be in hospital, too badly injured to complete the hateful task. I saw myself facing the shopkeeper, whimpering apologetically as though I was to blame, begging him to be so good as to replace the rotten spuds. He would look at me stonefaced, with the martyred expression of one pestered by a fool. Oh please, God, make him change the fucken spuds!

God gave me Frank for deliverance. He was coming home from work, striding along in his heroic boiler suit, whistling one of the jolly airs they sang around the scout campfire. I went to him, burbling my woes; he smiled and shook his head, looking down on the weakling brother he would have to support for the rest of his life: 'Come on, be a man. Stop whinging.'

I claimed Mother was afraid to take the spuds back herself. But Frank said, 'She's doing it for your own good. She wants to make a man of you, wants you to stand on your own two feet. You've got to face these little trials if you want to succeed in life.'

However, he was prepared to help me just this once. 'We'll go and see this cheating scoundrel together.'

He carried the spuds and I walked by his side as if beneath the shade of a great tree. When we reached the shop, he confronted the shopkeeper. How squat and squalid the man looked beside Frank's clean-limbed youth and uprightness! He swore I had not bought the spuds from him – 'You've got the wrong shop, son. I doan sell rotten spuds' – but Frank stood his ground, unafraid, demanding satisfaction. It came from knowing he was in the right. He possessed a calm strength, the invincible assurance of virtue. It came from knowing he was loved. And the shopkeeper, sighing self-pityingly, changed the spuds. Frank thanked him gravely, with a mature hint of irony. There were some apples being sold cheaply, they were bruised and going bad. 'Fades', we called them: 'Gorr'any fades, mister?' Frank bought one for a halfpenny and gave it to me. I bit into the corruption and spat it out, eating what was left.

Mother had just finished ironing his Scout uniform when we got home: his khaki shirt with its badges, and his neckerchief. She put down the iron and greeted him with a loving smile. I took the spuds into the back kitchen and counted them into the vegetable rack. One was mouldy – that wily scoundrel! – so I hid it at the back. In the kitchen, Mother laughed as Frank regaled her with an amusing account of my cowardice.

I sat at the kitchen table beneath the budgie in its cage, drawing aeroplanes with bombs falling out of the fuselage. They were bombing that place in Spain. General Franco is saving Spain from the Communists. What was on the wireless? Arthur Askey and Stinker Murdoch, Elsie and Doris Waters, The Western Brothers, Joe Loss and His Orchestra. It was cold and Mother sat at the fire with Maggie and

Jessie. Maggie was dark-haired, Jessie had her fair hair set in a Marcel wave. Dad was away at sea and Frank was with the Scouts doing some good deed somewhere. It was better that way; I have always preferred the company of women, no matter their cruelty. Maggie was reading one of the crime books she got from Boots Library, tuppence a book; she wouldn't use the public library, you never knew where the books had been, they might have been borrowed by people with scabby hands, nits in their hair.

Jessie asked Mother if there would be a war; Mother said Mr Chamberlain would keep us out of it.

She was quite old already, forty-four. For a working-class woman in those days, that was getting on. It would have made a difference had she been younger and softer. I used to dream of such a mother – one more loving, obviously; but if that was too much to ask, then at least educated and intelligent. I have envied those young men blessed with handsome, intelligent mothers, with whom they could talk about books they've read and people they've met, art and science and the curiosities of religion, history and psychology and the best ways of living. I could never discuss such things with my mother. We never had a discussion as such; communication was usually one-way and took the form of commands or instructions, or life-weary platitudes that I instinctively distrusted.

'You're never satisfied,' Maggie said. 'Stop picking your nose, it'll turn into a pig's foot.'

'You don't know when you're well off,' Jessie said. 'Take your elbows off the table.'

Alternatively, I wouldn't have minded some blowsy innocent whore of a mother – one of those tragicomic characters like Carol, forever falling down and laughing helplessly, picking themselves up with a broad smile that made you think they loved generously. I used to imagine how I would shepherd such a mother home from the pub, pitying the shameless drunk; how I would forgive her when she confessed to yet another slobbish love affair, and vowed to reform. I could care for her, that was the point, I could love her.

The others didn't have this problem. Mother had probably never raised her hand to Frank, never needed to; but she had hammered the girls in her time.

'You don't know you're born, sunshine,' Jessie jeered. 'She gives you a thick ear and you think it's the end of the world. You're spoilt. You never get the hidings she used to give me and Maggie. When she was young and still had her strength, she'd keep you off the floor with left hooks.'

'She'd knock you into the middle of next week,' Maggie confirmed.

But they felt it was her right and duty and that they probably deserved what they got. Wiser and more compassionate than I shall ever be, they loved her without difficulty, bought her chocolates and flowers out of the few coppers she allowed them from their wages and always excused her tantrums with the formula 'Me mam's had a hard life, God help her'.

There were remarkable facts in her past which explained her lifelong struggle to achieve respectability safely beyond the common people she despised. Her own mother was actually of the petty Irish gentry, the daughter of a family in Wicklow, had her own pony to ride, a devoted nurse and plenty of pence to spare for the poor. But when she was of an age for such foolishness, she fell in love with the stable lad and eloped with him.

'That was her downfall,' Maggie said through her serious spectacles.

The couple fled to England and holed up in a room in a stinking court with a communal privy and one pump in the yard for everyone. Endless, wearying squabbles over who had dirtied the toilet and whose turn it was to lambaste the pump for a stuttering gush of impure water. The stable lad hoped to become a jockey, they would have oodles of dosh once he got a mount; but there were no mounts to be had in Liverpool, and work was scarce for Irish immigrants unless the priest found you a job. The best he could get was driving a horse and cart, which he did with bad grace, often sloping into the boozer before rolling home to bash his wife in drunken self-pity. He was a country boy and city life was too much for him; he soon went to the dogs, drifting from one job to another, often unemployed. Then they had to beg the parish for a few shillings, pride and shame preventing my grandmother from seeking the help of her family. She couldn't cope with poverty, her housekeeping was hopeless; she would spend money on flowers and lace doilies when there was scarcely dripping to spread on the bread; she would tell her wondering daughter stories of her grand life in Wicklow while the landlord booted the door for his rent. She never learned to cook cheap, nourishing food – pig's trotters, a sheep's head – but instead, longed for balls at the Assembly Rooms, her pony and her dear old nurse. After a few years, as though life had had quite enough of her whinging, a runaway carthorse kicked her in the head and killed her.

Her family had to be informed, but the stable lad dared not return to Wicklow. Holy Christ! they'd skin him alive. So Mother went alone, a bony, dark-haired chit of sixteen, sitting up all night on the deck of the Irish boat wrapped in her mother's shawl. In Dublin, she counted the coppers in her purse and took the train to Wicklow. She presented herself at the great house, its drive curving around a lawn and a shrubbery. A maid answered the door and sent her to the servants' entrance but eventually she got to meet her grandparents, and sundry uncles and aunts. They stood in stiff clothes defending their hearth, ranged mightily above her as she sat on the edge of a chair and told them of her mother's death. She said nothing of poverty or degradation, for her mother would not have wanted it known. Her relations sighed and muttered and were downcast. They offered her a cup of tea, slice of soda bread, and handed her a couple of quid for the journey home. She never saw them again and all contact was soon lost.

When I heard Mother's story, I claimed her mother for my own. Wasn't it a well-attested fact that particular traits – refinement, intelligence, call it what you will – sometimes skipped a generation and graced the next? It explained my superiority to the rest of the family, my sore yearning for something quite beyond them. I thought of my grandmother often and studied the one photograph we had of her: her pale daunted face, her wounded eyes. I knew how she must have felt, exiled to Liverpool, surrounded by a coarse mob who did not understand her and derided her flinching sensitivity. I was uninterested in her husband, my grandfather, who had reformed to some extent after her death. He had died some years ago, being cared for in his last years by Mother, who was nothing if not dutiful.

The house in Wicklow was not unlike the small mansion in Woolton where she had worked as a housemaid, bossed and humiliated, overworked and underpaid – 'But it wasn't like that!' she would tell you. Hard work never hurt anyone, and she had grown to admire, even to love, the people she served, whom fate had set over her, real ladies and gentlemen. Oh and the frolics, the great gatherings she had enjoyed from her below-stairs perspective! Splendid dinners and parties, and the glass of sherry they offered her while she curtsied at the door. She had become the servant who might once have served her mother. But this was unsurprising, given her impoverished, slapdash upbringing (more slap than dash). She needed the security her place as a valued servant gave her, the protective shade of a social class over her. 'They weren't just bosses; they were good to me. I'm not like you and your dad, too proud to accept that there are people higher up than me. There's always got to be a top, a middle and a bottom to society.'

We were not at the very bottom, lowest of the low, but clung like a plaster on a boil to the bottom of the lower middle class.

Was my father any better? Worse in a way, for he was a hypocrite, admiring and fearing the boss class while affecting to despise them. It was the impoverished, powerless past that was to blame. He had married young, his wife as young; it was a rash step in 1914 and his family had warned him against it. But he was a cocky young man with a naïve belief in luck and the future. Shortly afterwards, the war had begun. He hadn't wanted to leave his wife's side, his job, the little house they were renting, but social pressure proved too much and he submitted when the great boss voice of England, supported by a pious whinny from the pulpit, told him that he must enlist. In the event, he had a cushy time, first as a batman, then as a cook in a cookhouse behind the lines.

The war had brought him close to the upper classes for the first time in his life and he fell in love with those he encountered: the gallant lieutenants, the monumental majors. He loved their appearance, their uniforms, the beauty of their polished Sam Brownes, their holstered revolvers, their fox-hunting boots and jodhpurs, the British Warms and martial trench coats they wore when inspecting the trenches, their medal ribbons and those pips on their shoulders, magic buttons galvanising you into submission. He admired the way they held themselves, their purposeful stride, the insouciant courage with which they faced death. It formed him for life, ensured he would never make common cause with his workmates in defiance of the boss; yet, at the same time, and quite genuinely, he loathed the upper classes. I harbour a similar ambivalence.

After the war, it was difficult to get a decent job and there was always the threat of the sack should you object to working overlong hours for little pay. In those days, you had to give the chef a regular backhander to get a job in a decent kitchen, and he couldn't do that; partly because he couldn't afford it and partly from a ridiculous pride, a pained sense of justice. Then his wife became pregnant. The child was sickly from birth and it wasn't long before it became seriously ill. They did not know what ailed it; it seemed simply to lack the disposition to live. Eventually, his wife wrapped it in her shawl and took it to the hospital. In the crowded Outpatients department a doctor looked at it and felt it as though it was a chicken he was reluctant to buy, shook his head and said there was nothing he could do. It was winter, icy slush in the streets, and she walked all the way home, carrying the child, to save a halfpenny tram fare, her thin boots letting in the wet. She sat with her baby in the bare, damp, smelly room before a weak fire which Dad kept alight with bits of torn cardboard and minute pieces of coal. Then the infant seemed to stretch itself as though it was yawning, and she thought, Oh, it's waking up, I'll have to feed it. But it was dead.

They were overwhelmed with grief and guilt, and she was angry; she raged against the hospital; the child should have been looked after, given the care they could not themselves provide. Although Dad couldn't have taken it back like a bag of rotten spuds, she wanted him to go to the hospital and complain, see one of the higher-ups, whoever was responsible, and give them a piece of his mind, make them see the anguish they had caused. But he pleaded with her, mumbling abjectly: 'It wouldn't do no good, you can't go telling these big doctors their business, they'll just say it's our fault for not looking after it properly ...' She had stared at him, head inclined, waiting to hear a more positive response; when he shrugged helplessly, she realised the sort of man she had married.

We were two of a kind, me and my dad, constantly falling short of her expectations.

Yet they had come through. To prove it, we had moved to a bigger and better house – one of a terrace of tall houses facing a public park, the rent twelve-and-six a week, which we could afford now that Frank and the girls were bringing home a wage. There were two reception rooms on the ground floor inhabited by the best furniture, but we lived at the back in what we called the kitchen – a good-sized room with a fireplace for everyone to sit round. Cooking was done in the back kitchen. There was a scrap of garden at the front of the house and a flagged yard at the back, enclosed by brick walls. Beyond the rear wall was the back-entry with its litter of tin cans and soggy newspapers, dead cats and old boots. Jordan territory. It connected our road with a street of smaller terraced houses, allowing me to choose either the park's green illusion, where I could climb mountains and tramp through a jungle, or the backstreet full of kids yelling and pulling each other about in racing games – those who were not humpbacked, who didn't wear an iron brace on their legs or would never leave the sickbeds in which they would soon die.

The day after we moved into the house, I went into the backyard and found some kids standing on the wall staring down at me, Smidger and Copey and the rest, their impudent Scouse faces. 'Gerrup on dis wall. Are yew fucken scared or what?' they said, picking their noses, wiping their noses on the sleeves of torn jerseys.

From the dustbin I heaved myself on to the roof of the outside lavatory, then on to the backyard wall, scraping my boots on the bricks as I did so – 'What have you done to your good boots?' – and ran along the wall with the lads. It was six feet from the ground and no more than a brick wide. We ran across one backyard after another, the women in their back kitchens glaring at us: 'Those damn lads on the wall again!' We jeered at the women, fingers waggling at our noses, bums stuck out derisively.

Was I really one of them? A part of them, yet apart from them.

They had a strict set of beliefs to which you subscribed if you didn't want a smack in the gob – an ideology that gave coherence to the world, enabling you to appreciate where you stood and whose side you were on, on the wall:

Everton FC is the School of Science; Liverpool FC couldn't kick a hole in a wet *Echo.*

All Catholics will go to heaven when they die; Proddy-dogs won't.

Boy Scouts are brave and resourceful; the Boys' Brigade are a bunch of Protestant wankers.

BSA make the best bikes; Raleigh bikes fall to pieces.

Joe Louis is the greatest heavyweight, Nel Tarleton the pluckiest lightweight, Don Bradman the best batsman, Harold Larwood the fastest bowler, Dixie Dean the greatest centre forward. In the world.

Amy Johnson is the best woman pilot, George Formby the funniest comedian, Gracie Fields the greatest entertainer, Ronald Colman the best film star. In the world.

The Face at the Window is the most frightening film ever made; they will pay you to spend a night alone in a picture house watching it.

The Coronation Scot is the fastest train; the Queen Mary beats all other ocean liners.

Mussolini is a joke; Hitler is Charlie Chaplin.

The Loyal Orange Lodge is a conspiracy of crooks and bullies.

Jew boys have all the money. Niggers have dicks eighteen inches long. The Irish are thick as two short planks.

The Pope is infallible; he cannot tell a lie.

Freemasonry is a secret plot to rule the world.

Mrs Simpson is a smelly Yank; Edward should have been king.

Dr Marie Stopes is a wicked woman.

The pips in raspberry jam are made of wood.

General Franco is saving Spain from the Communists.

If a bulldog bites you, it cannot let go …

What happened to them, the lads who ran along the wall? Did they become high-wire dancers, circus riders, acrobats, trapeze artistes, mountaineers, steel erectors, test pilots, nerveless speculators …? Most came down off the wall in time, finding their fate in the backstreet. Some died in the bombing. But I've been scampering along a wall ever since.

They made up jeering jingles – *Jordan the Warden, he broke his mother's cordon* – and did me the honour of making one in my own name: *Peter Leape, he made his mother weep.* It was Dad's name: was I destined to the same luckless fate? Had they tried to impose the name on Frank, he would have rejected it indignantly. I would not have been surprised to discover that at baptism he had chosen for himself a name that eminently suited his upright nature: *Frank the Swank, he broke his mother's bank.* It was good the way the words curled round each other; and the rhythm – Da, da-da, da-da-da-da-da-da!

Stan (*the Man, he's a Desperate Dan*) was leader of the gang – half a dozen boys in jerseys and short pants forever running somewhere, or fighting, or calling each other names, playing marbles in the gutter, wrestling in the gutter and, when the war came, hunting for shrapnel in the gutter. Guttersnipes. I went along with them, much to the distress of Mother and Maggie. It was partly from mateyness, partly from fear. When we weren't running along the walls or playing in the street, we had fights with other gangs, hurling obscenities and stones at each other. Led by Stan, we stole into the railway yard and searched empty wagons for anything edible that might have been mislaid in unloading – broken biscuits, sweets in dusty corners, damaged fruit – stuffing our pockets until we were chased away.

Frank had never run along the walls or looted a railway wagon. He enjoyed wholesome outdoor pursuits like the Cycling Club, young men and maidens riding through the countryside of a Sunday, maintaining a perfect formation, banking and soaring like swallows at a bend, heads and shoulders skimming the top of a hedge. They rode racing bikes with dropped handlebars and lean saddles, they wore shirts and shorts, the girls wore felt berets with a stalk growing out of the crown. They scarcely made a sound as they hissed along, legs revolving effortlessly, faces glowing with a purity of purpose. They took a curve with a rapt alignment of body and machine, freewheeled downhill, then dropped a gear and steadily mounted the other side.

Frank took great care of his bike; he squatted in the backyard cleaning and oiling it. His dark, lean face was bent over the sort of task he loved and I loathed.

'Give us a ride,' Jessie said. 'Go on, be a sport. I won't damage it.'

'Your fat bum wouldn't fit on this saddle!' he laughed, and nudged me, inviting me to share his boy-scout scorn of dizzy females.

He was going to be a priest. Although he was past the age when boys generally entered a seminary, Mother was convinced he had a vocation; he would make up his mind sooner or later, then she would be able to show him off to relatives and to the ladies of the Mothers' Union: 'My big son, the priest!' But could she bear to part with him? Wouldn't she rather keep him beside her always? But that was impossible; he was so good-looking, such a good boy, some designing female would be sure to grab him sooner or later. Better surrender him to the church to be preserved in the amber of celibacy than lose him to some rival.

Why did he want to be a priest: to do good? There was more to it than that. The world was a fallen world, he informed me, choked with human sin, and it was the heaven-ordained task of priests to battle with this corruption, to cleanse the world for God. They were like knights of old, he said, and I could see a Roman Collar, God's gorget, already fastened about his throat. He wanted to rescue man from his iniquity, raise him up and lead him back to God. People needed to be led, he said; they could not be left to their own devices; they had to be told what to do and what not to do. 'And told off, if necessary!' he added jovially.

But I was more spiritually-minded than Frank; I was genuinely, you might say scientifically, interested in God. I lay awake at night in my room at the top of the house, listening to the meditative clank of a shunting engine in the railway yard. Whenever a car passed on the road below, its headlights spread a fan of light that slowly traversed the ceiling like the unrolling of a mystical scroll. The lonely clank of the engine and the wheeling light somehow put me in mind of eternity. I would imagine the world spinning round and round in space; then my mind would set off, racing back through all the ages of the world, man and ape and the great reptiles of the encyclopedia, seas rising and falling, mountains erupting through the earth's crust, back and back at breakneck speed in an attempt to find God's beginning, my mind tearing out beyond the world and the solar system, beyond the Milky Way, beyond the very creation of the universe. I was dizzy with intellectual vertigo, imagining so many worlds and suns reduced to their beginning and then to nothingness – yet still God was somewhere beyond. He had existed before creation and would continue to exist long after the universe had passed away, scintillating in lonely majesty for all eternity.

This is a trick I can no longer perform.

'Who made you?' the teacher would ask, resting his bored face on a pudgy fist; and someone would be picked on to answer – 'God made me.'

It was arse-faced Jones, a scabby kid everyone loathed. God made him? I was scowling beneath the crucifix at the back of the class in a Catholic elementary school fit only for dullards.

'Why did God make you?'

'God made me ... God made me ...'

Jones didn't know the answer. The teacher looked at me and I reeled it off: 'God made me to know Him, love Him and serve Him in this world, and to be happy with Him forever in the next.'

It never meant as much as the roller-coaster ride to eternity in my head.

Sometimes dad was away for so long that we almost forgot him. But he made sure we remembered him with the presents he brought back. Jessie was his favourite, the first he looked for whenever he came home. 'Aye-aye, there!' he would say. 'Here we are again!' hefting his big suitcase over the threshold. 'The bad penny returns!'

It was practically an apology. We were both intruders. He was a thin, wiry man with a lined face and an uneasy grin, his head cocked with mock aggression. He was all nervous movement, jerking about, heading an imaginary football, dancing a few steps or sparring with me, leading with his left and for some reason, as though it was part of a professional boxer's repertoire, knocking his nose with his cocked right thumb. Jerking about and dancing and always on the hop, as though afraid that if he stayed still for too long someone would confront him and demand an account of his life.

I had his mousy hair. I had her bony cheekbones. I had his naive blue eyes. I had her melancholy. I had his wit and imagination.

His smile for Jessie was loving, and I would catch a bit of it before it faded at the sight of Frank, who had inherited Mother's talent for making you feel as though you must have done something wrong. He would heave his suitcase on to the table and we would gather round for the presents, which he distributed like Father Christmas, demanding a kiss before he handed them over. His bristly cheek, the smell of Woodbines, the joy of having me dad back again ...! There were nylon stockings and a mouth organ, a prayer book with a mother-of-pearl cover, a penknife, a pair of boxing gloves, a box of candies, a coconut with the face of an Indian carved among its bristles. But as important as the presents was the bric-a-brac that clung to him, incidental souvenirs from a fabulous land across the sea: a bus ticket from Manhattan, a book of matches from a bar on 42nd Street, a postcard featuring the Statue of Liberty, a packet of razor blades made in the USA, a Hershey Bar, a copy of a newspaper with its different paper and print – glamorous detritus that convinced me America, the fabulous land of swing bands and crooners, skyscrapers and gangsters, actually existed.

After the presents, he would bring out the food he had stolen from the galley, maybe a chicken, a bag of sugar, a joint of beef, a medicine bottle of brandy abstracted from the officers' mess. 'I wish you wouldn't,' Mother would say, shaking her head with a suffering smile as he piled the stuff into her arms.

'They won't miss it. Should see what some a them pinch.'

'It's stealing, you know,' Frank informed me when we were in the backyard. 'He calls it "pinching", as though that makes it all right, but it's really stealing. It's like a servant, a slave, stealing his master's goods behind his back. How can you have respect for a father like that?'

'He's a case,' I said.

A case was someone who could be relied upon to do the jokey, unexpected thing. But it could also mean a madcap failure. Then there was a head case and a hard case. Frank was a hard case.

Dad enjoyed being at home, sitting close to the fire in winter, holding his hands to the blaze with a sigh of satisfaction before opening the *Liverpool Echo* and reading the local news – 'Let's have a sky at the scandal!' – his lips moving as he read. He would light a Woodbine, hiss out the smoke with relish and then nip out the cigarette when it was only half smoked, tucking the rest behind his ear.

He took me on board his ship and showed me around. It was probably only a rusty travel-stained freighter, but I felt highly privileged when I set foot on its cluttered deck, the steam-hissing steel-clanging deck of a ship that had battled its way through mountainous seas to fabulous ports: Buenos Aires, Valparaiso, New York. There was nothing to compare with a ship; it was a world of its own, framed in rugged steel and seasoned wood, slung with tarry ropes and cables that smelt of oil and the salt sea.

Singing beneath his breath – he was rarely without an absent-minded song – Dad led me down a narrow passage like a dimly lit tunnel, and showed me his cabin. 'I get a cabin to myself now I'm second cook and baker.'

There was a bed and a porthole, and a let-down table where he wrote his letters home, always in indelible pencil with the tip wetted for purple passages. The walls were of riveted steel, coated in white paint, gleaming with condensation. Bulkheads. And the stairs you called "the companionway". A ship had its own language.

He took me to the Officers' Mess, which was empty. I had never encountered such luxury before: a polished mahogany dining table riveted to the deck, a sideboard with silver dish covers and a blaze of cutlery, a drinks cabinet gleaming with exotic bottles, make you tipsy just to look at them. The very air seemed different, smelling of nautical tobacco and brandy in goblets. I could imagine the officers seated here, their gold-braided uniforms, the languid drawl of their talk, their confident laughter. An existence glowing with privilege.

'This is where the officers hang out.'

'Wouldn't you like to be one?'

I wished he was.

For his first meal home, Mother would cook him a steaming plate of bacon ribs, his favourite dish. We sat round, toying with our own plain tea, watching as he stripped pink meat from the bones with a clash of false teeth and spoke of his latest trip. This time they had called at Buenos Aires before sailing on to New York, and – 'We had a coupla' greasers along with us, real Liverpool Irish buckoes. You know the sort of article, all brawn and no brain. Well, soon as we get to Bona Zers, these two beauties go on the razzle and a'course they get in trouble. They'd been drinking and got into a fight over a woman or summat. Anyway, they struggled back on board and I was the first person they come across. (I'd not gone ashore; I've been in Bona Zers before; there's nothen there.) Well, our friends were in a fright, I can tell you, big blubbering clowns! They were scared outta their wits and beggen me to help them. Me! Act soft and I'll buy you a coal yard. The police were after them, and the police in those parts make ours look like tarts in frilly dresses. As for the jails –! The greasers were afraid they'd be locked up: "Kill us in der, dey will!" But I told them, there's nothing I can do for you, lads; you got yourselves in trouble and you'll have to face the music. Well, if looks could kill! I thought they were gonna jump me and I had the big frying pan handy just in case! Just then, big noise on deck, the police arrived. My stars, shoulda seen them run! They charged outa the galley, but before they got off the ship, the police copped them and took them away, and we never saw them again. Sailed without them.'

He went to sea but he wasn't a sailor, a jolly Jack Tar. Like many in Liverpool, he was simply a working man who could get no other job. He feared the sea, never having learned to swim, and loathed its eternal emptiness, its menacing lack of meaning. He looked forward to the end of a trip, yet when he got home he found a family of strangers, children who had grown always a little different in his absence, with whom he could never establish a continuing relationship. He was loved, nevertheless. I loved him: he was a case. Maggie loved him, though he generally ignored her, preferring pretty Jessie, who teased him boldly.

What of his wife: did they love each other?

'He's dead scared of her!' Jessie laughed.

They would dress up – his pale, narrow face above a white muffler; her felt hat pulled down on her head – and go into town and spend his wages, searching for bargains in Blackler's, tea and a scone in the Kardomah café. She did not go with him to the football, though he sometimes took me – Everton FC is the School of Science – but they played cards and went most nights to a whist drive organised by the parish church. We played cards at home: Newmarket, Rummy, halfpenny in the kitty. Mother played intently, eyes sharp for every card that was shown, lips bitterly tight when she lost. She was not a good loser.

On Sundays we all went to church. During Mass, Dad's face had a pondering expression that had little to do with prayer. Mother's careworn face was wistful. She had once told the girls that when she was young she had wanted to be a nun. She would have liked to retire into quiet contemplation, safely locked away from the fret of the world. She had not a great capacity for enjoyment and I cannot believe she was ever in love, ever sexually aroused and satisfied; more likely, she resented the sexual demands made on her. Yet she often gave the impression of being harried by unrealised and incomprehensible desires, grittily suppressed. She was melancholic, never expected things to turn out well. She felt obscurely that life was unfair, that she hadn't had a square deal; but she never turned this into politics. She preferred religion, she believed quite literally in heaven; that was where she would finally receive her just reward. When Frank was killed, she felt quite sure that they would meet again in heaven; though this did not prevent her from grieving terribly.

Each time Dad came home there were problems to be dealt with – the rent had gone up, there were mice in the kitchen, the dog had run away. On one occasion, it was my boot.

'Have you seen the state of this lad's boot?'

Mother grabbed my ankle and lifted my foot as though I was a horse being shod. The sole of my boot had come away from the upper ('Gerrup on dis wall'), and wearing it was like having a duck-billed platypus on my foot.

'Now that's not right, is it? I know he thinks we're made of money, but even on his worst days he couldn't have done that much damage ... if the boots had been properly made in the first place.'

Dad nipped out his Woodbine and tucked it behind his ear. He stooped to examine the boot.

'The other's starting to come apart as well,' Mother added.

'By crimes!' he sighed. 'Don't you ever look at the things before you buy them? Where'd you get them, Paddy's Market?'

'It's not my fault!' she glared, releasing me and drawing herself up and away from him.

'Well, you bought the bloody things, didn't you?'

And they had a row. There were often brief, bitter spats when he came home; it was never easy to readjust to married life. Was she even pleased to have him back, just when she had grown accustomed to being by herself with her children, her beloved Frank? On his part there were naive expectations and self-pitying disappointment. But he was ready to return the boots to the shop; he would take out his frustration on whoever had sold them.

'They're not gonna get away with it! I'll give them a piece of my mind.'

'Are you sure you can spare it?'

He took me with him to the shop, the platypus flapping and quacking as I walked. He wanted me for evidence, also perhaps to instruct me in the art of making a forceful complaint. (Had she told him about The Spuds?). The boots had been bought at a department store in town; it was crowded with shoppers but Dad pushed his way through, dragging me along, muttering and cursing, quivering a little. What he didn't know was that there was something dodgy about the boots. I knew it, but I didn't tell him for fear he would shout at me, he was in such a rage.

'D'you see this?' he snarled when we got to the Boots and Shoes, and he hoicked my foot up on to the counter like giving a Nazi salute with my leg. 'I'm not standen for this! I wanna replacement, a new paira boots.'

I expected the counter assistant to blanch with fear and replace the boots without further ado, amid profuse apologies. But he remained unimpressed, even when Dad worked the sole of my raised boot back and forth. 'Look at this! That's not right.'

'When'd you buy them?' the assistant asked languidly.

Dad was not prepared to go into details with an underling. 'I wanna see the man in charge, not his snot rag.'

'You don't have to insult me,' the assistant said. 'I'm only doing my job.'

He would not disturb the manager for such a trivial matter, but he fetched a shopwalker. He was a tall man, taller than Dad, stiff and straight like a guard's officer, and he was unmoved by Dad's bluster, treating him with contempt. He glanced disdainfully at the boot and told me to remove my foot from his counter. I obeyed at once. Then he questioned Dad as though they were in court: Had he bought the boots here? When had he bought them? Where was his receipt? How long had the boy worn the boots?

'This is hardly a matter of fair wear and tear, you know,' he concluded. 'In any case –'

And this was where the boots were dodgy, for although they had been bought at the store, Mother had not bought them; a neighbour had bought them and later sold them to Mother for half a crown when her own lad had grown out of them, although he had crunched about in them for a while. I knew this and should have warned Dad; it was my fault he was being steadily crushed into humiliation. Eventually, he was forced to admit that he hadn't got a receipt, that the boots were, well, not exactly bought here, but – The shopwalker smiled scornfully. He was not moved by Dad's tearful rage, his whining demand for his money back, his threat to "go higher up" and even "write to the press".

'You should be ashamed of yourself, carrying on like this in front of your boy.'

'Never you mind about that!' Dad bawled, though it came out as "Neh you myn bow da!", because of the sobs of rage and mortification he was stifling.

Some shoppers were looking on with interest; one woman tut-tutted to another, 'Carrying on like that in front of the kid!'

Behind the shopwalker's back, the assistant was sniggering furtively.

'Now be off with you,' the shopwalker said. 'Unless you would like me to call a bobby and have you put in charge for causing a nuisance.'

Trapped in a hopeless situation, and almost as though he sought punishment now for his stupidity, Dad refused to give up – 'Is this what you call service?' He appealed to the crowd: 'Have you ever seen anythink like this, where they won't give you a square deal? I'm never ever gonna shop here again, I can tell you!'

'Thank God for that!' the shopwalker laughed.

He walked away. The assistant was joined by another and they ushered Dad towards the exit, each holding one of his arms as though he had been arrested. They forced him along, stifling giggles and shaking their heads, telling him, 'You've not gorra case, y'know', while I trailed behind through the crowded store, convinced more than ever that taking an article back to a shop was never a good idea.

In the street, Dad strode along furiously, dragging me with him, hiding his face. We left the main street and began to descend towards the waterfront, into an impoverished and disreputable district. Dad stopped outside a grubby shop, its window piledhigh with junk. He gave a throwaway laugh and, drawing me into the shop, asked whether they'd a pair of boots to fit his lad. They had everything in that shop. The shelves were piled to the ceiling with second-hand clothing, most of it sold for coppers by drunken seamen who had spent their pay, and desperate people who were broke. There was a bay where boots and shoes were piled in a heap, pairs tied together with string. The shopkeeper rummaged through them and returned with three pairs of boots.

'These look good,' Dad said. 'They're as good as new.'

The shopkeeper knelt before me and jammed one of the boots on to my foot. It was too small. The next boot was too big. I felt like Cinderella's ugly sister. There was only one pair left and I was cold with anxiety: what if they didn't fit, either? They weren't a perfect fit, but I could walk in them.

'New boots are always stiff at first,' Dad assured me.

'But these aren't new, Dad.'

'Buy them new,' the shopkeeper said, 'and you'd be paying guineas. A young lord wouldn't be ashamed to wear them boots.'

'We'll take them,' Dad said. 'How much?'

'Half a crown.'

The shopkeeper threw my old boots into a bin and I hobbled at Dad's side in the young lord's boots as we left the shop and sought a tram stop. Mother was out when we got home. When she returned, she faced Dad peremptorily. 'Well?'

He told her that the store had submitted to his demand for an exchange. 'They cudden' give me a new pair, of course, but the ones we got are as good as new.'

I know this because I was listening behind the door. It wasn't the first and it would not be the last time I would eavesdrop. An intruder, a usurper, a disappointment, and now an eavesdropper on other people's lives.

Jessie took me to New Brighton, the seaside resort across the river. We went on the rides in the fairground and she bought me some crisps and an ice cream. We sat on the beach among a swarm of holidaymakers – parents with their kids picnicking on banana sandwiches gritty with sand, a child toddling forth and falling over, a dog racing across the beach, barking at the waves. There was a frisson of joy in the air, in the sunlight, the blue sky, glossy sweep of the river. It was freedom; we were all having a day away from the boss. Jessie changed into her bathing costume and sunbathed while I read a comic; she frowned when young men passed and admired her figure.

'Did you see that feller give me the eye? He's got a nerve!'

I went down to the water's edge and paddled cringingly, fearful of treading on something ghastly; I stared at half-naked girls in their bathing-costumes. When I got back to Jessie, she was asleep. How big girls' bodies look when they're lying down; they seem to swell with sleep. Bored, I dug in the sand. On the surface the sand was warm; below it was cool and damp, packing itself around my hand like something living. Eventually, Jessie woke up, brushed herself down and changed back into her blouse and skirt. It was time to go home.

'Well, we've had a lovely day out,' she said, as we made for the ferry.

We sat at the stern on a slatted wooden bench that, a notice claimed, would serve as a raft should the boat sink. The creamy foam of the wake tumbled thick from the propellers and frittered out delicately over glassy green water. 'The Captain is doing his washing,' Jessie said.

In the glow of a sunset barred with soft grey clouds she confided in me her great ambition. She spoke of it in a low, serious voice, her fair hair lifted by the breeze. She wasn't going to work in no factory for the rest of her life, she'd been taking dancing lessons on the q.t., tap-dance a speciality, and she meant to go on the stage, become a showgirl.

'You'll be a star, Jessie!'

'I may not get that far; but if I can get into the chorus, I'll be happy. It's always been my dream.'

There was a show opening in the Isle of Man and she had applied for an audition, it was her big chance.

'What'll me Mam say?'

'I don't give a good gosh darn, kid! She ain't gonna ruin my life like she's ruined Maggie's.'

I admired her courage and determination; the glamour of the stage filled my head with glittery spun sugar. My sister a showgirl! Nevertheless, leaving home, escaping from Mother, would not be easy and I decided to pray for her; I would begin a novena that very day. I was not devout, but I was familiar with the benign economy of prayer and knew there was a greater chance of impressing God if you prayed for another rather than for yourself. There was no doubt the novena helped, for although Mother objected strongly, Jessie was unshaken; and after the usual rows, tears, Jessie belting upstairs to fling herself on her bed, Mother declared that she could do nothing with the girl, (for she was no longer of an age when she could be slapped into submission). She packed her case and set sail for the Isle of Man singing *Cal-i-for-nia, here I come!* Who was to stop her? Dad was away at sea and might even have encouraged her had he been home, for he would sometimes declare he should have gone on the stage himself ('Scrubbing it,' Frank would murmur), and would do Fred Astaire to prove it. Frank knew nothing of Jessie's plan and Maggie actually subsidised it with the few pounds she had been saving for a new bike.

How had Mother ruined her life?

Maggie had left school at fourteen and was working in a warehouse packing toys, twelve hours a day. Waking one morning and feeling ill, she wanted to stay in bed and begged to be allowed to do so. But Mother, fearing she might get the sack if she failed to turn up for work, refused to believe she was ill and sent her off on her bicycle, the bony, ill-nourished girl wearily pedalling her way to work in the heavy sleet of a winter's morning, 1933. The next day she was bedridden, seriously ill with rheumatic fever. She was ill for a long time and though she eventually recovered, she was never to be as well as she might otherwise have been.

I realise that getting drenched won't give you rheumatic fever, but what mattered at the time was having something else to hold against Mother, vindicating my failure to love her.

Later in the summer Maggie took me to the Isle of Man to see Jessie in the show. She wanted Mother to come as well: 'We can have a nice day out.' But to have seen the show would have implied that she had forgiven the disobedient girl, so she refused. She had her principles and she held on to them grimly, even though she would dearly have loved a trip to the Isle of Man.

At the Pier Head, Maggie held my hand tightly, gulping palely whenever she had to ask directions. Beneath her raincoat she wore a fashionable white and brown polka-dot frock. In the crowd milling about the landing stage there were lots of excited polka-dot girls. The young men with them wore their shirt collars open over the collars of their jackets; their hair was slicked back, sleek with Brylcreem. Few were without jackets, it wouldn't have been proper, and many carried raincoats folded over their arms. When the gates at the far end of the landing stage were opened, the crowd surged towards the cruise ship, which was larger than any ferryboat, and we set off on a rollicking Sinbad voyage through a sun-splashed sea. The decks were crowded with holidaymakers, some on their wakes week from the cotton towns. They drank from bottles of beer and danced the Lambeth Walk, they sang *I'm the Sheik of Araby!* It was summertime and we were off to the three-legged Isle of Man. Landlubbers, we stared at freighters we passed riding at anchor in the estuary. The vessels ignored us, they were impervious, self-absorbed, committed to the voyage ahead. In one ship there was a seaman at the rail, heroic in a singlet, who spat reflectively into the water. The ship's hull was rusted at the waterline, but above the deck the superstructure of the bridge rose like a fortress, glittering white in sunlight.

The land fell away beneath the horizon and was succeeded by a blankness at which I stared nonplussed, my bearings lost. Haze obliterated the division between sea and sky; one might have been in God's pearly mouth, in danger of being swallowed. But we reached Douglas safely and flocked ashore. It was the grandest place I'd ever seen, opulent in the sunshine, with a golden beach, a long promenade and a towering rampart of hotels facing the sea. Behind the hotels was a maze of narrow, crowded streets with plenty of pubs and cafés, and shops selling rock and ingenious ornaments made of seashells. A piano played in one of the pubs and people were singing. The buildings cast shadows half across the road, then you emerged suddenly into blinding, rejoicing sunlight.

In a crowded café we ate fish and chips with thin slices of bread and butter and a pot of tea. Maggie carefully extracted the bones from her fish, her spectacles intent. Afterwards, we walked along the promenade, looked at the shops, bought Manx kippers and spotted a Manx cat, the kind with no tail that brought good luck. But the sunlight was deceitful;

clouds had gathered, grey and ominous, by the time we went to the theatre.

I had never been in a theatre before. You couldn't see as well as you could at the pictures and I couldn't make much sense of the musical-comedy plot, but I was charmed whenever the chorus of half-naked girls appeared, with Jessie among them. They formed a line with their arms round each other, bared shoulders gleaming. They marched and pranced and kicked out their legs, bellowing a cheery seaside song, smiling appealingly at the audience:

> Sing as we go!
> And let the world go by!
> Singing a song, we'll march along the highway!
> Say Goodbye to sorrow!
> There's always tomorrow!
> To think of today!

We went backstage afterwards, we were actually allowed backstage, and Jessie emerged from a crowded dressing room pink with giggling, shrieking girls. She took us to a late-night snack bar and mugged us to a milkshake and American doughnuts, her voice teetering on delirious high heels as she spoke of the exciting life she was leading.

'And what will you do when the show ends?' Maggie asked.

'I'm going to London with some of the other girls, We'll get work there.'

We returned to Liverpool on the midnight boat. A storm had blown up and the sea was choppy, the gangway swayed, the ship rocked alarmingly. A man stumbled, drunk, as he came on board; he dropped his kippers, which skittered across the deck and dived into the sea. Maggie huddled in the saloon when the ship left the harbour, but I stayed on deck. Too much had happened that day and was still happening – for the storm seemed an extension of the stage spectacle – to waste it in the safety of the saloon among green-faced women, fretful kids and snoring drunks. The night was black, the wind roared and flung spray and rain in my face, the vessel reared and plunged. Passengers tottered from larboard to starboard, coats flying and bodies twisted in grotesque attitudes as they clawed the air for support. The steel plates of the hull groaned, lanyards whipped and snapped, the few lights on deck flickered feebly. I had been scared of facing the shopkeeper, but here I was not afraid, confident that the good ship would carry us safely home. I stood beneath an awning, holding on to a stanchion, smiling as the storm battered the ship. It was like being flayed alive and enjoying it.

A group crouched in the lee of one of the lifeboats, men and women singing to a piano accordion played by one of the men. Music wheezed from the instrument. The "box", they called it. He's smashing on the box. There was laughter and applause when the song ended, then bottles were tilted, cigarettes were lit and another song begun: *Sing as we go ... Red Sails in the Sunset ... Tumbling Tumbleweeds.* The accordionist worked the bellows, producing an uneven gush of sound. He was unmoved by the storm, his face calm and steady above his instrument, his hair flying, fingers reaching confidently for the keys. And the night, the plunging ship, wet gleam of the planks, the shrouded lights, the thunder of the storm and the figures crouched around him in a circle – ! Undaunted, the accordionist played and people sang, their voices borne to me on the wind, snatched away by the wind.

CHAPTER TWO

The day the war started I was in the park lavatory with the backstreet lads. We were seeing who could piss highest up the stinking, green-slimed urinal slab, when a kid entered yelling, 'The war! The war's started!' and we all rushed out and began killing each other. We grabbed handfuls of soil and flung them in the air, 'Gu-doom!,' for a bomb exploding.

We weren't afraid, we knew Great Britain would win and we were excited. A momentous event, a kind of snarling Christmas, was suddenly upon us. The grown-ups were not excited; the men were glum, the women anxious. Young men and girls, buttoned up in uniforms, were constantly on the move, burdened with kit, kissing loved ones goodbye. We pestered soldiers for regimental badges, polished them golden and mounted them on a belt,trophies of war.

People who had been neglected for years suddenly found they were needed, they were important, they were making history. The government exhorted them with martial slogans: FREEDOM IS IN PERIL, GUARD IT WITH YOUR LIFE! ... YOUR COURAGE, YOUR CHEERFULNESS, YOUR RESOLUTION, WILL BRING US VICTORY! Hitler's pale, mad face was everywhere; people laughed at him, they jeered at the Nazi swastika. In the newsreels, grey ranks of Germans goose-stepped their way across Europe; Poland was invaded; Stukas dive-bombed helpless refugees; German tanks raced across Denmark and Norway, Belgium and Holland. The war was getting closer, but there was too much going on to be afraid. Life swarmed with novelties, gas masks and stirrup pumps, tin hats and identity cards, ration books and a post office bank account once the war began to pay off in higher wages. An anti-aircraft gun appeared in the park 'Lukud the fucken gun!' and an air raid shelter was built in the road. There were searchlights and EWS tanks, ramparts of sandbags. People criss-crossed their windows with strips of paper to protect them from bomb blasts. In the blackout, masked torches wavered uncertainly, pedestrians bumped into each other and were killed crossing the road.

One day I flew my Spitfire, the next I piloted a bomber, then I was an air-gunner shooting down a marauding Messerschmitt. Alternatively, I could be the commander of a tank squadron (I was invariably an officer) or the plucky first mate of a corvette. These absorbing adventures were more to my taste than charging upon Germans with the backstreet lads. But the war oppressed Mother; she didn't think it was good for me. She obeyed the government when it advised evacuation and sent me off with other kids to the safety of Wales.

'They'll never bomb Wales,' she said. 'There's nothing there worth bombing.'

I was away for a few months, then she brought me home. Couldn't she bear to be without me? I had wanted to stay with my foster parents, they had no son and they had made a loving fuss of me; but Mother feared their influence.

'You know what the Welsh are like,' she confided in Maggie. 'You can't trust them.' They were chapel-goers and would have corrupted my Catholic innocence given half a chance.

Some of the schools were closed and kids ran wild in the city. As a temporary measure, Father Doonan, the parish priest, foraged up some sort of an education for those kids who were not evacuated. Classes were held in the church hall, boys and girls being taught together. How clean and obedient the girls were! How disdainful of the uncouth boys they were forced to sit near. Father Doonan and a teacher brought out of retirement instilled discipline, but could only teach the same dull stuff as before – long-division sums, the catechism, kings and queens of England, the British Empire. Classes rarely lasted more than three or four hours, then we were dismissed and could get back to the war.

Dad was rarely home and Frank had joined the Air Force. 'You're the man in the house now,' Mother said.

'Just tell me what you want doing.' I was eager to help win the war, even felt capable of taking spuds back to a shop now.

'Well, you can kill that hen for a start.'

There were four hens in the backyard, scrabbling about on a bit of earth that had once been a neglected flower bed. It was fenced with chicken wire sagging from poles that Dad had waywardly hammered into the soil. One of the hens had stopped laying and should be killed; a nice roast chicken for Frank when he came home on leave.

'Come on,' Mother said. She pressed a hatchet into my hand and I entered the enclosure. Muck and feathers lay about the dun clay of scratched earth. Something like brackish water began to drip inside me and there was a metallic taste in my mouth. The hatchet hung useless from my hand. 'Get on with it!' Mother said. She swooped and seized the doomed hen and thrust it upon me, a flurry of bulky feathers, scaly yellow feet scrabbling at me frantically. I dropped the hatchet and clasped the bird. How light and warm it felt! There was nothing beneath the dusty feathers but fragile bones and a beating heart. Mother was chanting something, instructions presumably; something about wanting me to place the hen's neck on a brick so that its head could be chopped off. But I couldn't do it. I envisaged the gritty 'ding' the hatchet would make, iron jarring on stone with a baffled ring as the blade came down, severing the bird's scrawny neck; the beaked head with its eyes shut lying squandered on the earth.

'Oh, give it to me,' Mother wailed, 'if you're such a coward!'

But as I moved to obey, the hen thrust its head under my arm with a pitiful, trusting impulse, burrowing blindly into me for protection. My heart wrenched and I let it go.

'Now look what you've done, you soft thing!'

The hen squawked away down the enclosure with an aggrieved ruffle of feathers, then forgot its terror and began to peck aimlessly here and there.

Maggie was helping to win the war. She got up early and went to Mass before going to work, praying for victory. She hauled at a great lathe in an aircraft factory, but the work was too hard for her and she became ill, although she still doggedly turned up for work every day. When they discovered she could spell and add up, she was transferred to the office and became a progress chaser; she studied figures and charts and spoke to foremen on the telephone, nagging them into faster and more efficient production. At the other end of the telephone, case-hardened men swore at her and said it was impossible; when they realised she wasn't to be moved, they pleaded for understanding and indulgence. But she drove them unmercifully, pledged nunlike to the task, her pale fragile face, her uncompromising spectacles, insisting on greater effort, targets surpassed. It was the happiest time of her life. She was getting good wages, she had a responsible job and Mother admired her, not least because she could make sense of rationing and knew exactly where the Germans were at any given moment.

Jessie had gone to London to dance in a revue and she stayed there throughout the war, making only occasional visits home. Confronted with Mother's exasperation and Maggie's silent reproach, she would explain that her work made as great a contribution to the war effort as anyone's. 'Someone's got to keep the public's spirits up. And we're there for the boys when they're on leave; we give them a show that cheers them up. We carry on right through the air raids until the bombs get close; and even then, when we go down to the cellars with the customers, there's sure to be a bit of a song and dance.'

I admired her more than ever, a showgirl with platinum hair and painted fingernails, her dainty figure clothed in black market finery. What did she mean about being there for the boys when they came on leave? Frank would have suspected a sin. But what mattered to me was the aura she brought home of a gallant wartime world, the glamour of the London Blitz and a showgirl's life, a hasty cigarette and a slug of gin, then into her sequinned dress and on with the show. The gaudy stage, the troops roaring their love at her, the bouncy tunes and patriotic chorus routines, the troops clustering at the stage door afterwards and then perhaps dinner at the Café Royal with a Spitfire pilot handsomely weary from shooting down Germans in a dogfight. Then a party, a dance until dawn. What a life!

Dad was less impressed, for their visits home rarely coincided. He missed her and felt neglected. 'She knows I'm home,' he said bitterly, 'she could come and see me if she wanted.'

His wages were swelled by danger money and we acquired new possessions on the strength of it: a radiogram, a three-piece suite, a new carpet. He smiled and shook his head wonderingly, remembering the few sticks of furniture in the impoverished house he had known as a child, the flea-ridden bed, the mice and cockroaches, the damp and mould. 'We've come a long way, no question. God, if me poor mam was alive today ...!'

Yet the new things barely made up for the frights he suffered at sea. I prayed for him, we all prayed, and it is a fact that he came through the war unscathed, was never once on a ship that went down. That did not prevent him bleating and sighing, cursing spivs and black marketeers, unions threatening strike action – 'While us poor sods go in danger of our lives to keep the country from starving!' I thought of his ship tiptoeing across the Atlantic, a U-boat skulking beneath the surface and a vessel in the convoy suddenly exploding, slipping beneath the waves, many poor sods drowned, their tragic wails lost in the surge of the waves. 'Shoulda seen it go down!' he exclaimed, wide-eyed. 'Just outta nothing. BOOM! And a sheet of flame. Keep them prayers going for us, kid.'

I grew tired of the backstreet lads. I couldn't bring myself to be close friends with them and doubted whether they really liked me. They were a gang and moved as a unit, fiercely loyal to each other. They thought alike, grabbing fistfuls of clichés from the backstreet store, and were intellectually incurious, content with their comprehensive backstreet philosophy. But I had begun to doubt whether Jew boys really had all the money, whether niggers had dicks eighteen inches long. In any case – niggers, Jew boys – there was something wrong with the names, even though my family used them freely.

I sought a different pal, someone I could talk to without having to wade through obscenities or a fug of depressing banalities. I wanted to get to know Benny Golding, whom the lads despised, for he didn't run along backyard walls or join the gang raiding wagons in the railway yard, lighting fires in the park, stealing from Woolworths – exploits I had enjoyed but which he considered puerile and antisocial. He was called Red Benny because his father was a communist, the scandal of the backstreet. He was three inches taller than me and eighteen months older, with a dark thoughtful face beneath stiff, dark hair, a wide loose mouth good for jeering, and sharp eyes sometimes softened by a lightly scoffing affection. I was interested in his Jewishness and admired his proud loneliness, his refusal to go with the crowd. I thought he would be flattered by my advances (wasn't I prepared to rescue him from social isolation?), but it was only with reluctance that he accepted my friendship and he was never as close a pal as I would have liked. His mother was dead and he lived with his father and younger siblings in a house whose backyard was just across the entry from ours. He was an intellectual, enjoyed reading and the cinema. Not the pictures, the cinema. 'Have you seen *La Grande Illusion*? Have you read *Huckleberry Finn*?'

Eager to contribute to a literary discussion, I warmly recommended *King Solomon's Mines,* which I'd read more than once, enthralled by the trek to Sheba's Breasts, the fighting, the diamonds, the spear-carrying savages both noble and beastly, and the great Dark Continent where nature raised great tangled jungles and killing deserts against the puny impertinence of man. But Benny scoffed at Rider Haggard and treated me to a communist diatribe on the looting of Africa, the cruel exploitation of its peoples by the British Empire. I was amazed and appalled, never before having heard the Empire criticised. A map of the world liberally splodged with red occupied a place of honour in my classroom, alongside Jesus crucified on the cross.

Making Benny's acquaintance was like being on the Isle of Man steamer again, the weather both stormy and exhilarating. Yet there was no need to feel intimidated by his superior age, height, knowledge and intelligence, for he suffered an ultimate disadvantage of not being a Catholic and seemed quite unaware of the danger to his immortal soul should he persist in following his father's atheistical example.

I sometimes went to his house and he taught me how to play chess, though I was never very good at it.

'You're too impulsive. You don't think logically.'

'At least me dad's not a Communist.'

I boasted of my gallant father braving the U-boat perils of the ocean, my elder sister gamely serving the war as a progress chaser, and my younger sister, the glamorous star of some saucy revue in the West End. Benny was impressed for once. 'I would like to meet her. Of course, many Jews are in show business.'

His house made an effort not to appear impoverished and all the kids had their household duties, one to wash the dishes, another to sweep the floor, while their father stood at the stove concocting a huge pan of scouse. He called his kids amigos. When he met me, he said, '*Buenas dias, amigo!*' It came from the Spanish Civil War, where he had fought with the International Brigade. (General Franco is saving Spain ...) His wife had died while he was away and he had returned home to look after his kids. He was a watchmaker by trade, but his income was uncertain; he sometimes lost jobs because of his politics. He was a thin, dark, bony man, who could be sarcastic and did not appear to enjoy life; there was too much wrong with it under capitalism.

There were books all over the place in Benny's house, pictures on the wall of Lenin and Josef Stalin. Frequently, the parlour was jam-packed with communists arguing and laughing in that evil way they have, there were even girls present. I had never imagined there were female communists.

'They're discussing the Stalin–Hitler pact,' Benny said once when the noise was especially loud, curses and harsh jeers battering the air. 'What are your views on the invasion of Finland by the Soviet Union?'

He was immensely knowledgeable and advanced. It must be his father; an intelligent father could tell you things like that, keep you informed on world events. And then there was his Jewish grammar school, vastly superior to the brainless muddle of my elementary school. It was depressing and made me more than ever discontented with the family I was stuck with. They in turn disapproved of my friendship with Benny, which they had discovered despite all my efforts to conceal it.

'It's a sin, being friends with Communists,' Maggie said.

'They'll make a little Jew boy of you!' Jessie laughed.

'Why can't you play with Catholic lads?' Mother said. 'You're always so contrary.'

'I'm going to convert him,' I said.

The question of religion had arisen already, and he had offered to lend me *The Martyrdom of Man*, by Winwood Reade – 'What's it about?'

'The suffering religion has caused mankind.'

'No thanks.'

It would not have been quite so bad if he and his father had been practising Jews attending the synagogue in their yarmulke things, but they were out-and-out godforsaken atheists. I had never met atheists before, and at first it was as though Benny was a leper, unclean and infectious. I wondered how one could possibly live without the security of religion. 'You mean you don't believe in God?'

'As Laplace said, I have no need of that hypothesis.'

How could you explain the universe without God? 'You can't, can you?' I challenged, desperately hoping he couldn't.

And indeed, all he could offer was the lame excuse that science had not yet resolved that problem. 'But in time it will all be explained,' he assured me. 'In the meantime, I don't choose to rush into the supernatural for an explanation. As for the Bible – surely you don't believe in Adam and Eve and the Garden of Eden?'

I suppose I must have accepted something of the sort at some time, just as I had once believed Liverpool FC couldn't kick a hole in a wet *Echo*, although I had never examined either concept closely. But did I really believe in the Bible account? Benny's scepticism was like being threatened with checkmate in a merciless game of chess.

The air raids began with a couple of false alarms that had us hopping out of bed and racing for the shelter – a crowded, dimly lit place with scarcely room to walk between people who sat on hard wooden benches, facing each other. Benny's father had sent his younger kids away on the evacuation but Benny stayed with his father, not only because they were close to each other but also because he did not want his education disrupted. He never came to the shelter. He claimed he suffered from claustrophobia and explained what that meant: but wasn't it just as claustrophobic crouched with his father beneath the stairs in their house? I suspected he was too proud to join the neighbours in the shelter. It was also the case that he and his father were not well liked; some even suspected they might be covert Nazis. It was a German name after all, Golding.

We carried coats and blankets to the shelter, along with something to eat and something to read, a torch, rosary beads and an attaché case that contained everyone's important papers. Sometimes, when Maggie was working nights, I had Mother all to myself. She would put her arm around me and urge me to say Hail Marys. The raids were a novelty while the bombers kept their distance and it was exciting to be up in the middle of the night, huddling scared with thirty or forty neighbours. Everyone had their accustomed place in the shelter, the oldest inhabitants nearest the exit, and no one took another's place. Strangers entering for the first time were regarded with silent disapproval – why had they left it so long before seeking safety? – and would be sent to the rear where the light was poor and it was damper than elsewhere. Many had to go to work the next day and they would try to catch whatever sleep they could, lying curled up on the wooden benches or wrapped in coats and blankets on the concrete floor. Small children were put to bed in this manner while the rest of us sat and waited for the bombers, backs against a cold brick wall with a limey smell, a fuzz of white stuff on the bricks. Some chatted in subdued voices, others played cards or tried to read.

Chapter Two

I read stories of boys in a public school, their chums and japes and midnight feasts in the dorm. The masters wore chalk-smeared gowns and mortar boards; there was usually a fussy Frog who taught French, a fearsome maths teacher, Old Stinks who taught chemistry, and the Head, whom everyone respected despite the lickings he was obliged to administer from time to time. The fine old ivy-covered school – Hurrah for the School! – had a quad and a tuck shop, fives courts and playing fields where the sun always shone and the boys seemed to spend most of their time. Among the boys there was always a jolly decent chap who was a born leader, who occasionally got into scrapes but would always own up to a misdemeanour, taking his caning like a man; there was a smiling Indian of princely descent and a bespectacled swot and a plucky fag, a sneak and a cad and a sixth-form bully. They were a racy tribe whose enviable existence I shared imaginatively while lamenting that such a life, far from the backstreet, would never be mine.

I couldn't even get as far as the life Benny shared with his school friends. I had met some of them, but they were snobbish and considered me an ignorant kid. There was a girl as well, altogether lovely, with curly black hair and a broad smile. I wanted to be friends with Benny's friends, attracted by their intelligence, their bland shrugging insouciance, but they didn't want me. They seemed disparagingly amused by Benny's acquaintance with the goy kid.

About this time, Carol and her kids came to live next door. The house was let off into flats and theirs was the basement flat. The woman didn't seem very respectable – 'Where's her hubby?' Mother asked Maggie.

'In the army; or so she says.'

'Tell us another!' Mother sniffed.

When I was not hanging around Benny trying to attract his attention, I spent a lot of time in the backyard throwing a tennis ball against the wall and, when it bounced back, walloping it with a chunk of wood roughly hewn in the shape of a cricket bat, imagining I was Don Bradman, shamefully possessed by glorying daydreams. The advantage in playing alone was that I always won, and it was while doing so that I first became aware of the kids next door. The boy was about ten, the girl eight, and she was nagging her brother for a drag of the cigarette he was smoking: 'Go on, Eric. Ah, go on.' The wall between the backyards was six feet high and I couldn't see them, and nor could I see Carol when she came into the yard and yelled at them.

'Wharra yeh playing at? Smoking at your age, you should be ashamed!'

'You smoke,' the boy pointed out.

'Aye, but I'm a grown woman and I buy them, I don't pinch them from me mam. Give it here. Cheeky bugger!' she laughed, presumably taking the cigarette from her son and smoking it herself.

She laughed! No violent outburst, and no thick ear, which I would have earned had Mother caught me smoking. I was amazed. Carol spoke with a strong Liverpool accent and her tone was bright and bouncy, with often a gurgle of laughter.

'I doan know what I'm gonna do with you. You'll grow up a hardened criminal.'

'Don't be daft,' said the boy.

To his mother! Don't be daft. And she laughed!

The next time I heard her, I was in the yard with Dad; we were trying to strengthen the wire framing the chicken run. 'Now I know what they felt like when they built the Pyramids,' he said, dropping his hammer and lighting a cigarette. He cocked his head alertly when Carol's voice sounded from next door's yard. Then he grinned at me, fetched a box and stood on it to peer over the wall.

'Who are you lucken at?' Carol said, with her laugh.

'Oh dem big, big eyes!' Dad said, jigging about on the box as though he was a Nigger Minstrel, though all Carol would have seen were his shoulders and hands and his Al Jolson smile.

I got to know Eric, flattering him with an elder's friendship in order to reach Carol. I envied him having a mother so young and pretty, and before long I had persuaded him to take me home with him. The rooms were dark and damp, half underground, filled with a muddle of second-hand furniture, and usually a heap of clothing waiting to be washed – 'It'll have to fucken wait, an all,' Carol would say, preparing for a night out.

They never seemed to eat properly, usually it was baked beans on burnt toast, chips and tinned sardines, or a blob of tinned spaghetti. At home we ate well; meals were always on time and were fully furnished – a roast and two veg, followed by a rice pudding. Mother was a dutiful housewife, and though she couldn't put much love into her perfunctory kisses, her meals proclaimed a maimed affection. On the other hand, Carol was a wonderfully attractive woman. Childbirth hadn't given her the weary belly-sag that marked many mothers. Her body pressed softly against her clothes, her bright eyes fixed you amusedly, a tip-tilted nose gave her face a winsome gleam. She often went out of an evening, leaving Eric to mind his sister and the dog, the cat and its kittens. I kept him company for I loved to see his mother dressed up: a little fur cape draped about her shoulders, a black velvet skirt that reached just to her knees, hair glittering with shampoo and her face precious with make-up. They said she couldn't manage, owed money everywhere and spent what she had on glad rags and a good time. What did she care? She was off to the Grafton Rooms where Mrs Wilf Hamer's band played for servicemen on leave, sailors ashore for the night and girls radiant with excitement. It was all there in Carol's jazzy perfume: the dance floor surging with couples clutched in each other's arms, lights gleaming in a haze of cigarette smoke and the band playing a favourite of mine, *In The Mood.* The music stops and you think it's the end, then the drum kicks off, the saxes breeze in and everyone goes to it once more, the men swing their partners, the girls shriek and laugh.

Carol would kiss her kids goodnight before she left. 'Come on,' she would say. 'Let's give you a big smoochy one.' Eventually, I got a kiss as well, a big smoochy one.

She was different from any woman I had ever known – my mothballed aunties, or the draggle-haired neighbours gossiping on the doorstep. She was easy-going and capricious, and could rage savagely at times, yet I never knew her to be meanly critical of others. Live and let live. It was probably no more than moral indolence, but it impressed me at the time; it was better than the stringent code by which Mother and Maggie lived. Carol didn't care how she lived, nor did she give a curse for the boss or the church. She had a variety of jobs – assembler in a factory, packer in a warehouse, waitress in a café – and either walked out of them or was sacked sooner or later. Much of the time she lived on the dole and whatever additional benefits she could scrounge. Her husband had left her. He was an Irishman – 'Oh, miles above me in education! But once I had the kids, he began to feel trapped. He was ruining his life, he said, married to me. Called me an ignorant Liverpool slut. That wasn't very nice, was it, Peter? I know I'm not educated, but I don't think I'm stupid.' She stared hard at her smouldering cigarette. 'He slammed out of the house one day and I've never seen him since.'

I told Benny of her, glowing with love, and he gave me a glance of amused pity. I kept going next door, couldn't get enough of her. It worried Mother and Maggie.

'She's a bad influence. Religion? She's got no religion.'

'Midnight Mass at the Grafton Rooms, that's the only religion she knows.'

'And her kids. It doesn't look like they ever get a good wash.'

'And what's she do for a living? How does she support her kids?'

'There are ways and means. I've a good idea how she earns her pocket money,' Mother sniggered.

Frank, home on leave, added his admonition. 'Don't get too familiar with her. Don't keep going round there. You know what she is.'

He wore a white flash in his forage cap to show he'd been selected for aircrew training. They didn't want him for a pilot despite all the balsa-wood aeroplanes he'd made, so he was training to be an air gunner. He would eventually become a sergeant and his pay would be eight shillings and sixpence a day, with one and six danger money when he was flying, the price of twenty fags. The rough blue serge uniform, which sometimes made a man look an oaf – ill-fitting jacket, wrap-around trousers, perky forage cap – made Frank a man; he had the strength and hardness of a man, together with rugged male preoccupations. He answered questions laconically, implying that he knew more than he was allowed to tell, and he ate huge meals, all of our rations. He killed the chicken and it rapidly disappeared down his gullet. He had begun to smoke, Capstan Full Strength; smoke poured from his nostrils, carrying away all his Boy Scout uprightness. His body had grown heavier and thicker; he filled the house like Field Marshal Goering. I shook my head with pleased disillusion, for there was no doubt that service life had coarsened and corrupted him. I hoped Mother would be repelled, but the daft cow loved him more than ever. She and Maggie crouched beneath him with a gloating female submissiveness.

From my bedroom window I saw him in the street with Carol, then they turned a corner out of sight. He must have been warning her off me. But when next I saw her, all she said was, 'He's a bobby-dazzler, your big brother.'

She was teaching me to dance. She was always singing and dancing, the wireless was tuned permanently to the Forces Programme and she had gramophone records of Yankee dance bands, Glen Miller, Tommy Dorsey. 'Come on then!' she said. She held out her arms, I closed with her and we foxtrotted about the kitchen. I looked up into her eyes, into her teasing, ambiguous smile; I could feel the warmth of her body, the curve of her back beneath my hand. The tips of her breasts just touched my chest and something begin to stir inside me. What was happening? What was this great gross thing rising up in my groin? Embarrassed and confused, I arched myself acutely away from her. She let me go, laughing.

She sat opposite us in the shelter, an arm round each of her kids, smiling at me roguishly from time to time. The air raids usually began at around midnight and might last until dawn, though the bombing occupied only a fraction of that time. The bombers came in waves and each wave might last a quarter of an hour, fifteen minutes of heart-stopping terror and then a lull, followed by two or three further waves of bombing, followed by a longer, exhausted lull until the "All Clear" finally sounded. Some nights it was hours before anything happened, and people began to hope it was a false alarm. 'They're not coming for us tonight,' they said. Soon after we would hear guns firing in the distance, hesitantly at first and then rapidly, in a panic, like great dogs barking. People chattered nervously, cursing the war and the government. The warden asked them to be quiet and they told him to shut up; one man threatened to sock him on the jaw; we all hated the warden. Then everyone fell quiet, straining to listen. A few bombs fell, but the explosions seemed to be quite far away.

'Going for the docks,' a man said.

We softened with relief. The docks were miles away. But then out of nowhere and as though we were being punished for presumption, a stick of bombs fell close, exploding in a torrent of unearthly shrieks and bangs that seemed to swallow you.

'Going for the railway,' the man said.

'They'll go for the bleeden railway and get us!' a woman wailed.

We crouched in the gloom and the bangs swarmed about us, the enormous engulfing roar of high explosives, all the more terrible in the dark. Suddenly Carol got up, she glanced about wildly and began to sing. She went up and down the shelter, gesturing in her loving way, getting people to join her in the song. A number did so. I sang loudly out of loyalty: *There'll Always be an England, Wish me Luck as you Wave me*

Goodbye, There'll be Bluebirds over the White Cliffs of Dover. And Carol swinging her backside up and down the dim, crowded shelter while the air raid raged outside. 'Making a show of herself!' Mother muttered.

Neither she nor Maggie joined in the singing. But in the heightened perilous atmosphere, I loved Carol passionately and wished she was my mother. What fun we would have, how involved with each other, what heartbreak she would cause me!

There was a lull, the bombers droned away, the guns were silent. Carol returned to her seat and everyone sat very still with their heads bowed as though they were thinking deeply; mothers hugged their children and whispered to them; a couple of pale-faced girls sat holding hands. I thought of Benny crouched under the stairs with his father. Eventually, the "All Clear" sounded and we got up, yawned and stretched, smiling at one another. We were proud to have been bombed.

The next morning there was shrapnel to collect, and it was strange to discover these spent fragments of the night's raid, these relics of danger. Truants from school, we moved slowly along the gutter, eyes downcast, stooping every so often and seizing a prize. Some of the shrapnel might have been pieces of bombs or bombers, but mostly they were bits of anti-aircraft shells that had exploded high in the night sky.

'Imagine,' Smidger said, holding a sliver as sharp as a dagger, 'one a these comes whizzen down, dongs into your skull and shoots outta your bum!'

Benny never joined me in this pursuit, he found it distasteful. But I loved the shrapnel. It was gold and silver, it was barbaric jewellery. I patrolled the gutter of a morning after a raid when the sky seemed ashen from the night before, rapt with the excitement of the search. Some pieces were scarcely an inch long, the biggest was hardly more than six inches, but all were heavy for their size. They were of steel nearly an inch thick, dull silver in colour and often incised with lines. Beneath the surface the metal was grey or brown and tightly clenched into itself. Some pieces were stilettos or Palaeolithic axe-heads, some were tiny gods or demons of fierce iron. If I was lucky I might find five or six pieces, which I'd stuff into my pocket, tearing the lining; other times I returned home empty-handed. Any shrapnel I found was cleaned and polished carefully, and I was saddened when one or two pieces were so hopelessly rusted they had to be discarded. The rest I wrapped in tissue paper and laid them in a box that had once contained Ballito fully fashioned stockings.

In the first week of May, Liverpool was raided every night and nearly 2000 were killed, twenty ships were sunk at the dockside and many houses were destroyed. The morning after the first raid, I sought out Benny and chided him for not coming to the shelter. It was foolhardy. Surely he could conquer his claustrophobia in order to save his life? And what would happen to his immortal soul if he was killed? It troubled me. The consequences were serious if you died an atheist.

'I'll bet you've never even been inside a church, have you?' I said, seized with a sudden idea. If I could just get him inside a church and in the presence of God, a miracle conversion might occur. 'I just happen to be going along there myself,' I lied. 'Why not step along a-ways with me, pardner?'

'You want me to go to church with you?' He smiled incredulously.

'Just to see what it's like inside. You're not scared, are you?'

'What is there to be scared of?'

'God.'

'You've got God in your church? Where do you keep Him?'

'Why not come along and see?'

He shrugged and accompanied me to church like humouring a child. A late Mass was in progress and the church was half full. The priest droned his Latin, the congregation coughed and shuffled in the dimness of the nave. We entered a pew and knelt down, Benny wryly accommodating himself to the unnatural position. He seemed interested in the altar, the candles, the priest's vestments and the nature of the congregation.

'Well?' I enquired, when we left at the end.

'Sociologically interesting,' he conceded. He was alert, smiling, intellectually intrigued. 'I may specialise in the sociology of religion, after university. Like Durkheim, you know. The whole business of ritual and belief interests me.'

'Anyway, will you be coming to the shelter tonight?'

'I think not. It seems somewhat cowardly.'

'Cowardly!'

'Let the blighters do their worst, is what I say!'

'Well, look, the thing is …'

'What?'

'Just in case you're in – you know, in danger; there's a prayer you can say.'

'You want me to say a prayer?'

'It's called *A Short Act of Contrition,* and if you say it in an emergency, it wipes away all your sins.'

'Really? You're sure of that, are you?'

'What you say is, Oh my God, because Thou art so good –'

'– art so good. I see.'

'– I am very sorry that I have sinned against Thee and by the help of Thy grace I will not sin again.'

'And I'm to remember all this?'

'I've written it out for you.'

He accepted gravely the folded slip of paper I offered. 'And what exactly will happen if I'm dying and I say this? Will I be whipped straight up to Heaven?'

'You have to say it as though you really meant it.'

'Rather difficult, that, I'm afraid. And if I'm only to say it at the point of death, what's the point of promising not to sin again?'

I crouched in the shelter with Mother and Maggie, our hearts sinking into a weary depression when we heard the bombers overhead, the droning rise and fall of their engines, the dreadful unflagging persistence of their approach. They were coming for us, they were searching us out, stealthily feeling their way across the night sky, absently evading searchlight beams, the flak popping harmlessly about them. The bomber crews were not distracted, they sat at their stations: pilot, navigator, bomb aimer. They murmured to each other in German, precise observations and instructions. They had a deadly Nazi calm about them, born of contempt for inferior nations. And it was all enacted in darkness. They flew in the night; we huddled in the dark below.

Carol got up as before and began a song:

'Who does she think she is?' Maggie muttered. 'Gracie Fields?'

But no one felt like singing and she sat down again. Then the bombs began to fall, the screeching, tearing noise of their descent like an express train howling through the dark, a huge heavy train hurtling down upon your head – for the noise seemed to extend the bomb as though it was the length of its noise – a dreadful iron mass making for you, packed with explosives. There was a startling, heart-stopping

BANG! and then the roaring, slithering crash of masonry collapsing. How many in the shelter were wetting their kecks? I was. And praying hysterically. If there was a direct hit on the shelter, it wouldn't blow everyone apart but would fuse us all together, body meeting body and all crushed in a hideous sticky mess – a nauseating mass of compressed flesh, bruised and bloodied, all identity obliterated.

There was a lull in the raid, the firing of the guns faltered uncertainly and you could hear the alarm bells of fire-engines, the screech of an ambulance, blasts of a warden's whistle. Searchlights scanned the night, glanced off the silver skins of barrage balloons, found nothing. Was the raid over? Or was another wave to be expected? We prayed for the lull to continue, straining with all our might, as though it was possible to prolong the lull by sheer willpower. We were huddled and intent, gripping the silence with our wills and holding it fast, determined not to let go.

Eventually I let go, fell asleep and awoke suddenly into a nightmare, to bombers overhead and desperate gunfire. People prayed aloud as a stick of bombs fell close, seemingly on top of us, BANG! and BANG! and BANG! A torrid blast shook the shelter and there was panic. People got to their feet and ran about, unable to stay still, desperate to leave the shelter, fearing they were trapped. 'That's our house!' they cried as BANG! and a BANG! 'They've got our house!'

A Civil Defence worker entered and spoke to the warden.

'What is it?' people cried. 'What's he tellen you?'

The warden looked grave. He said some houses in the backstreet had been bombed.

'Oh, Jesus, Mary and Joseph!' a woman cried.

No one dared leave while the bombing continued, but as soon as it stopped, some people barged out of the shelter, seeking their homes. Maggie asked the warden whether our house had been bombed; he thought not. We left the shelter as the "All Clear" sounded. The sky was ruddy with flames and there was the alarming smell of smoke. Fire engines raced past, headlights dimmed, bells ringing wildly.

'Thank God, it's still standing,' Mother muttered, fumbling for her front-door key.

We entered the house and Maggie switched on her torch, afraid to switch on the electric light until she knew the blackout was secure. The serious damage was at the back of the house. All the windows had been shattered, the glass driven like daggers into the furniture; many slates had been torn from the roof and a chimney pot had been flung down into the yard.

'Oh, look at all my lovely furniture!' Mother wailed, as Maggie moved the torch beam from one piece to another – the new easychairs shattered, the new dresser pierced with shards of glass, the table sagging on broken legs. Pictures had been snatched off the wall and lay smashed on the floor – Our Lady of Lourdes; the Sacred Heart. An enemy had broken in and destroyed whatever he could lay hands on.

'Oh, they've even broken that lovely vase I got for a wedding present!'

Mother's face ran with tears and I longed to comfort her. But how ... how was I to do that? Pretentiousness got the better of me and I chanted solemnly, 'The war giveth and the war taketh away.'

'Oh, don't be so damned stupid,' she said.

I hurried into the backyard, flaming with embarrassment and misery. Why could I never get anything right with her? I ran along the entry. In the backstreet, many of the houses had been reduced to heaps of rubble. It was as though half the street had been lifted high in the air then slammed down concussively, scattering its contents, knocking houses aside, bending lamp posts, uprooting the pavement. Upper rooms had been torn away from walls that nevertheless remained standing, a fireplace and rags of wallpaper clinging to them. Glass and broken slates littered the roadway, bricks and spars of wood; water leaked from a burst drain and there were fragments of charred paper everywhere. An ARP warden, steel helmet pushed back on her head, face smeared with dirt, sought to comfort an old woman who sat on the kerbstone clutching herself and rocking back and forth. Further down the street, a body was being carried into an ambulance. Civil Defence workers were clambering over the wreckage; firemen were putting out fires still alight.

Although I guessed at once that Benny was dead, I searched for him – muttering, crying, shaking my head – among the huddled groups of people standing about, some with bits of belongings they had managed to salvage. His house was a heap of smouldering bricks, out of which a few floorboards jutted upwards. How could anyone have survived? Yet the rescue workers persisted with their search, picking away at the bricks with their hands, clearing a space and calling down into it – 'Hello? Anyone down there?'

Benny's father stood outside the bombed house, draped with a blanket; his arm was in a sling, his face was smeared with blood and grime, and there was white dust in his stiff, dark hair. He stared at me without recognising me. He had been scrabbling desperately at the wreckage, calling his son's name, until pulled away. Neighbours clustered about him, trying to comfort him, forgetting they had once despised him; but he was not aware of them, his face as of stone. He and Benny had been in the house together, sheltering beneath the stairs; the bomb had dropped just as he had left to go to the toilet, the blast hurling him clear of the house. Some of his clothes had been blown off and he had fallen badly, breaking his arm. Otherwise, he was unharmed.

Benny had been killed, but I had been spared. The revelation poured over me. Had the bomb-aimer released his bombs a quarter of a second sooner, they would have fallen on the shelter, killing us all. But I had been spared; the Angel of Death had passed over me and killed others, Jordan among them. From this point I began to believe that a special destiny awaited me.

Maggie came and took me away. 'Was it your pal? Ah, the poor lad!'

But when we reached home, I broke away and went to Carol next door. She was in the furthest reaches of the basement putting her children to bed. We met in the dark passageway, I told her of Benny and she took me in her arms, holding me close to her soft, warm body while I wept. Then she sent me home: 'Your Mam needs you.'

I joined Mother and Maggie in the shattered house. There was no electricity, but the gas was functioning and Maggie was making a pot of tea while Mother sat helpless, moaning about her ruined furniture. When we had drunk the tea – Maggie forcing it into Mother between her sobs – we went to bed, shaking window glass from the bedclothes.

Late the following day, Father Doonan called to offer his priestly comfort, the wisdom of a God who had spared the righteous while smiting the ungodly. I asked him about Benny and whether there was any hope ... His heavy Irish face grew solemn. He knew of the family, the communist father, and he held out little hope for the poor lad. Even had he managed, in the agony of death, to stammer the Short Act of Contrition I had passed to him, would it work for a non-Catholic? What about Limbo, I suggested, the compromise between Heaven and Hell? But the priest, weirdly pedantic, pointed out that Limbo could only be defined as *limbus patrum*, the state from which Christ had released the souls of Old Testament worthies, or *limbus infantium*, reserved for the souls of mental defectives and unborn babies. There was no arrangement for atheists, however sincere. Indeed, the more sincere, the more surely damned.

'My thoughts are with the poor father,' he went on. 'I shall remember him in my prayers.'

I felt sick and dizzy, my mind drawn up to where God reared huge and terrible like a fixed sheet of lighting charged with inconceivable power; something altogether beyond the human. It had scornfully swatted poor Benny aside and, in the process, punished his father for his absurd atheism. I thought of Mr Golding standing outside his ruined house, his face as of stone. How terrible to be denied the consolation of religion at such a time, denied the comfort of believing his son was with God! How feeble the insolence of atheism confronted by the sudden, thundering power of death! And Hell, there really was something called Hell, a place of perpetual darkness and unceasing anguish, indescribable torment. Though God's infinite mercy must never be doubted, Divine Justice was implacable; there were rules and they must be obeyed; there was one God, a Catholic God, and one must believe in Him, obey Him, love Him, and beg His forgiveness.

I was evacuated again, to the green peace of Wales and its mountains, calm forests, stony brooks, banks of wild flowers, fields jumping with white lambs. But I went unwillingly, reluctant to leave Liverpool. I was homesick for the war; I wanted to be with the others in the shelter, sharing their terror, an experience that nevertheless glittered with pride and defiance. I missed Carol and eventually wrote her a passionate letter, telling her how I admired her, praising her cheerleader singing in the shelter and the zest and love with which she met each day, the bold freedom of her existence. I wrote at length and with surprising ease, the words piling up in my pen and flowing on to the page. I waited anxiously for a reply but none ever came, and before long I was cursing her for a heartless slut. She did not care for me, she had never cared for me, she was simply amusing herself with me! When a parcel came from Mother containing a cake and a bar of chocolate, a pair of socks and *Tom Brown's Schooldays*, my feelings somersaulted and I wept over the letter she enclosed, her ungainly handwriting and grammatical uncertainty:

> We are getting along alright, keeping our chin up and slowly getting things back to normal, the windows and the roof patched up ect. But of course I miss my little son and only wish we had been closer and done more things together while you were here.

My poor mother with only Maggie to keep her company, most of the time! I thought of her heartbreak the night of the air raid, the destruction of her lovely new furniture, which had meant so much to her; and my crass comment, 'The Lord giveth …' I had always been such a disappointment to her. I had never appreciated her goodness to me, the muffled love that had shown itself in daily care since the day I was born. Had she been present at that moment, I would have rushed into her arms and we would have loved each other at last and for the rest of our lives.

I was continually unhappy, homesick, mourning Benny and profoundly confused about God, horrified by death. Although the countryside was refreshing, the village to which I'd been evacuated was a dull huddle of mean houses beneath a great quarry cut into a hill. I had been placed in the care of a fat, young woman and her lean, hard husband, a quarryman. Foster parents, they called them. They took me for the money, half a guinea a week from the government. They had a yowling baby and I was expected to mind it, pushing the thing in its pram. The school was little more than a shack and I knew all the long-division sums on the blackboard, I'd stared at them for years in previous schools, too bored and frustrated to bother getting them right. There was little to read; there wasn't a public library and there were no books in the house – 'Make your eyes bad, reading,' my foster father said. Village culture was a tin chapel and a pub. The couple often went to the pub, leaving me to mind the baby while they were out.

I hated the woman especially, her swollen legs and gross belly, the loose fat that hung from her upper arms; I feared her slovenly drawl, occasionally followed by a casual clout across the head. She and her husband sometimes argued when they got back from the pub, and in my bedroom in the cramped council house I would hear their raised voices and then perhaps a thump and a cry as the man whacked her, burying his fist in her fat gut. Give her one! I thought viciously. Give her another!

The winter was cold, the country was deep in snow. We plodded to school, the snow coming in over the tops of our wellingtons. In the woods, snow clung crystalline to black branches, the mountain was a white mass, icicles hung from rocks in the brook. I stood in a winter's dusk in an immense silence, skeletal trees black against a pearly sunset. Ah, what was that ... beauty? I felt like crying. I had been in a sombre mood for weeks, brooding over Benny's death and contemplating God – not in any pious sense, but with profound unease.

There were more raids on Liverpool. 'It'll clear all your slums away, anyhow,' the quarryman consoled me. 'That's where you come from, the slums, isn't it? Must be where you learned to wet the bed.'

Mother came to see me. She brought chocolate biscuits which I devoured at once, fearful lest my foster mother gobbled them. I had not seen her for months and she had grown old in the interval, harassed with anxiety for Frank, for Dad away at sea and for Jessie flaunting herself on the London stage. I wished there was something I could do to cheer her. To get away from the house, I took her to a neighbouring wood, a favourite place of mine. After walking for a while, we sat on a fallen tree trunk and she asked how I was. I poured out my complaints, exaggerating for good measure; I begged to be taken home, but she did not seem to be listening. Her face was wan and listless; I feared disaster. Me dad. Was me dad all right?

'As far as I know. It's your damn brother!' she burst out.

Frank? Had something happened to Frank?

'It seems,' she said, looking away along an avenue of trees, 'he no longer wants to be a priest.'

I could have told her that, years ago.

'Now he's in the air force, all he wants is to get flying. He wrote and told me he's lost his vocation. So he won't be going to be a priest after all – if he ever really meant to! I've sometimes thought he never really meant it. But of course I believed him, and told everyone he was going to be a priest. What are they going to think of me now? Your Auntie

Lizzie and Auntie Florrie, Father Doonan and all my friends. I'll be the laughing stock.'

'I'll go,' I said.

'What do you mean?'

'I'll go in his place.'

'You?' She gave a slighting laugh.

'I've always wanted to be a priest.'

It seemed incredible, but she gradually grew used to the idea. It wasn't as ridiculous as it had seemed at first, and it would save her face with Father Doonan and the nuns at the Cenacle convent, not to mention the ladies of the Mothers' Union. By the time she was ready to return to Liverpool, it was settled that I would become a priest. At least it'll get me away from these buggers, I thought, for she had agreed to take me home with her. That was part of the bargain.

My foster mother objected, fearing the loss of money. 'You can't do that, it's against the law.'

She was bigger and younger than Mother; but Mother wasn't a coward and life had hardened her. In any case, she had always contemned the Welsh. 'He's my son and I can do what I like with him.'

It was past midnight when we got home. The house had been shakily put together again after the bombing: the roof had been repaired, the chimney pot replaced, windows had been glazed or boarded up, and hundreds of bits of glass had been removed from the furniture. Maggie was already in bed and Mother did not wake her. She made some cocoa and fixed me a thick sandwich, half the cheese ration. We sat at the kitchen table and she gazed at me, shaking her head wonderingly. 'You're a good lad. I never would have dreamed ... But you must be sure you've really got a vocation, y'know. Don't just say it to please me. Once you've decided, there's no turning back.'

'I'm sure,' I reiterated.

I wasn't sure, but how could I admit that now? What mattered was that I had gained her love, she was proud of me, I had saved her from despair. In the days that followed I said nothing more about becoming a priest, hoping she would forget about it. But she broadcast the news at once, telling everyone, blithely trapping me within a bristling fence of public expectation. Jessie, home for a visit with a parcel of black market delicacies, was amused and faintly incredulous; but Maggie was pleased. For years she had been praying that I might become a priest. 'I always fancied you for a vocation rather than our Frank. He's too big-headed, whereas you've always had a thoughtful look. God has chosen you, Peter. Isn't it exciting!'

Dad didn't like the idea. 'What's he wanna to be a priest for? You've been getting at him, havven you? I thought your darling Frank was going to be the Holy Father?'

He appealed to me when we were alone: 'D'you really want to go, son? It's a big decision, y'know.'

But whenever people doubted the sincerity of my call from God, I was obliged to defend it as though they had impugned my courage and honesty. Also I enjoyed the attention it aroused. I had always felt myself to be different, and the interest people now took in me seemed to confirm it. Mother was proud of me, I had become a charmed object in her eyes, a boy dedicated to God. She refrained from pressing me on the subject, however, in case I changed my mind. She showed me off to the ladies of the Mothers' Union – my big son, the future priest!' – made sure I got the best of the rations and bought me new clothes, whatever could be found in the shops for clothes coupons. It was like embellishing a noble victim chosen for sacrifice. I had her love now, as much as I had ever wanted: but had I purchased it at too great a price? In any case, her love was no more than borrowed; I would soon be gone from her and my career as a priest would inevitably put a distance between us. There was also the thought that, because of our relative worth, she could more easily sacrifice me than she could Frank. Maybe she was even thankful to be rid of me, by means that flattered her Catholic devoutness. Such suspicions never ceased to plague me.

I had looked for Carol and her kids as soon as I returned from Wales, but they no longer lived next door. When I asked what had happened to them, Maggie and Mother smiled a shared joke.

'Your girlfriend has skedaddled,' Maggie said.

'She's done a flit. Left owing money everywhere.'

'She took her kids with her, thank God, so they won't be cluttering up the place no more.'

'I told you she was no good,' Mother said. 'Seems she even robbed the gas meter before she left. No one knows where she's gone, but you'll never see her again, that's for sure.'

Chapter Two

Father Doonan had found a seminary that might take me; it was run by a missionary order and one of its priests travelled from Richmond in Yorkshire to meet me. 'I am called Father Kirsten.'

He had been a missionary for some years in Africa. He was jovial, weathered and tough – the kind of priest who might have accompanied Allan Quatermain to King Solomon's Mines. He told me of the seminary. 'It is a nice place, very nice. In the heart of the country, you know. Very nice. Look, I show you. I have here some photographs. Here is the house. We call it the 'House', though, as you can see, it is really a castle! And here are some of the boys enjoying themselves.'

'Zuh boys enchoying zemselves.' He was a foreigner.

The boys appeared to be laughing at some sally their priest of a teacher must have made; they were in a classroom with large windows open to a sunny day. In other photographs they were bowed over their desks in a study period, then one saw them sitting at long tables in the refectory, a large bright room, the same sunny day, the boys gazing rapturously at what seemed a good pile of grub. They were shown walking in the extensive grounds of the castle, and also playing football and cricket.

'Our boys work hard, but also they enjoy themselves, as you can see.'

Such boys, if they had what it took to become a priest, and it took hard work and not a few sacrifices, ultimately became servants of God in the missionary field. As such, they wore white tropical cassocks and pith helmets. One photograph showed a priest, cassock tucked up, riding a motorbike; in another he was surrounded by black kids, all grinning. Father Kirsten appeared in some of the photographs, a commanding figure in tropical gear. In one particular photograph he was directing some blacks in the construction of a large wooden shack –'You know, when you go to a new station, at first there is nothing, so you have to build your own church!' In another, he was cheerfully spooning medicine into an assortment of natives, all of them grinning gratefully.

I began to believe I had a vocation after all. Previously, the prospect of a priest's life had been vague and dull, largely taken up with saying Mass, visiting the sick and consoling the dying – not a career likely to attract a lively lad. But that was the life of a parish priest, and I was to be a missionary, one of God's elite warriors, living in the wilds of the Dark Continent, wearing a pith helmet, riding a motorbike, courting danger and gaining the love of hundreds of blacks, who wanted nothing better than to be baptised and made members of the church.

Father Kirsten spoke of his role at the seminary. 'I am what they call in Hollywood a talent scout. Yeah, sure! I have been to Hollywood, you know. Oh, I am not a film star! But the bishop took me to Paramount Studios and I shook the hand of Bing Crosby. That's so! Bing Crosby himself. We are looking,' he continued, 'for that special boy whom Almighty God may have called to the priesthood. There are very few of them; even those who are chosen, do not always stay the course. It has to be a very special kind of boy. I am not speaking of a little holy-holy, you understand. It does not have to be a boy who is always going round, you know – ' Fr Kirsten parodied a little holy-holy with prayer-joined hands, eyes lowered reverently. I laughed politely. 'No. The boy is often what you call a regular guy. He gets into scrapes perhaps, he has fights sometimes, he may even run wild. Tom Sawyer. He loves to play games, loves his parents; he even loves God! This boy is something of a leader among boys, and he is a clever lad. It is not with him all play and no work. He is intelligent, he loves to study. And he is a boy who may be troubled by deep thoughts – How and why the universe was created. For what are we put upon this earth? These are the thoughts such a boy might have. He seeks answers. He wants to change the world for God. He wants peace on earth, and justice for all; the tyrant to be humbled, the sick and lonely to be comforted, and everyone brought to the knowledge and blessings of Our Lord Jesus Christ through His Holy Catholic Church.'

I was thinking of the seminary (a fucken castle!), the large bright classrooms, the boys bent over their books in the study period or playing cricket, their white flannels gleaming in sunlight. I seemed to hear their voices: 'Oh, well bowled!'...'I say, you chaps, the tuck shop's open.'...'What was it Old Stinks was chunnering on about in Chemistry?' Could I be one of them? Was I a leader among boys, intelligent and resourceful, not a little holy-holy, sometimes getting into scrapes but always honestly owning up? I thought of myself as a missionary in a white cassock and a pith helmet, riding a motorbike through the jungle, administering medical care to sick and destitute natives, a white man surrounded by adoring blacks. There was also the point that in entering the seminary I would leave behind the wartime world, the grubby backstreets, the backstreet mind, escaping into a secure, superior world of study and play, my life dedicated to the austerity of a noble calling. Was this what my life had been spared for? As a priest I could also, I thought somewhat confusedly, pray and say Mass for Benny's imperilled soul.

Father Kirsten had spoken of God's Plan. God had a plan for everyone, and mine was perhaps to become a priest. I was taken with the idea; it had never struck me before, despite its obvious truth. Everyone and everything was a part of God's plan for the world. Nothing was accidental, everything had purpose and meaning. You might think you were thinking for yourself, but you were really being thought, with every event conspiring to shape your life to some God-ordained end. Although it might seem restrictive, there was the great advantage of knowing that your life was significant and meaningful. God was aware of you, He had your best interests at heart, a destiny that figured both in this world and in the next.

Nevertheless, once Father Kirsten had gone, taking much of the romance of missionary work with him, it was sometimes difficult to reconcile myself to God's Plan, for whenever I dared to think seriously about it, I was seized with doubts and sought the convenient conviction that I was not worthy of the priesthood.

'That is what the best of us might feel,' Father Doonan said, 'when facing the choice between this fallen world and the glory of God's service; and it's a good sign ... a good sign; it shows you have the right humility.'

An examination was arranged for prospective candidates, which I passed easily, all part of God's Plan. Then I found myself bound in a social straitjacket fashioned by the desires of others, and I was unable to move to save myself. Though specific advantages awaited me – I would be living a jolly boarding-school life and would get a good education – I still feared at times that I was making a mistake. But what could I do about it? Was I to tell Mother and break her heart? She had told everyone that her youngest was to become a priest, and I couldn't let her down. I was trapped in an implacable social process, reinforced by my own timidity and uncertainty, and there seemed no escape.

I had finally succeeded in impressing Frank and he was full of encouragement. 'Mother's so pleased, she's really proud of you. And I can see now that you're much more spiritual than I ever was. You'll make a much better priest than I ever would. All I'm fit for is squatting in a rear turret, shooting down Jerry!'

Many kids had returned from evacuation and the school had reopened. It was towards the end of the term and everyone was bored and restless, including the teacher, who sometimes relieved his boredom by thrashing us with a leather strap, a short thuggish thing stiffened, they said, with whalebone. I strove to enliven the boredom with my skill as an entertainer. In a backstreet gang you could either be a bully or a buffoon, a leader or a wanker, a good mate or an entertainer. I would have preferred to be accepted as an intellectual, but that was out of the question and I became an entertainer; at least it allowed me to exercise ingenuity, and when I let myself go I could amuse my pals with a variety of antics, comic voices, goofy walks and hideous faces, together with a hilarious line in mimicry. I often performed in class while the teacher's back was turned, provoking sniggers and muffled guffaws that caused him to turn abruptly and fling the board duster at me.

There was a gang of boys who were leaving that year, the sort any school is glad to be rid of. You know the sort of article, all brawn and no brain. They hung round the dustbins and sacks of salvage in the playground, smoking and sometimes drinking if they'd found a bottle in a bombed-out house: big tough louts, talking and sniggering, fucking and blinding, full of lewd tales. I was scared of them, but also fascinated. They had hair-raising tales of the air raids.

'Der was dis one I heard,' one said, and they would all gather close, their shaggy heads bowed, thoughtfully digging the stubby toes of their rubber wellingtons into the asphalt. 'Seems like der was this vicarage got hit, like. A vicarage, gorra direct hit. An when the ARP gets der, they found the owl vicar all right; he was sitten der, cuppa tea in his hand an his fucken head blown off!'

The gang reeled about, helpless with laughter, whimpering, 'Fucken head blown off!' and 'Cuppa tea!' Then they came together for the rest of the story.

'But when they cum to look for his missus, like, cudden fucken find her anywhere! Den one a them, one a the ARP, looks up and der she is – embedded in the ceiling! Blown up by the blast an embedded in the fucken ceiling in her nightie, fat tits dangling down an her hairy old cunt winken its eye at you!'

'One I heard,' another said while the gang were still wiping tears of merriment from their eyes, 'der was this aerial torpedo – a aerial torpedo dropped by a bomber an it ripped through three cellars, three fucken cellars, before it got to dis one, where there was like about twenny people, all sheltering. Then it blew up; killed the fucken lot!'

'An wharra bout,' a third offered, 'that feller an his tart, like, in a doorway; musta been havven a feel, maybe a stand-up shag; then this bomb bursts an the blast, the blast, like, glued em together! They cudden get em apart; the bodies was like melted into each udda, an they hadda bury them that way.' And again the grotesque blossom of shaggy heads reeled apart, spluttering in hilarity, arms gesturing wildly, one youth stooped over and coughing laughter, another grimacing helplessly with mirth.

I exorcised my appalled fascination by mimicking the gang to my mates; I had their voices and mannerisms off perfectly. 'Der was dis vicar, see, dis vicar!' I would say, making apish gestures, all hunched up and lumbering about, grimacing and grunting, spewing laughter, my shaggy head bent.

Unfortunately, someone gave me away; an enemy told the gang of my mockery and they cornered me after school. There were four of them; big, strong fuckers. I was terrified. Many convenient murders must have been carried out during the war, the body buried in the ruins of a bombed-out house, only later discovered and assumed to be the victim of an air raid. And these lads knew their way about bombed-out houses; they were the first out of the shelter after a raid, foraging among the rubble for loot.

They surrounded me, their snarling faces and tangled hair, stink of Woodbines, clothing matted with dirt. Their viciousness and stupidity made me feel I was a delicate and intelligent youth, sensitive and civilised, menaced by grunting, squinting Neanderthals. They drove me back across the playground until they had me in their favourite lair by the dustbins.

'Ahr, ey, look, fellers,' I faltered. 'I've got to get home ...'

But what did they care? A cosy, loving home was not in their experience. One of them pushed me and I fell back against the dustbins. Another thrust his face in my face: 'You bin making fun of us, la.'

The others joined in: 'Make fun of us now!'

'Go on, whack, give us a show.'

'You're a birrava comedian, aren't you?'

'Give us a show now,' they chorused.

They wanted me to perform my artistry here, on the spot, among the dustbins? All I could think of was escape, and it made me a blubbering coward. 'Ahr, ey, fellers, let me go, please! I won't do it again, I promise. I'm sorry!'

Yet even at this abject moment an observer within, cool and detached, deplored and despised my moral collapse.

'Ahr, come on,' one of them said, growing bored. 'Let's go. The caretaker'll be along in a minute. Give him a good hiding and let's scram.'

'Break his arm!'

'Shit in his gob!'

'Tie his dick in a knot!'

Excited, they pressed close, laying their hands upon me. It was loathsome, I felt hot and sick, the hideousness of their hands mauling me, their snuffling laughter as they bore me back upon the dustbins; and someone, who was presumably myself, shrieking and wailing, begging for mercy.

'I gorra better idea,' one of them said. 'Grab 'is kecks.'

'Yeah, grab 'is kecks!'

They closed upon me; their terrible, knowledgeable hands searched me; they raised me aloft to snorting guffaws. Someone ripped at my braces and removed my short pants. My body writhed desperately while they fingered my dick, my bottom. My eyes blotted with tears and someone, some little boy with a broken voice, was wailing pitifully.

Then suddenly they were gone. Or was it that I had fainted and was not aware of their departure? I was alone, flung among the dustbins; the evening was growing dark and I was without my pants. They had taken my pants away and I had no underpants; nothing but the skimpy tail of a shirt to cover me. I was shamefully naked and what was I to do? How could I get home?

The caretaker, locking up, found me and found my kecks hanging from a nearby lamp post. I seethed with shame and self-pity, struggling into my pants, hating the gang. Thank God, I would soon be rid of them all, all the stupid, lumbering brutes of the backstreets. I would be gone from them forever.

CHAPTER THREE

The seminary had some admirable features, but sooner or later these shrank and disappeared behind the black serge of Father Prefect's cassock. He was in charge, he dominated our lives and we hated him.

He was German; the priests were mostly German; it was a German order. That was strange. After all, we were fighting the Germans ... Although the seminary had been established in England for some years, the priests had been rounded up at the start of the war and interned in the Isle of Man. Because they were German and despite being released as harmless aliens, they were still regarded with suspicion by those locals who were not Catholic: They might be priests, but they're still bloody Germans! However, the seminary could survive without local support; it was virtually self-sufficient, most of its needs being supplied by a farm that was part of the estate. Some boys were sent to work on the farm of a Saturday afternoon – it was either that or cleaning the house from top to bottom – and it wasn't long before I found myself gathering spuds in a muddy field on a leaden, autumn day, hastily scrabbling them into a bucket while a tractor turned at the end of the row and approached once more, remorselessly unearthing another row.

'We're just their slaves,' Rennet moaned.

It was cold, the gritty spuds raised segs on my hands and the bucket was arm-yankingly heavy. The farm work was supervised by lay brothers, whose labour maintained the seminary. We thought of them as failed priests. They, too, were German, their peasant profiles proclaiming a knobby innocence. There were also a few nuns, who cooked and did the laundry, heavy-bodied women with wimpled faces that had long since abandoned femininity.

We lived in a castle, but it lacked pedigree. It was a nineteenth-century reproduction owned by a stockbroker who had bequeathed it to the order on his death. Approaching the entrance you were faced and questioned by a high wall that marched away on either side of formidable stone gateposts. The gates themselves had gone, they were now probably part of a battleship, yet they remained in principle, firmly shut to the outside world. Beyond the entrance a drive swept through extensive grounds to the castle, referred to as the "House". It was three stories high, battlemented in places and furnished with sundry turrets for defence, but it was difficult to comprehend as a unit and doubtful whether any boy had ever done so, for we were not allowed to linger at the front, it was out of bounds. Why?

'It's because,' Rennet said, 'once you're at the front, you might be tempted to escape down the drive.'

It was sickening the way he was always talking of escape, the sneaking levity with which he referred to the seminary and the priesthood. If he didn't want to be here, why did he stay?

'He can't take it,' Jim Kapowski said.

My friends despised Rennet because he couldn't take it.

'He's a weasel,' Simon Parker said. 'Those weaselly front teeth of his.'

Clearly, Rennet had not been chosen by God.

The castle's entrance hall was imposing and the rooms on the first two floors were spacious and well lit, their ceilings were high and handsome, their windows of noble proportions. The boys' dormitories were on the third floor where the ceilings were low and the windows no more than utilitarian. It was where the servants had once slept and it had not featured in Fr Kirsten's photographs.

We couldn't leave the seminary grounds, Richmond was out of bounds except for escorted visits, and we went home only once in a year, when the priests reluctantly set us free for a few weeks in the summer. There was an airfield nearby and we often heard bombers on their way to Germany, where most of the priests' relatives still lived. We were in bed when the bombers passed overhead, but I sometimes stayed awake to hear them, thinking of Frank crouched in his gun turret, saying a prayer for him. Then I would fall asleep, only to be jerked awake at half past six by Father Prefect's terrible bell. It was a brassy handbell, which he swung vigorously while striding from one dormitory to another – Ga-dang! Ga-dang! – his glasses shifting in a humourless grin, his ruddy face blazing between his black cassock and the black, winged biretta planted firmly on his head – Danga-danga-dang! Danga-dang! It was an image that would stay with me for the rest of my life and it was two-dimensional; I could not imagine the sort of man that might exist beneath his Father Prefect persona. Perhaps there was no one beneath. Perhaps he was Father Prefect through and through, his individuality petrified into a function. The Boss, we called him. Father Superior was head of the seminary, but we rarely saw him. It was the Boss who mattered.

You had to get up the moment the bell rang – it was like leaping out of bed at the clamour of an air raid siren – no one ever stayed in bed long enough for Father Prefect to catch him. I would slump down on my knees, gabble a prayer then make for the washbasins in the corridor outside, to wash in icy water. At first, horrified, I scarcely dipped my fingers in the water, smearing damp hands over my face. But it was impossible to deceive Father Prefect; that was the one great lesson one learned at the seminary: like God, the Boss would always find you out. Every morning after early Mass we had to stand in line, stomachs churning with fear and hunger, while he examined first our held-out hands and then – heads bowed submissively – our necks. When I was caught with an unwashed neck, he marched me to the showers and stood guard while I undressed and took a cold shower, the water shrieking its iciness down upon me.

After you were washed and dressed, and before you went down to Mass in the chapel, you had to make your bed, and this was a further cause for anxiety. If you had not made your bed as Father Prefect had taught you during your first week – blankets tucked in tightly, sheet turned over precisely twelve inches, pillow smooth and stationed exactly at the head – you would find when you returned to the dormitory that he had made his rounds, had spied a fault and hurled the bedding in a heap. You were then obliged to make your bed all over again, fretting in case it still failed to meet his exacting standards. Sometimes, a bed that had been remade was turned over yet again, the culprit quivering with fear as he made his bed for the third time while his companions stood about, making jokes.

The first time my bed was assaulted, I gazed at the wreckage appalled. I thought I had made it correctly, but the Boss had passed like God in a whirlwind and had wrathfully torn it up. My poor bed was devastated, and the debris – swirled blankets, ravelled sheets – suggested a fearful tornado of anger, even hatred. That blazing, ruddy face above the white dog collar – did Father Prefect hate me, hate us all?

There were never more than fifty boys at the seminary; every year some returned to the world, gleeful rejects, while five or six new boys appeared in their place; and it was these who were Father Prefect's especial prey. We were viewed as ignorant, unruly urchins it was his duty to discipline – though he preferred self-discipline. 'Self-control!' he was constantly hissing at us, 'self-control!', which made you think the whole tormenting exercise was essentially designed to vanquish the sin of self-abuse. Those boys who had survived several years of his regime and no longer provoked his wrath had become his collaborators. 'His Gestapo,' Rennet said. They were prefects who spent much of their time keeping order among the younger boys and inscribing their misdemeanours in a notebook, which they presented to the Boss once a week.

In the refectory, the younger boys sat at two long tables running the length of the room; the senior boys, and four novices in their black cassocks (they had taken minor orders after some years at the seminary) occupied a table running the width of the rear wall. Friday was a day of fasting; for supper there was nothing but a bowl of pea soup (good thick stuff, however) a chunk of bread and a glass of water; and it was after this repast that Father Prefect would open the prefects' notebooks and proclaim everyone's wrongdoing during the week – the breaking of one or another of the rules set down in the Rule Book every new boy had been given. Everyone had his face raised to Father Prefect as he read the charges: 'James Kapowski, talking in the corridor; Peter Leape, making faces behind my back; Sidney Tooley, hands in pockets; Brian Leyland, fighting; Michael Murphy, swearing; Simon Parker, running on the lawn ...'

One never forgot Father Prefect's voice, the curt accent to his very correct English, the admonitory intonation, the slight hiss of his delivery. It came to seem like the voice of the seminary itself. He sat on a raised dais at one end of the refectory and presided over every mealtime, his biretta always placed on the same corner of his table, a book beside his plate. The food we were given was plentiful and nourishing: porridge for breakfast; soup for dinner, with a big bowl of spuds as well as meat or fish; bread and cottage cheese for tea, and a substantial supper at seven o'clock – except for Fridays, when Father

Prefect bent his face over the notebooks, then raised it to fix his glance on one offender after another, his nose wrinkling to shift his glasses higher on the bridge, a mannerism I had parodied when making faces behind his back, for which I was given No Tea for a week.

This was the punishment he relied on, for we were never beaten; you could hardly call it being beaten when he swung you about by your ear. If you were given No Tea, you had to sit in your place at one of the long tables, facing an empty plate, while the others in your section went at the food with gusto. There was only dry bread and the same watery cottage cheese for tea every day except Sundays, when jam took its place. No one liked the cheese, but they gobbled it greedily, often grinning and skitting at your misfortune while you sat there starving. *Schadenfreude.* I enjoyed learning German and would search through the dictionary for the longest and harshest words I could find: lexical masochism.

After tea, the boys were allowed half an hour's free time before the two-hour study period. As I wandered dully about the grounds, achingly hungry, stuffing my hands in my pockets for comfort and then hastily withdrawing them in case a prefect saw me, I was accosted by Rennet, who, after furtively looking round, drew a cottage-cheese sandwich from his trouser pocket and gave it to me. It was pretty soggy, for it had been in his gungy pocket, and I wondered what his motive was. Was he trying to make friends? These reflections occurred to me while, hiding behind a tree, I savaged the sandwich, swallowing gruntingly. When I had eaten, I remembered to thank Rennet, and the boy – upper lip raised above rodent teeth – offered to bring me another sandwich tomorrow, even though, if discovered, he would be condemned to No Tea himself.

But I shook my head: 'No, thanks. I only ate that one because you'd gone to the trouble. Don't bother doing it again.'

He would have had to balance a slice of bread on his lap beneath the table, smear cottage cheese on it and cram another slice on top, working furtively and feverishly in case he was seen by Father Prefect or one of his Gestapo. What was more, it was two slices out of his own ration and he'd had to go without. Nevertheless, I didn't want him for a friend; he had a sneering face and no one liked him; he was always moaning and couldn't take it – for when we were not suffering from it, we tended to regard Father Prefect's regime as an assault course designed to prepare us for the noble rigours of missionary life, and were proud that we could take it, take all that he could dish out. Until he dished it out.

It was a strange existence. The moral climate was never settled; there were sunny days, there were storms, there was prolonged drizzle. Some priests were cheery and kind, and would comfort you if you were miserable, but some frustrated bastards were woundingly sarcastic. There were boys it was good to be with, a few pals for grumbling together, and there were some surly bullies. It was like any boarding school in that respect. The only thing missing was sex – at least I never encountered a priest or older boy who tried it on; I had to go beyond the seminary for that. There were games of a Wednesday afternoon; the rest of the time there were lessons, some of which I enjoyed. I discovered poetry and classical novels in English lessons; I listened to records of classical music the music teacher played for us; I was charmed by the pretty altar in the chapel, its tall candles rising out of a colourful froth of flowers through which shone the gold of the tabernacle, and the voices of celibate men soaring in plain chant.

At every meal, every item of food was shared out rigidly and the boys had rules of their own for this. The tables in the refectory were organised in sections of four. My section included Rennet, Simon Parker and Mick Murphy. The breakfast porridge was fairly easy to manage. Each section had a bowl for four and each boy was entitled to one ladleful of porridge. But after four ladlefuls had been taken, there was always some left in the bottom of the bowl. Everyone wanted it but there was only enough for one, so lots had to be drawn. A boy chosen by the section, never the same boy twice, would show, secretly, to a boy in the next section, a number made with his fingers from one to four, which the others had to guess, whoever guessed correctly being entitled to the cold and congealed remnant of porridge. If no one guessed correctly, then the boy who had made the number took the porridge himself. The same drawing of lots took place, automatically, obsessively, in every section among the younger boys and even, as a languid habit, among the seniors. But even when the food was scrupulously divided, there were still problems. The meat at dinner, for instance: suppose there were four slices on the plate, so one slice each. Yes, but what if one slice was larger or thicker or leaner than another? The section had a way of solving this problem also. One boy would shut his eyes while another turned the plate until the one with eyes shut cried 'Stop!' Then the piece of meat nearest to you was yours. Yes, but could you be sure the boy had his eyes tightly closed? Perhaps he was peering beneath slyly half-closed lids and crying 'Stop' when the best piece of meat was nearest him. Rennet was capable of that, and could one be absolutely sure of Mick Murphy? He was Irish, after all. As for myself, observing shrewdly while my eyes were apparently shut became a specialised skill.

The method of sharing frequently led to quarrels, and the refectory often seethed with the vicious bleating of boys. But whenever the noise grew intolerable, Father Prefect, glancing up from his book, would ding sharply the little bell on his table, imposing instant silence. The quarrels were often resumed once we were out of his sight, and they occasionally led to fights – muffled, graceless affairs in some corner unseen by prefects. However, skitting was the favoured method of combat; boys were constantly jeering insults at each other. The best skitters were masters of the art and delighted in reducing their victims to pitiful, blubbering wretches – their intelligence ('Where were you when they were giving out brains?'), physical appearance ('Where did you get that nose – in the jumble sale where you got your ears?'), parents ('When are they letting your dad out of jail?') and hometown ('Bolton. They have to keep the bolt on so no one escapes!'), all mangled to a ludicrous parody much relished by onlookers. Fighting was prohibited, but verbal insults did just as well, and it had never occurred to Father Prefect to make a rule against skitting.

Even if it didn't lead to a wrathful bout of skitting ('Of course you cheated, you're always taking more than your fair share, that's why you've got such a great belly!'), the obsession with sharing out the food affected everyone. Sometimes I couldn't sleep for wondering whether Rennet had really had his eyes shut when the plate of meat had been turned; there was also the suspicion that Mick Murphy had an understanding with the boy in the next section to whom he showed numbers with his fingers. Could you be sure the boy was telling the truth when asked to confirm the number Murphy had shown him? Like most of the junior boys, I awoke each morning hating Father Prefect and his merciless bell; I attended chapel and said my prayers worrying whether I would get my fair share of porridge.

Was it for this that I had entered the seminary? Was I to progress to senior boy and then to novice, and thus to ordination and a post in the mission field, eternally wrangling with myself and others as to whether I was getting my fair share of food?

The boys rarely spoke of becoming priests, though I was sure Paul Chisholm contemplated his God-given vocation with reverence. He had that sort of face. I wanted him for my friend, and wished I could be like him. He was taller than me, with rich brown hair and the sort of face you kept looking at, wondering what made it so attractive. I was dissatisfied with my own face, my thin nose and mousey hair.

Paul never criticised seminary rules, nor did he hate Father Prefect – 'He must have been a boy like us once. And think what he must be going through with his family in Germany being bombed.' His mother was a grammar-school teacher and I had met her briefly the day our mothers had brought us to the seminary. Her face possessed a serene refinement; her warm smile and gracious manner made me ashamed of my own mother, and I had wished she would disappear.

'Do you love your mother, Paul?'

'Yes, of course. Don't you love yours?'

'I suppose you've got lots of happy memories? You know, cherished ... cherished moments you had with her.'

'You haven't?'

'I can't recall one.'

But if this was an appeal for pity leading to a close friendship, it didn't work.

We did not go home for Christmas and to make up for it, the festival was celebrated with a brief glide into Germanic forest-and-fairytale sentimentality. We got an extra half-hour in bed and were wakened not by the customary crashing bell, but by the gentle jingle of the altar bell used at Mass; and Father Prefect, patrolling the dormitory, had pasted a special Christmas grin on his face. There was music also, a string quartet – two priests, two senior boys – played carols at the foot of the stairs. In chapel they played the Sinfonia from Bach's *Christmas Oratorio* and inevitably everyone sang *Stille Nacht, Heilige Nacht.* The food throughout the day was plentiful and exceptional. There was butter, there was roast beef and home-brewed cider, Christmas pudding with threepenny bits and a plate of sweets for each boy, the priests having donated their sweet ration for this purpose. Father Christmas – Father Langen, the youngest and most popular priest – distributed parcels from home. After dinner we were allowed to roam the woods adjoining the seminary grounds and normally out of bounds. We played racing games in and out of the black trees and were grateful to the good, kind fathers.

Then we returned to the normal routine, to six hours of classes five days a week, and even two hours on Saturday; there were two-hour study periods most evenings and a regular grind of homework. The priests taught us Latin and German, maths, a little physics and a Catholic version of history that was strong on the persecution of Catholics, hard on the Lutheran defection. But though there were superficial resemblances, the seminary was never the public school I had longed to enter. There was no funny French teacher, no Indian princeling who played sublime cricket, no tuck shop or midnight feasts in the dorm. Instead, there were hours in the chapel and a constant fear of Father Prefect.

With the exception of supervised trips to the playing field, we could venture no further than the seminary grounds for recreation; we were too closely supervised to slink away for an illicit afternoon in Richmond. The lawns in front of the House were out of bounds; we were confined to the rear, where there was another lawn, with an ornamental group of trees at its centre. But only priests were allowed to walk on it, reading their breviaries.

'Some day,' Rennet vowed, 'I'm gonna race across it starkers, and shock you all!'

A gravel drive encircled the lawn and boys were allowed to walk there, but only one way round and it must always be clockwise. What would happen if a boy had a brainstorm and walked along the drive anticlockwise? 'It's like being in the army,' Rennet said. 'They make you obey all sorts of daft rules just for the discipline.'

'Why do we put up with him?' Simon Parker asked, as we walked around the drive in a clockwise direction.

Yet we needed Rennet, he was an escape valve, sulkily venting the protests we felt but rarely voiced. He made me uneasy at times, provoking troubling questions to which I had no answers. But if I had been truly virtuous or at the very least law-abiding, a priest in embryo like Paul Chisholm, I would have been unaffected by his cynicism; and although I assumed this necessary virtue would assert itself in time, I rarely felt spiritually or morally uplifted when I contemplated my vocation.

When he wasn't being Father Prefect, Father Prefect taught botany and was known as Father Kripps (aka "Crippen"). Because he was caught up in the subject, his manner was lenient; he smiled at the class and even attempted jokes. He took us into the park and showed us various plants, explaining the function of pistils and stamens, the features that distinguished one flower from another, and the wonder of pollination. It was easy then to gain his approval by discovering an example of a plant he sought, asking a question and appearing amazed at his knowledge. Unaware of sycophancy, his guard lowered, his love of the subject shone forth in a way that was almost naive. He smiled shyly, his gaze bent on the flower in his hand, and for a moment it was possible to see the simple, vulnerable man beneath the cassock of Father Prefect. But this we resisted.

Then it was spring and the trees in the park glittered with bright leaves, the lawn was a brilliant green, the hills surrounding Richmond glowed in strengthening sunlight. The bombers still took off for their flight to Germany, but I was usually asleep when they droned overhead. In any case, the longer I remained in the seminary the more remote seemed the world outside. We did not have access to a wireless and rarely heard the news. It was easy to ignore the war in the crowded, sternly regulated seminary day, given one's overriding preoccupation with lessons and marks gained, skitting and sharing out the food, No Tea and Father Prefect. But the war surfaced briefly when Frank, as a special concession, was allowed to visit me.

He was burly and suave in his RAF uniform, which bore the insignia of an air gunner, and I was proud of him. It would have been even better had he been an officer, but at least he carried with him all the tragic glamour of a bombing raid – dusk and the bombers looming black on the airstrip, the encumbered crews walking to their aircraft, the engines firing into life, the bombers lumbering down the runway for a wobbling take-off.

He examined the seminary with wry curiosity. 'I might've been here myself,' he observed. And after I'd introduced him to some of the priests: 'Christ! We may have bombed some of their relatives.'

His swearing disturbed me. He smelt strongly of cigarettes (I hadn't had one since entering the seminary) and smoked one after another. He looked older and appeared nervous and apprehensive, peering with strained eyes as though he had not slept for some time. We sat on a bench in the park and he told me of bombing raids on which he had flown, admitting to stomach-churning fear, and I was with him in the rattling, vibrating aircraft as it droned its way ever deeper into enemy territory, a vast empty space beneath us. 'I'm often shit scared, we all are, except for mad buggers who never believe they'll cop it, and are usually right. Only the good die young.'

I might have been hearing his confession – Bless me, Father, for I have sinned – and I recommended prayer to combat his fear. He laughed in a jeering, hopeless way.

'Oh, I pray all right! I have like a diarrhoea of prayer sometimes, especially when the flak is bursting round us, the aircraft shaking itself to bits; or when a snapper zooms at us and I can't get him in my sights, the guns firing at nothing. I pray then all right, it all bubbles out of me. Please God, don't let me die! Please God, let me survive to drop this load of shite on those Jerries down there, killing as many as possible. And look, here I am! God saved me so that I can go back and drop more bombs another day!'

I was alarmed. He had become quite a different Frank.

'Anyway, the war can't last much longer now the Russians have turned the tide.'

'The Yanks – '

'Fuck the Yanks. They're all talk and big dicks. It's the Soviet Union that has made the big difference. Stalingrad! They've got Jerry on the run.' His face brightened. 'And once it's over, I've got plans. Get married, raise a family; but I'd also like to, y'know, do summat for the workers. I've made some really good friends in the Raff and they've made me aware of socialism. That's what we've got to work for. Everything must change once we've won the war. A fairer society, the redistribution of wealth ...'

He went on and on, boring politics, atheistic Communism and how he meant to work for the engineering union when the war was over – help the workers to a better life. Then, crushing the stub of his cigarette into the pristine gravel of the path, he changed the subject, surveying me curiously. He wanted to know about life at the seminary. I told him a little – 'It seems to be nothing but rules,' he observed. He thought about lighting another cigarette, but desisted. 'Are you sure you've done the right thing? Are you sure this is the life you want?' He smiled affectionately. 'You know nothing of the world outside and how good it can be.'

I was not sorry when he left.

Before we went home for the summer vacation we were addressed by Father Superior, a priest so rarely seen that some of the first-years wondered who he was. He generally secluded himself behind the green baize door that led to the priests' living quarters, where boys never ventured. He did not teach but was purely an administrator, spending his time hunting down money – loans, grants, legacies – to maintain the seminary. He was a small, elderly man, wearily benevolent, speaking so quietly that those at the back could scarcely hear. He wished us all a pleasant holiday but warned of the temptations we would face in the world to which we were returning.

'Pleasures of the flesh,' Rennet grunted. 'Just let me get at them.'

'Our friend has been advised to leave,' Paul Chisholm told me later. 'They don't want him.'

'He couldn't take it,' Simon Parker said.

We were going home for a month. The senior boys, having for several years had the virtues of self-control hammered into them, greeted the fact with no more than the bland smile that would serve them well as priests; but the rest of us were excited, couldn't keep still and kept packing and repacking our suitcases, voices clattering jokes and jeers. Rennet was ignored and I felt obliged to cross to his bed and say goodbye. His weasel face looked as though he had been crying.

'I'm chuffed,' he assured me. 'I've been trying to get them to sack me all year. It'll be good to be back in Civvy Street. I'll get a job with my uncle, he's a baker. First thing you know I'll be managing the place. And girls, I'll have tons of minge.'

'I'll never forget the first time I was given No Tea and you smuggled me out a sandwich. That took guts.'

'You're the only one I'll miss. The others never liked me.'

'But why did you come here in the first place?'

'It was my mum.'

A bus took us all to the station in Richmond, where we boarded separate trains. Rennet went off to Birmingham, Paul Chisholm headed further south. I had hoped he would invite me to stay with him in Dorset, but he had not suggested it. I travelled with others to Liverpool, where we parted, laughing and skitting.

Mother was waiting at the end of the platform and I summoned a shamefaced smile; tender gratitude warmed her kiss. She touched me as though unsure whether this handsome stranger could really be her son. It was practically a year since I had been home and I was returning not to the old patched-up house, with its backyard full of stale fantasies, but to a place I had not seen before.

Mother was excited: 'Just wait till you see it!'

We walked to a tram stop, past the ruins of bombed-out buildings and, after waiting in a queue, caught a tram to a suburb I had rarely visited, although I knew it as one of the most desirable in the city. It was where well-off people lived. And were we living there now? Leaving the tram, we walked along a pleasant avenue planted with trees, with narrow lawns between the pavement and the roadway. Birds sang and hopped in the trees, the front gardens were bright with flowers; the back gardens would be given over to vegetables. DIG FOR VICTORY! I was conscious of a sunlit serenity, air one could only call balmy. None of the houses had been bombed, there was scarcely a trace of the war. Nothing nasty, you felt, could ever happen here.

'Here we are,' Mother said, stopping outside a large detached house with an ample garden.

There would have been railings and a garden gate had they not been taken for the war. A drive led to the front door. How was it we were living in such a splendid house? Had Dad won the Irish Sweep? Mother led me up the drive; but just before we reached the front door, she swerved to the right, where steps led down to a basement. 'We go down here.'

'We live in the basement?'

'You don't call it a basement round here. It's a Garden Flat.'

'Who lives upstairs? Whose house is it?'

'It belongs to Professor and Mrs Willard. He's got a Chair at the university, so you have to call him "Professor". They're both very nice. I'll introduce you to them.' She opened the front door. 'Come on.'

It wasn't fully underground; when you looked out of the window your eyes were on a level with either the surface of the front lawn or the back garden in the region of the bins. It made you feel as though you'd been buried standing up. The ceilings were low and at first I was conscious of the great weight of the house pressing down on us. They were up there, moving about, eating their meals, Professor Willard and his wife. If I'd X-ray eyes I could have looked through the intervening floors right up her skirt to her knickers. The flat had a living room and a kitchen, two bedrooms and a box room that just accommodated the bed where I would sleep. There was little room for my belongings, but I wasn't expected to live at home; they had moved to this place without taking me into consideration. The seminary was my home now.

After the castle's spaciousness, the rooms seemed small and confining, crammed full of furniture brought from the old house. It was strange not to be surrounded by boys, not to be ever alert for the swish of Father Prefect's cassock. I missed the old house, the freedom of my attic room, the cockpit of my Spitfire, the bridge of the destroyer I had commanded, the fantasies that had overflowed my room into the outside lavatory, which had served as a tank or a submarine; and the backyard where I had made centuries as Don Bradman – and Carol, my lost love! I remembered her with anguish. If she had not absconded, would I still have gone to the seminary?

After tea I was taken upstairs to meet Professor and Mrs Willard. There was no back entrance to the flat; we had to leave through our front door, climb the area steps and enter by their front door, to which Mother had a key. The rent was low for such a splendid flat in such a desirable neighbourhood and she was expected to make up for it by doing some cleaning (the stairs, the hallway, the front steps) and the washing. 'They've got a lovely washing-machine. The work's nothing; I enjoy having something to do.'

It had also been suggested that Dad might do some gardening when he was home, but this condition had been dropped when he had hastily shown he couldn't tell a pansy from a dandelion.

We entered the quiet splendour of the Willard hallway, parquet floor, grandfather clock ticking sonorously, hallstand with coats and umbrellas, even a walking stick. I thought of the professor striding across a moor wielding his walking stick. And why I was so stupidly nervous when meeting new people? It was as bad as taking something back to a shop; I was congenitally insecure. A number of rooms led off from the hallway; Mother tapped at the first door on the right and a voice cried, 'Come in!'

The room overlooked the front garden. They would have seen us entering, creeping into their house like awed pilgrims at a shrine. The first things I saw were a grand piano and a wall lined with books. They took my heart.

'So this is your son!' Mrs Willard said.

'How do you do, young man!' the professor said.

Both spoke with a forced heartiness, apparent also in the energy with which they wrung my hand.

'Do sit down!' Mrs Willard said.

We sought chairs that would not object to being sat on.

'Well!' the professor said. 'So this is Frank.'

'Peter,' Mother murmured timidly.

'Peter? Of course.'

He was a lanky, middle-aged man who constantly held himself back as though to avoid intimate contact. 'Well, young man, this is a ... um ... a singular profession you've chosen for yourself! Do you enjoy being locked away in a seminary? You must tell me all about it some time.'

We got away as soon as we could. Mother scolded me for not looking people in the eye when I spoke to them. 'There's no call to be afraid; they're really very nice people. He's a real gentleman and she's very ladylike. They're really just like friends.'

Becoming familiar with them, even as a cleaner, must have given her the feeling of inhabiting her own mother's early life. Chatting to Mrs Willard during a pause in the hoovering or while scrubbing the front step, she may have felt they were practically equals, that the lady obviously realised she was more refined than her situation would suggest. Oh, poor Mother! I could imagine the Professor jovially chiding his wife for encouraging good Mrs Leape's pretensions: 'Really, my dear, you've got the poor old thing believing she's a friend.' I was developing the habit of extemporising in my head scenes like this, complete with dialogue. I did it without being aware of it, the scenes arising unbidden.

'What's he a professor of?'

'Some science thing or other.'

I had looked forward to the vacation; yet now I was home, especially given my strange new home, I was dissatisfied, disorientated. Mother and Maggie did not know how to treat me. It was as though I was already half a priest. I had been given to the church and they no longer considered me part of the family. My alienation, begun seemingly at birth, was complete.

Most of the time only Maggie and Mother were at home; I saw Jessie and Frank only briefly. Jessie was amused by the garden flat, but it induced one of Frank's finest scowls. Dad was home between voyages – 'When you're a priest it'll be like your dad calling you "Father",' he observed – then he joined a ship on a convoy to Russia, which gave him plenty to moan about in his pencilled letters home. Mother took me visiting and showed me off, but I was no longer a remarkable exhibit. The nuns of the Cenacle petted me absently, the ladies of the Mother's' Union barely glanced up from the balaclavas they were knitting, and Auntie Ann's teenage daughter examined me as though I was a freak. We were like a music-hall turn that had made a round of the halls once too often.

I had plenty of pocket money; Mother gave me some, Maggie gave me more, and I spent much of it going to the pictures alone, seeking out lavish Hollywood musicals. They were not the sort of films I should be watching, and I stared at a luscious technicolour harem of girls. Rita Hayworth! Dorothy Lamour! (Lucka dem tits!) I ogled them, a Players cigarette at my lips, the wicked habit resumed as soon as I had returned home. Smoke issued from my nostrils like steam. Most boys my age would not only be smoking, they would be drinking, they would have jobs with money of their own, they would be making dates with girls. I had never in my life kissed a girl and now I never would. 'I'll have tons of minge!' Rennet had said.

Expected to keep up with my studies, I had brought books home with me, but delayed opening them. Instead, I read the Old Testament – were we really supposed to believe all this? Little wonder they scarcely referred to it at the seminary. Then I found some books that were not in the seminary library: *The Golden Bough, The Martyrdom of Man* (dear old Benny's recommendation) and *Lilliput Magazine* for the sex. I was restless and often wandered about the neighbourhood looking at girls. There were such lovely, refined girls here. I followed at a distance as they strolled in dawdling couples to their tennis club, their nude legs lovely in white shorts. Sometimes, I lingered in the front garden. The window of the front room was open and I could hear Mrs Willard playing the piano, Chopin floating out and nestling among the flowers. The professor had suppressed his desire to hear all about the seminary and I had not been invited to visit him again. But the Willard living room – its piano, its books, the pictures, and most especially its leisured, cultured atmosphere – clung to my memory. It was even better than the officers' mess.

One day I went down to the landing stage – it was crowded with kids, with laughing girls in summer frocks, men in uniform – and took the ferry to New Brighton. Large white seagulls with cruel yellow beaks hovered above the stern, riding the air on outstretched wings, crying plaintively, yapping and laughing. We passed ships that had been bombed and sunk in midstream, their masts and funnels showing above the surface. And how many drowned bodies in the green dimness below?.

It was a different New Brighton. On the beach, the seaweed-plastered rocks I had once flown over, my goggled face peering down at a mountainous plateau from the cockpit of a plane, were reduced to dull humps of sandstone no more than a couple of feet high. It was a sunny day and couples and family groups were laying claim to plots on the beach, chattering and laughing. Men paddled meditatively at the water's edge, trousers rolled up; mothers distributed sandwiches and unscrewed vacuum flasks; girls took off their frocks, stepping out of them insouciantly and kicking them aside. They lolled on the sand in bathing costumes, bare legs glistening, breasts soft and loose. Half-naked young men joined them and together they sang the latest songs, smoked cigarettes and told jokes. Before long, the girls were flying, shrieking, across the beach, the young men chasing them. Uniformed servicemen lay with their girls, hugging and kissing. On the promenade, GIs in sleek, tailored uniforms strolled past. They smoked Lucky Strikes, tossing them aside half-smoked. It was July, the Allied invasion of Europe was under way, the end of the war was in sight.

I went to the fairground racketing on its hill like a battle in toytown. People hurled wooden balls at effigies of Hitler and Mussolini; they squeezed into cuddly carriages and were whirled away on fearsome rides, shrieking and laughing. Eventually, I found myself at the waxworks. It was at the rear of the fairground in a shaded, disused area, a shabby old enterprise that for some reason I loved. Maybe it was the comforting sense of failure. It was crowded with wax figures, few of them well preserved: the Royal Family, Winston Churchill, George Formby – the usual bunch. Some of them could no longer stand erect; they leaned to one side or craned forward, greeting the visitor with a pained smile. Winston Churchill looked drunk, George Formby was caught in a cramp, Mae West's tits were sagging. The waxworks brought the famous down to my own undistinguished level.

The best part was the Chamber of Horrors. It was down a narrow flight of stairs that seemed to seal itself up behind you as you descended. Down there, the air was unnaturally cool and the lighting was feeble, no more than a dim, greenish glow. Luckily, there were few visitors, for you had to have silence and stillness, a clammy compression of evil, to really appreciate the Chamber of Horrors. And they were all waiting for me, smiling cruelly: Jack the Ripper, Bluebeard, Dracula, Landru ... In addition, there were tableaux of prisoners being tortured with the rack, the boot, or the water torture. The place oozed suffering and terror, decay and death. Each of the exhibits occupied a cell and you peered through the bars at them: you were visiting the condemned. Some of the figures had lost their stuffing, their period clothing was dusty and threadbare; but that only served to strengthen the impression that they had been caught in the act and were preserved forever at the height of villainy.

Ignoring the other visitors – a soldier; a giggly couple who soon left – I began my tour of inspection, greeting each old friend in turn. Jack the Ripper glared stonily, a razor in his hand and a woman at his feet, her bloodied throat half sawn through; then there was Dracula – opera cloak, bloodstained fangs – then Bluebeard and his heap of slaughtered wives.

'Historically incorrect!' a voice cried suddenly.

I was shocked. Had one of the exhibits spoken? But it was the soldier; he stood two cells away. 'Bluebeard might have had plenny of wives in Perrault's Mother Goose, but in reality he murdered children,' he added, as he approached. 'Know who the guy really was? Gilles de Rais, that's who he was, a nobleman who once fought at the side of Joan of Arc. Can you beat that? He killed little kids because he needed their blood for some scheme he had for making gold. Alchemy.'

It was the first American I had ever met, and just my luck to get an untypical specimen, for this wasn't some handsome wise guy in a film star's uniform, manhandling a cigar, glowing with a Yankee suntan, chewing gum, reading the funnies – this was a failed American. He was slightly built and somewhat crooked, as though he, too, had lost some of his stuffing; his uniform didn't fit well and he wore spectacles. Probably some lowly clerk from the supply base at Burtonwood.

'You get a kick outta this place? Me, too. All this crap –' His gesture took in the forlorn tableaux, the musty smell and half-hearted lighting, the rigidity of murderers caught forever in attitudes of crazed malignancy. 'You got an unintentional truth here, y'know? Everything is third-rate and falling apart, so it conveys exactly the sordidness, the mediocrity, of evil.'

I was impressed; the GI was an intellectual. His sallow face seemed to go from side to side, rather than from top to bottom, an effect instigated by his wide, lively mouth. He was probably a Jew, and for that reason alone I was prepared to like him, for Benny's sake and to atone for the casual anti-Semitism evinced by my family.

'Then take these scenes of torture. Have you noticed that in most cases the victims are dames? Look along here, the water torture.'

We examined the water torture. It was in a corner cell. A woman was bound hand and foot, her body stretched to straining over a low stool, and two men were pouring water into her – at least there was a funnel jammed into her mouth, a bucket tilted over it. 'The victim is forced to swallow gallons of water,' the GI read from a card attached to the bars. He turned to me. 'What are we thinking here? We're both wondering what happens, right? Gallons of water, for Chrissake! Does she keep pissing it out or does her bladder simply swell up and burst?'

I was both horrified and fascinated; the images danced a lewd cancan in my mind, scintillating with voluptuous cruelty. I was both the torturer holding the woman down and the torturer pouring water into her; I was even the woman herself, struggling frantically, the funnel jammed down my throat, my eyes imploring mercy.

The GI gripped the bars. 'It's pornography. Know what I mean? We're in there with her. We're the torturers, gloating as we pour it into her. It's a rape, right? We're raping her with water.'

Of course he was a Yank. No Englishman would have spoken that way, as though his dick was attached directly to his brain.

'All these hopeless monsters – !' His gesture included a dame stretched out on the rack and a dame being pressed to death, with large stones placed on her chest. 'They hadda torture and mutilate women because they could never achieve a normal, loving relationship with them. That's why we unnerstand!' he hissed at me through his glasses. Then his lavish self-contempt subsided. 'Let's get outta this place.'

I followed him up the stairs. Outside, the air was fresh and glittering; the fairground vibrated in sunlight, churning crowds and colour in a whirligig of noise and movement. We stood together. I did not know what to do next. The GI shuffled cigarettes out of a pack of Lucky Strikes and gave me one. We lit up and I inhaled. My head reeled.

'What gives over there?' he asked, and I followed him past a couple of stalls to the Crazy House.

It was a gimcrack structure, architecturally insane, with a jumbled roof and lopsided chimneys. Idiot faces stared out of celluloid windows, and a crowd stood waiting for girls to walk across a balcony open to view. Whenever they did so, a blast of air blew their skirts high, the girls tottering and shrieking as they sought to cover themselves, underclothes flaring.

'Jesus!' the GI groaned. We both stared as the girls scuttled screaming across the balcony, raped by a column of air. 'You got an erection? I sure have.'

That was what it was called, then: an erection. I drew heavily on my Lucky Strike. I felt hot and wild, staring at the girls, their stocking-tops, the froth of underwear.

'Where's the john?' the GI asked. I thought he was enquiring for someone named John. 'The can!' he exclaimed, writhing. 'Whadda you call it? The Gents!' It seemed an odd time to want a pee.

I led him to the lavatory. It was a nasty stall open to the sky, located beneath the skinny, trembling scaffolding of a roller-coaster. As we entered, a train of carriages thundered overhead, darkening the sunlight. The carriages careened by on flimsy rails, trailing the shrieks of excited girls. There was a legend scrawled on the lavatory wall: *man with hole in pocket feels cocky all day.*

'Got to get rid of this thing,' the GI grinned. He undid his flies and brought out, as one might manoeuvre a tall beam under a low doorway, a huge red erection. 'The last pathetic resort of inadequate personalities! You'll help me with this, huh? Mutual aid.'

I expected a policeman to appear at any moment. Closing upon me, the GI mumbled of girls and what their underwear concealed and how we were two of a kind, both sensitive and intelligent, both inadequate personalities doomed to the mundane evil of jerking off. He pushed me into a cubicle with hardly room for two and closed the door. He had his dick in his hand and was offering it to me as he crowded me against the wall. 'Where's yours?'

I protested weakly as he undid my trousers. I was appalled, yet not merely appalled; helpless, yet not really helpless. He took my hand and closed it about his cock, took my erection in his hand and kissed me.

'You're a sweet kid, ya know that?'

My lips parted in horrified amazement and he pushed his tongue between them. Good God! I was gagging on the brute of his tongue, the water torture; I was that helpless dame, crushed against the wall in the reeking cubicle, my bottom caressed by his free hand, while his other hand jerked and his mouth kissed with his fat, slimy tongue. Then he stooped and popped my dick in his mouth. I had never imagined anything so depraved (in his mouth!). It would be terrible if anyone entered and pulled open the cubicle door, found me with my pants down and this great sucking leech clinging to my loins. Then he clasped my bottom in both of his hands and stuck a finger up me. The assault was so unexpected that I jolted wildly, dislodging his spectacles, which then hung from one ear. At the same moment, as though I was roasting in flames of hell that were nonetheless luscious roses crushed between female thighs, an astonishing golden happiness streamed out of me into the GI's gobbling mouth. I threshed his cock alarmingly and sperm flew everywhere, all of it spurting from the GI as he spat out my contribution and as his cock spat his.

Cursing, he cleaned himself as best he could then wrenched open the door of the cubicle and went off without a word. I slumped on the lavatory stool, amazed and fearful. It was the most original experience I had known since the Germans had bombed Liverpool. I loathed what had happened and was horribly ashamed, though it would not be long before I would be putting into practice what I had been taught. Apart from anything else, I was disillusioned. I had begun to anticipate a valuable friendship with the GI; he was an intellectual and must know many things. But all I gained was a fag, a wank, and the conviction that I was an inadequate personality.

I returned to the seminary in a mood of weighty bewilderment that had nothing to do with guilt. Father Prefect greeted each boy as he arrived, wrinkling his glasses up on the bridge of his nose. My lips curved in response, in the usual urge to please him. Tyranny made sycophants of us all. I had a bed and locker in a different dormitory, and the fact that I was now a second-year gave me superior status. A toughened veteran of the regime, I would be able to boast to the new kids of how many No Teas I had suffered, how often my bed had been wrecked; I could dogmatise on the rules for sharing out the food, I might even indulge in a spot of skitting, and I would frighten them with tales of Father Prefect's monstrous cruelty. That was something. It was good, too, to see my friends again and tell each other what we had done in the hols – well, actually, I got wanked by a Yank. But I had told no one of this, apart from a priest in confession, receiving as a penance the Five Sorrowful and Five Joyful Mysteries of the Rosary.

'Let us inspect the new sprogs,' I suggested to Paul Chisholm.

They were clustered on the lawn with their mummies, bewildered twerps with heads that bulged at the back, set on stalk-like necks. 'I wonder how many of these will be able to take it?' I sneered. 'I wonder if they realise it's the only time they'll ever be allowed on the blessed lawn?'

Paul was disturbed by my tone.

Although the mothers were sacrificing their sons to God, it might have been parents' day at any boarding school. But most fathers were absent in the forces and women were in the majority; mothers and sisters, some young and good-looking.

'I fancy that one,' I muttered, earning another dismayed glance from my friend. I was beginning to enjoy shocking him. Wipe that sanctimonious smirk off his face.

The women – their clothes, their bodies – exuded a force that caught the priests off balance, reducing even Father Prefect to little more than a tentative smile. There were novices present also, remote youths in black cassocks who merely inhabited the same seminary as the boys, having nothing in common with us. In a few years they would be priests; the war would have ended and they could stride into the foreign missionary field searching for souls to save. I had scarcely noticed them before; but now, my perception debauched by the GI and his lavatory follies, I observed them closely as they chatted with someone's sisters, good-looking lively tarts – I wouldn't have minded seeing them cross the balcony of the Crazy House. Was that what the novices were afraid of? There was a kind of jokey, fluttery alarm in their manner. When anything amusing occurred, they shied away from the girls, neighing laughter and flinging pale, narrow hands before their faces, swinging themselves about as though they were tethered. It was pitiful and repellent, and made me decide that I no longer wanted to be a priest.

Yet for some time I did nothing about it. The thought of Mother weakened my resolve: her fury – the raised hand, the thick ear – her scorn for my failure, her misery, her shame before the Willards and her friends in the Mothers' Union. I was sure it would break her heart. And while I dithered, the seminary regime seized me once more and I was dragged along with it, submerged in it. The desire to escape persisted as a dull, nagging ache, but I procrastinated; I was afraid to face Father Prefect, and his incredulity should I tell him I wanted to leave. And what if he said I couldn't leave, I was promised to God now and there could be no turning back?

In November we were given a holiday to celebrate the birth of the founder of the order. It was a bright, cold day and Father Langen took the second-years to Richmond for a treat, a smile on his lean, tanned face. He was an Austrian who had not been home for many years, a noted mountaineer who longed for the steepling freedom of the Alps. He led us across the town's great marketplace, past the castle and over the bridge, then on a path through the woods. The river ran alongside, glinting silver through the trees, falling away as the path rose steadily. The trees were tall and stalwart, sycamore, ash and beech. They had lost most of their leaves.

'Do you know this story, boys? It was a long time ago. Some soldiers found an underground passage running from Richmond Castle, and they wondered where it led to. Yes?' Father Langen halted and we clustered about him. 'This passage, it was too narrow for a full-grown man, so they sent a little drummer boy down with his drum. "Keep beating your drum," they said, "as you go along; we will hear you from above." So the boy, who was a good boy, not like some of you fellows! This boy, he gets down into the passage and he begins to walk along it in the dark. Well, perhaps he had a candle, but it would still be dark and frightening, yes? Anyway, he kept beating his drum as he went ... Now let us walk on. We are walking along the same path those soldiers took many years ago and they are listening hard, you see, they can just about hear the drum beats from the boy beneath. Now let us walk further. The drum is still sounding. Can you hear it, Kapowski? They say you can still hear it of a moonlit night if you're very, very quiet.'

Jim Kapowski howled dismally.

'Now we stop here. Do you know why? Do you see this stone? This is the very point where the soldiers no longer heard the poor boy's drumming.'

We stared at him. 'What happened, Fah?'

'It is not known. But the boy was never seen again.'

'They could have sent a dog down after him,' Simon Parker said. 'A dog would have found him.'

We left the wood, crossed a muddy meadow and came to the road that led to Easby Abbey. 'Founded in the twelfth century. But now it is in ruins, as you can see.' Massive limestone walls reared up from the grass, broken off at the corners. In many places the stone facing had fallen away, revealing crude inner masonry. There were gaping windows, some still retaining delicate Gothic tracery. 'This was once such a splendid place. Over there was the refectory; here is where the monks slept. Look at the thickness of the walls, boys! Think of those venerable men, the Premonstratensians. That is what one calls them. They came over from France and built this great abbey to the glory of God. That was in a time when Our Holy Mother Church ruled the civilised world.'

When we left the ruin, I sought Father Langen's advice. That was the way one usually put it, and he probably guessed what was coming. Back at the castle, he took me aside and listened to what I had to say. I confessed that I had lost my vocation. I had been mistaken, God had not called me, I no longer wanted to be a priest. He asked whether I was sure, had I thoroughly examined my conscience, had I prayed long and hard for enlightenment? I said that I had. He looked grave and said he would put my case to Father Prefect. 'He is the one you should have approached, you know; he is closest to you and, believe me, the best friend a boy could ever have.'

The next day, Father Prefect told me to come to his office; it was located among the classrooms on the first floor. I was frightened – I was so bloody cowardly. The spuds, the fucken spuds! – but the Boss treated me kindly, his ruddy face glowed with sympathy, the best friend a boy could ever have. He was distressed at the possibility of losing me. But it was only a possibility, he assured me, smiling warmly. Intelligent and thoughtful boys such as myself often doubted the genuineness of their vocation. Of course, if I was determined to leave, the seminary would have to let me go. 'We do not keep here a boy against his will.' But first I must pray hard, we would pray together, he would offer up a Mass on my behalf.

Now there was not only Mother to consider but also Father Prefect, who thought so highly of me, who was actually offering up a Mass for me and who would be most disappointed should I leave. And might he not be right when he claimed I was merely experiencing the sort of doubt any intelligent and thoughtful boy might feel? A doubt, he would not have been at all surprised to discover, that the Devil had placed in my heart.

I returned to my studies, plugged away at German and Latin, quarrelled about the sharing out of food, did my share of skitting and, when I could no longer resist the temptation, abused myself in the lavatory and was plagued with guilt afterwards. Then it was Christmas once more, the tinkle of Father Prefect's fairy-like bell, the lovely string quartet playing at the bottom of the stairs, the presents, the special grub, and a letter from Mother hoping I was well and happy – *I am really proud of my little son.* I felt myself sinking into a helpless acceptance of the seminary. After all, what was there at home for me, and what sort of life would I find back in Civvy Street? Although we now lived in a middle-class suburb I still saw life in terms of the backstreets – the backstreet mind crammed with bigotry and clichés; the Neanderthals who had humiliated me. The seminary, despite its niggling discipline and the obligation to love God, offered me beauty and learning, the safety of a circumscribed existence and the opportunity to dedicate my life to some noble, selfless cause.

In February, Dresden was destroyed in a thousand-bomber raid by the RAF. Some days later, Father Prefect told me I had a visitor. Normally he would give a boy this news in a tone that implied both he and his visitor deserved No Tea for causing a disturbance in the rapt seminary year, but on this occasion his manner was embarrassed, even solicitous. I found Maggie in the chastely polished room where visitors were segregated. She was, inevitably, sitting on the edge of a chair, slight and bespectacled, pale and distressed, overawed by the castle's austere grandeur. She got up at once and clutched me: 'Oh, Peter, our poor Frank!'

'What? What is it?'

Frank had been badly wounded while bombing Dresden. The crew had done all they could for him, but he was dead by the time they reached England – 'That's terrible!'

Frank, dead? It was inconceivable. His body had been returned to the family and I was expected home for the funeral.

I did not know what to feel. Why did I always have to examine my feelings and try and sort them out, the genuine from the spurious? Wasn't any feeling in danger of becoming spurious once you questioned its genuineness? And did everyone feel this compulsion? Not for the first time, I felt different from my family, I couldn't grieve for Frank as they did, my sorrow was not as unpremeditated as theirs. They were overcome by feelings they never questioned and it made me feel inadequate, a cold fish incapable of rising to the occasion. At the funeral, when I should have been oblivious to anything other than sorrow, I was distracted by the reaction of the bereaved: how Jessie's tears smudged her mascara, how red Maggie's nose was and how, when the coffin was lowered into the grave, Mother seemed on the verge of chucking herself in after it. I even questioned the verb I was using, rejecting "throw" (too dull), and "toss" (too flippant) in favour of the hard-boiled "chuck".

I had felt vividly for Frank when first hearing of his death. Empathy, I had experienced empathy. I imagined a Messerschmitt materialising out of nowhere, its bullets smashing the perspex of his gun turret and slamming into him, six or eight bullets in his legs and chest and one in his throat, his face ravaged by the most terrible anguish, eyes sinking into dullness as unconsciousness overcame him. But was that sorrow? It wasn't Frank I was imagining, it was myself; I was producing another of those plays in my head in which I was always the hero. I wondered if at the moment of death – already I was beyond his death and into fascinated speculation – he had recalled the religion of his youth, uttering the Act of Contrition that might save his soul from damnation. But he had jeered at the hypocrisy of prayer, he would have died unshriven. In which case, would God consign to hell this good young man, who had given his life that others might be safe? What sort of God could do such a thing?

Mother was overwhelmed with grief, bent over and barely able to walk from the graveside. Mrs Willard supported her – the upright middle-class patrician giving her arm to her faithful old retainer – and

Mother's grief was briefly tempered by gratitude: 'Actually attending the funeral of someone she'd hardly met. I was very touched.'

Although she had hugged me when I had arrived home and uttered some words of comfort – 'You've lost your poor, brave brother!' – she barely seemed to notice me thereafter. Dad was away on a long voyage, but Jessie stayed home for a few days. I wondered how long I might be allowed to remain at home. There was no doubt now that I must leave the seminary. I had taken Frank's place in going there, and now he was dead I must take his place at home. Surely, once she had recovered from the worst pangs of grief, Mother would want me beside her?

Back at the garden flat there was a subdued reception for the mourners, a few friends and relatives, at which the Willards put in a brief appearance. Jessie and I escaped as soon as we could, pulling on coats and going for a walk along the winter-bare avenues. She was as blonde and prettily petite as ever, and I was pleased and proud to be seen with her. She gave me a Lucky Strike and we paused to light up. 'I get them from my boyfriend,' she smiled.

She told me she meant to leave the stage once the war was over: 'I've had enough of it. It's not such a wonderful existence as I once thought.'

I was dumbfounded. How could she give up such a career?

She smiled at me, embarrassed. 'I don't get stage work all the time, you know; I'm not good enough, not really much in demand, to tell you the truth. Sometimes, I have to take other jobs just to keep body and soul together. I've been a waitress, a chambermaid. And when I do get on the stage, often it's just some crummy dance routine in an East End music hall.'

Her boyfriend was a sergeant with the American forces stationed in London. He wanted to marry her, take her back to the States with him. She had a Yank and a Yank had had me; she was leaving the stage and I was … I told her I wanted to leave the seminary.

'Oh, I think you should. I was never in favour of you going in the first place. You were too young to know your own mind. Me mam pushed you into it.'

'She did, didn't she? She pushed me into it.'

'She won't like you leaving, but you must be brave and stand up to her, like I did.' She flicked ash from her cigarette, its tip smeared with lipstick. 'I'm glad you're not going to be a priest. I've no time for them, myself.'

'Aren't you still a Catholic?'

'No fear.'

'What's it like?'

'Not being a Catholic? It's all right. Once you no longer have to worry about going to Mass and committing sin, life is really worth living.'

'Frank was an atheist.'

'Frank? How do you know?'

'He came to see me at the seminary. Do you think he's in hell now?'

'Of course not. God couldn't be that stupid.'

'You still believe in God, then?'

'Well, there has to be bloody something!'

The day after the funeral Mother said I should return to the seminary: 'They won't want you to stay away for long.'

I told her I did not want to return. I was rigid with misery and fear. 'I've lost my vocation,' I asserted, heart labouring. Such a coward! An intelligent and thoughtful young man, yet still afraid of his mother ... Nevertheless, preoccupied as she was with Frank's death, this really wasn't a bad time to make my plea.

She sighed and shook her head, but that wasn't a refusal, merely a resigned acceptance of the fact that I lacked the spirit to persist and succeed with anything. 'I thought it was too good to be true.'

I realised that the ordeal was over. It had lasted all of two minutes. I wanted to write a letter of resignation and not return to the seminary at all, almost as though it was some enchanted place from which I would never escape if I went back. But she said, 'Oh, you must go and tell them in person, a letter simply won't do,' once more forcing the bag of spuds into my hand, obliging me to stand on my own two feet. And for a moment Frank was there, he was taking care of me; together we took the spuds back to the shop and he bought me a halfpenny apple – I found myself weeping helplessly.

'Now stop whinging,' Mother sighed. 'For heaven's sake, they won't eat you! Anyway, there's your clothes; I can't afford to let them go, what with rationing and the cost of things as they are.'

I returned to the seminary the following day, and before Father Prefect had more than composed his face for commiseration, told him I was leaving. Now that my brother was dead, I was my mother's only son, I pointed out, and quite obviously she needed me with her. It was suggested, first by Father Prefect, then by Father Langen, and finally by Father Superior, that I should put God before family – hadn't Jesus implied as much? – and become a priest, taking Frank's place in the battle against evil, a rear gunner for Christ. My response was poignant reproach: surely they would not seek to detain, and trouble with further demands, a boy who had just lost his dear, brave brother? Eventually, they shook their heads and abandoned me to the world.

I expected my last day at the seminary to be the best I had spent there. In the event, my departure produced the usual mixed mess of feelings. Waking up was wholly delightful, there was something golden about it, enchanted. It had that roseate air of unreality that accompanies events of a magnitude greater than you feel entitled to. I rose for the last time to Father Prefect's daily bell, washed perfunctorily but made my bed as carefully as ever. If I hadn't, he might have hared after me, hauled me off the train and dragged me back to the seminary by my ear to remake it. I heard Mass in the chapel, and for the last time – a sentimental gesture – drew lots for the last scraping of porridge. After breakfast I said goodbye to my friends – Jim Kapowski seemed envious; Paul Chisholm was withdrawn, his handshake perfunctory – and brought down my suitcase from the dormitory. The others were going to their classrooms, but I was free. Free? Yet I could not fully rejoice until I was wholly away from the place, and right up to the last moment I feared some objection would be made, some clause found in the spiritual contract, forcing me to stay.

While I waited at the front door for transport to Richmond, Father Prefect crossed the far end of the great hall. He saw me, hesitated, then resumed his purposeful stride. Off to wreck some poor bugger's bed...The dog cart came round to the front and I got in, a friendly brother helping me with my suitcase. 'Going home!' he smiled.

As we clattered down the drive, I looked back at the house. It was stony and impassive, wanting nothing more to do with me. The seminary had turned its back on me.

CHAPTER FOUR

Dad had learned of Frank's death while at sea; he spoke of it to me when he came home: 'I never give him his due. He was a bloody hero, wazzen he? They've given him a medal. I'm so proud of the lad!' His eyes were red and wet. 'And what price bloody religion, bloody Loving God now, eh? You're the expert; you tell me what God was up to. Your mother and Maggie never stopped praying for him, for his safety, and it did no good at all! Well, that's bloody it as far as I'm concerned.'

'What do you mean, Dad?'

'Religion. I'm never gonna believe in it again.'

As though it was a horse he had backed that had let him down. Mother's reaction was more profound. Father Doonan, our former parish priest, who had known Frank as a Boy Scout and made a point of attending his funeral, had a hard time persuading her that his death was somehow for the best. She was wild and weeping, railing against God. 'It's a punishment, isn't it?' she cried.

I was eavesdropping and could see her face through a crack in the door, her draggled, grey-streaked hair and trembling mouth. Why should she feel God was punishing her? Perhaps she believed it was because she had not loved me enough ... I had always had to worm my way into it somehow.

Father Doonan was severe with her. Much of his career had been spent handling hysterical women, especially since the start of the war. He told her that Frank's death was a test of her faith. Had she imagined loving God was always to be easy and pleasant? Sometimes it was hard, very hard. But it was a challenge, a test. After all these years, was she about to doubt the Almighty's Goodness, His Loving Wisdom? She cringed beneath the touch of asperity in the priest's tone. We know

God is a good God, he insisted; therefore we have to believe all is for the best.

'But why did He have to take my lovely son?' Mother sobbed.

Father Doonan sighed, repressing a tremor of annoyance, and bent once more to the priestly task of finding excuses for God. It was more important to justify Him than to love Him.

Maggie's faith was shaken also. All those prayers, those Masses: the magic had not worked. And why Frank rather than another – some drunken, whoring oaf whose life was worthless? She was faced with a profound mystery, perhaps the greatest crisis in her life, and for a short while I wondered if both she and Mother might not abandon the God who had betrayed them. What a difference that would make! We might all three – and why not Dad as well? – find a new life beyond religion: more communicative, more honest, more generous-spirited, more loving. But what was there for Mother and Maggie beyond religion? How could they have managed their lives without it? Inevitably, when the sharpest pang of grief was dulled, their brief rebellion collapsed and their faith revived. They resumed their prayers for Frank. He was one of the "poor souls in purgatory" now. Unless he was in hell.

My future, now that I had failed to become a priest, offered a minor distraction. What was to be done with me? They gathered in the subterranean living room to decide my fate. As further education was out of the question – I was too old for elementary school and there was no chance of transferring to a grammar school – I would have to get a job. Dad thought I might follow him in his trade and become a cook, but Mother decided I must work in an office, much more respectable. I was indifferent, lounging at the kitchen table, gazing at the budgie in its cage. It was a new bird, the last having died of shock during the bombing. I knew what I really wanted to do and it had nothing to do with becoming a cook or a clerk. I wanted to ... ponder, examine and somehow recreate, the better to understand, what I thought of as significant factors in my life: the love I never got (never deserved?) from Mother; the confused feelings I had for Dad; my low esteem of myself; the impact of Frank's death, of being bombed by the Germans, mauled by the gang, abused by the GI; the experience of the seminary and the problems of sex, sin and religion. But I didn't yet see how this was to be done. In any case, I was glad simply to be back in the world, with a future that was open-ended. What a relief no longer to be burdened with that celibate, priestly destiny! I was ready for any job that would give me a way into the world, provide me with money to spend and the opportunity to meet some lovely girl, for I was free now to fall in love. Tons of minge? Heavens, no. The idea of fucking a girl, an ethereal virgin, was quite bestial.

A job was found for me with "the Corporation", as we called local government. I became an office boy. They are a vanished race now, you will never see them again; but at one time, in my time, the city centre writhed with them. They wormed their way through crowded streets, especially towards the close of the working day when, in a warren of offices, typists bent their aching backs to hammer out the last letters for the boss's signature, and senior clerks stretched and yawned, lit another cigarette and reached for the early edition of the *Echo*. Then a horde of boys, buttoned up in tight, cheap suits, collars askew about lurid neckties, hair slicked with Brylcreem, would swarm everywhere, clutching a wad of letters to be delivered to various offices in the city, for it was cheaper to use a boy than a postage stamp.

Attending the municipal offices for an interview, I walked up and down outside the large soot-black building a few times before daring to enter. Once inside, I had to find my way among a warren of offices, along corridors busy with clerks bearing important documents. It was early March, a dull yellowish day squatted beyond the grimy windows of the corridors, and the lights were on, making it seem as though broad daylight never penetrated here. Eventually I found the right department and was interviewed by the office manager, Mr Berry, who had his own "corporation", which is what we called a pot belly. Although I lacked qualifications, he was prepared to give me a job. The fact that I had been at a seminary worked in my favour, for it meant I had some education and was probably honest and trustworthy. That was what you had to put in your letter of application, Maggie said, standing over me as I inscribed, *I am honest, trustworthy and a good timekeeper*, loathing the brown-nosing fibs.

The building was full of departments: Parks and Gardens, Refuse and Salvage, Roads and Transport, Civil Defence, Rates, Planning ... I was in Housing. 'We're as important as any of them,' one of the clerks, Mr Renfrew, told me. Everyone was terribly loyal to their own department and fiercely jealous of its reputation. In Housing we were proud of serving the public, no matter how much we despised them, and were fond of telling other departments that despite being chronically understaffed and overworked, we did as good a job as any, and better than most. 'They're all peasants in Parks and Gardens,' Mr Renfrew said, 'hardy sons of the soil! And Roads and Transport wallows in chaos. Just run round the corner and get me twenty Players, will you? She keeps them for me under the counter.' He was a chain smoker. Small grey turds of cigarette ash rolled about among his papers, impelled by his breath.

'Our job is finding homes for people,' Mr Berry said, 'whether they deserve it or not. Eventually, Peter, you will come into contact with the public, and you will find the public can be an obstroculous beast, never satisfied no matter how much you do for them. We often have to deal with the lowest of the low, I fear; tenants who treat the homes we give them like pigsties.'

Part of my job entailed carrying files and documents, charts and plans, from Housing to other offices in the building, which was better than sitting on a stool at a sloping desk, adding up the figures in the post book and trying to make them tally. Walking along the corridors past windows criss-crossed with paper, red buckets of sand and water ready for incendiary bombs, I was aware of work in progress all about me. Clerks struggled with the panic of emergencies – 'Where's that file? What happened to Mr Jones? Where'd he go? Who's stolen my pen!' – they banged out of offices and raced away, dodging with a gasped apology important personages they encountered in the corridor, a senior administrator or a councillor, visiting industrialists, business magnates, Members of Parliament. It made me feel as though I was at the throbbing heart of a great city, a part of the task force dedicated to running it, however maligned by its denizens. Despite being despised, we continued nobly to carry out our duties, often under the most trying circumstances.

'You should have been here during the bombing,' Sarah said. 'That was fun. We never left the building for days.'

Apart from running messages both within the building and out in the streets, I had to keep the post book and operate the switchboard, make the tea and dust the office and fetch Mr Renfrew's under-the-counter cigarettes. My desk was close to the desks of two of the typists, Sarah and Vera. They typed letters and reports from the shorthand they had scribbled, fiddling with mucky carbon paper almost transparent with use, and cursing – 'Oh, damn!'; 'Oh, drat it!' – when they made a mistake, grimly erasing a mistyped letter with the small disk of an eraser. They made fun of me and were kind to me. Sarah showed me how to make tea for the department, a task which took precedence over any other duty. Tea in the morning, and again in the afternoon. Mr Berry had a china cup and saucer and two biscuits, the senior clerks had porcelain cups and one biscuit, the junior clerks a chipped cup and a biscuit. 'And us slaves get these rotten mugs.'

'Biscuits?'

'You must be joking.'

Two of the senior clerks were elderly men – Mr Renfrew and Mr Price – and two were middle-aged ladies, Miss Sutcliffe and Miss Tate. They had all worked for the council most of their lives. The junior clerks were younger and would have been in the forces, but for missing a hand (Ted Marlowe) and curvature of the spine (Willie Gregg). Some of the staff were friendly – Mr Renfrew kept winking at me; Willie Gregg kept on good terms with everyone so that they would not abhor him for being a cripple. The others merely used me to sharpen their pencils, fetch their cigarettes and evening papers, and run after them with an important document they had forgotten when they attended a committee meeting, though all they did there was set out papers and fill glasses of water.

However busy I was, I always found time to look up the typists' skirts as they sat at their machines, usually by dropping something and stooping to pick it up. Ah, God, their swelling thighs and the musky duskiness beyond! Their breasts – Sarah's pert brace, Vera's puddings – also proved instructive. Yet I was still nominally a Catholic and a certain consciousness of sin oppressed me; there were shameful goings-on in bed at night. I longed for some sweet, virginal girl to take pity on me and save me from myself before I went mad with masturbation.

Sarah showed me how to answer the telephone and operate the switchboard. It was a complicated arrangement of plugs and sockets, with small convex indicators that clicked awake like eyes whenever you put a call through to an extension. Sometimes I shoved a plug into the wrong socket and cut off the caller, leaving him submerged like a deep-sea diver with his lifeline severed.

The post book was ruled for pounds, shillings and pence, and I was told that I must account for every penny spent on postage. 'If there's any shortfall, it will come out of your wages,' Miss Tate warned me – a gnarled little woman with drab, tightly-rolled hair and a dust-laden voice.

'The last boy we had,' Sarah said, 'left in tears because of her. She led him a dog's life. So beware, young Peter!'

'I've known worse,' I assured her.

They dropped the bomb that ended the war. 'The end of the world, if you ask me, sunshine,' Caddy said, a tall, thin youth with a penchant for gloom. He, too, was an office boy. He worked in Finance and we sometimes went out together to deliver letters and other documents, leaving them at a number of offices in the city, a process that took at least an hour, given all the shop windows one had to look into. 'Carry on like that,' he added, 'drop any more atom bombs, and it will cause all the atoms in the world to disintegrate. The world will simply fall apart!'

'I'm going down Water Street,' I said. 'There's a tart in Tower Buildings who's madly in love with me.'

Dad left the sea and came ashore for good. 'What will you do now?' Mother asked.

He was fifty-three and it wasn't easy to get a shore job. He found one eventually in the kitchen of a hotel; but it was in Manchester, and he might not be able to come home very often. 'Should I take it?' he asked, a larger question in his voice.

Mother said he should take it. 'We don't want you on the dole,' she added, with her slighting laugh.

He remained gazing at her for a moment before turning away, busily lighting a Woodbine.

I had assumed they would draw closer because of Frank's death, but Mother had drifted away from everyone into a morbid meditation upon her loss. She nursed her dead son in her heart and sank ever deeper into a pensive, spiritual mood. Her listening manner, head on one side, became more pronounced, as though she was overhearing the dialogue of another world. With her husband dismissed and her children taken for granted, she virtually became the nun she had once wanted to be. I tried at times to engage her attention, but what chance did I stand? I had failed to become a priest and I could never hope to take Frank's place.

Dad repacked his seagoing suitcase and went off to Manchester, leaving me alone with two grieving women in the basement flat. I was glad to get out of it and go to work. Towards the end of most days, I set off through the busy streets with a handful of letters, passing abandoned air raid shelters and vacant lots, the sites of bombed buildings. I visited gloomy Victorian fortresses where, at a reception desk, an imprisoned princess might greet me with a smile. Yet how could I approach her, what would I say, how did one begin? Other boys chatted up the girls with ease. The dialogue was banal – 'Hello there, good-lucken!'; 'Who are you calling good-looking?'; 'Ain't you good-lucken, then?' – but I envied the insouciance with which they went about their flirtation, knowing I couldn't emulate it. I was fresh from the seminary and Father Prefect's dominance. For eighteen months I had scarcely been part of the world. I was disorientated, seething with inchoate feelings, constantly frustrated.

My ideal was a pure-faced virgin. I regarded such modest, ethereal maidens with awe and was incapable of sullying them with the thought of nasty, brutish copulation. At the same time, I was fascinated by the act of seduction. I imagined, with a prurient puritan agony, the deflowering of virgins and their faint horrified cries as, unable to resist the fatal charm of some suave seducer, they surrendered to desire. I could never have achieved such a conquest, it was surely a mortal sin, and in order to retain the image of virginity while enjoying the delights of seduction, I was reduced to seducing myself. In bed I became a girl, jerking off in a kind of narcissistic madness, imagining myself both seducer and seduced at one and the same time.

Then Jessie got married. It was a fait accompli; we knew nothing of it until she announced the fact. 'We got done in a registry office,' she told me. 'Don't tell me mam, will you?'

Mother was confused and distressed. Although Jessie had mentioned an American boyfriend, she had not yet introduced him to the family, and who could say what sort of creature he was? There was also the fact that nice girls did not go with Yanks. There was only one thing they wanted. And why marry without telling her family? Had she, by any chance, had to get married? In any event, it meant she would be carried off to America, to Seattle, thousands of miles away. Would we ever see her again?

Dad was upset. He loathed all Yanks on principle; they were everyone's weighty elder brother, and now one was robbing him of his favourite child. He came from Manchester to meet the man, Jessie having graciously condescended (as Mother would have it) to introduce him to the family. He strove, a surly father-in-law, to muscle up to the Yank; but Chuck, convinced that everyone must like him, failed to take offence. He was quite different from my Chamber of Horrors GI. He was a sergeant, large, handsome and benevolent, bending courteously to acknowledge his in-laws, treating Mother with a warm reverence. He boasted naively of Jessie's stage glamour and seemed to feel he had secured a fabulous prize. He was about to be sent home; Jessie would follow later. Established in Seattle, where Chuck would work as a partner in his father's store, she meant to start a school for little girls whose parents hoped they would become ballet dancers.

'But you were never a ballet dancer, Jessie.'

'I know the basic positions; I can even do them, after a fashion. Anyway, I'll soon get them on to tap and the kind of stuff they'll need for the chorus line.'

What did Maggie think of Chuck? Did she long for a husband of her own? She was approaching thirty and, having become somewhat vinegary, was unlikely now to be married. Although she devoted herself to Mother, Mother cared little for her; she had never possessed a winning appearance or personality, and was always outshone by Jessie. Yet her forbidding demeanour was no more than shyness, a fear of experience, which she had suffered throughout her life. When she felt safe, when she was with those she loved and admired, her manner softened and one saw then in her tentative smile an alternative self lurking like a prisoner, a self without Catholic bigotry or spinster repression, capable of joy and affection, which would never now be brought to fruition. For much of the war she had been happy and purposeful, with a good job, even a measure of authority, earning the respect of her bosses. This job had ended with the war and she had become a supervisor in Littlewood's Football Pools. I asked about her work and got the answer I expected: the girls who checked the coupons punters filled in once a week in hope of winning a fortune were as flighty and unreliable as fortune itself, although there were one or two, she conceded, after reflection, who were good hard workers. As for the bosses, the higher their rank the greater the respect she had for them, and I guessed that by paying her the slightest compliment they could easily persuade her to work any amount of unpaid overtime.

Chapter Four

Eventually, Jessie left for America, one of a chorus of GI brides in coats with blocky shoulders, hats like felt halos, boarding a liner and pausing on the gangway to wave goodbye to the newsreel cameraman.

Dad had come home to take leave of her. He had never approved of the move to the garden flat. 'We don't belong here,' he said, while we searched for a shop that might have cigarettes. But there were few shops of any sort in the neighbourhood; most of the residents had their rations delivered by Cooper's food emporium in the city. 'I mean, the neighbours are nice people, probably. Professional people, doctors and that. But you shudden be shoving in where you're not wanted.'

He rarely came home for more than a couple of days in a fortnight. 'Maggie thinks you've got a fancy woman in Manchester,' I told him on one of his visits.

'Oh, come on!' he sniggered. 'Who's gonna look at me, at my age?'

'Have you ever been unfaithful?'

He stared, affronted. 'What sort of a question is that?'

'What about Carol?'

'Carol? Who's Carol?'

'Carol next door, when we lived in the old house.'

'Oh, her,' he laughed. 'That's really funny, that is.'

'Why?'

'It was Frank who had Carol.'

'Frank?'

I remembered looking out of the bedroom window at Frank and Carol in the street below. '*Don't get too familiar with her. You know what she is.*'

'He told me about it, come and confessed, like, really upset. She was his first, you see.'

'He fucked Carol?'

'Don't put it like that, son. She was no better than she oughta been and I'm not sorry it happened. She was good for him, really; at least the poor lad got summat out of life before he died. It was probably Carol as much as anything that put him off being a priest. But she took it too seriously, wanted him to marry her, wanted him to take her on – her and her two kids! Act soft and I'll buy you a coal yard.'

'And I suppose when he rejected her, she left?'

'It was time for her to move on. She owed money all over the place. She even robbed her own gas meter.'

'I wonder what happened to her.'

'Women like that usually end up in the gutter.'

In the Housing Department, the older clerks were anxious, now that the war was over. Younger men were being demobbed and would be after their jobs. 'I don't see why they should get rid of us,' Ted Marlowe bleated, waving the stump of his missing hand; 'I can do the work as well as anyone.'

'They were glad enough of us while the war was on,' Mr Renfrew grumbled.

'We never let anything stop us, worked right through the Blitz,' Mr Price added.

But they were old and past it, couldn't they see that? Renfrew must have been at least sixty; and Miss Tate – 'I must have a job. I've got my mother to look after. She can't look after herself' – was surely in her fifties. I had little sympathy for them, contemning all old people as a matter of course, loathing and fearing the shaggy old buggers.

A couple of them were shunted into retirement eventually, and two recently demobilised men took their places. Time passed, it slipped by unnoticed, and in the new year of 1947 I was promoted. I became the most junior of the junior clerks and my duties assumed greater importance. I was now allowed to open all the correspondence that came to the department. Once the envelopes were slit open (carefully, so that they could be used again), I passed their contents to Willie Gregg, who decided which senior clerk should deal with them. Most of the mail consisted of uninteresting documents and official forms, but there were also letters from tenants or would-be tenants of council housing, and these I read before passing them on – *"I have not kep up with rent becawse my hubby has left me" … "We have been waiting for acamodation for 2 years now"… "The damp somethink terrible … mushrums growing on the walls."*

I was also detailed to answer the bell whenever a member of the public came to the counter, which was set apart from the office itself like a sort of quarantine. The bell sounded very like the bell that Father Prefect would ding whenever noise in the refectory became too loud, and I always answered it promptly. I might find a shabby elderly couple at the counter, fearful of authority, begging my pardon for bothering me while they explained their plight; another time it would be a burly snarling workman still in his overalls, who assured me, occasionally with a fist to my nose, that he knew his rights and would stand no nonsense. Then I had to return to the office and find a senior clerk who would attend to the enquirer: 'Oh, is it them again? I told them we can't do anything for them' ... 'That ugly customer? I'm not seeing him.'

Another office boy was hired in my place – more than once I was obliged to reprimand him for attempting to look up the typists' skirts – and I was given a raise. I could spend more on clothes; physical appearance became important. Though of a critical temper, I was not displeased with my appearance; I had finished growing at less than six feet, but my body was pretty well formed (I had all my limbs, my spine was straight), and my hair had become a richer brown. I had once feared I had a sneering face, but I had tried hard to bring down my curling upper lip, even if it made me look like a frog. I was now ready to believe my face was not unattractive, especially when I smiled, although my expression was often sombre.

'You look as though you've the troubles of the world on your shoulders,' Miss Tate said.

She had no idea of the trouble I was having with God and sex.

Mother was pleased with my promotion; a whimsical smile suggested that she was proud of me. But I was becoming indifferent to what she thought of me. I am not what I seem, I sometimes wanted to proclaim to the world, convinced that I was merely pretending to be a respectable clerk. It was all a facade, a subtly ironic performance, I assured myself. I am not really like this! And made a note.

I had begun to note down anything I considered significant, especially discoveries I made about myself. In fact, most of the notes were about myself. Even when I roamed impoverished and disreputable parts of the city and filled pages with compassionate observations, wondering if every youth I passed was a juvenile criminal, every girl a prostitute or a tragic deflowered virgin, my preoccupation was still egocentric; I couldn't get away from myself.

On one occasion an event overflowed my notebook and splashed on to a couple of quarto pages. One evening in November I had been on my way home when it began to snow. In no time the city was transformed and I stood staring up at the soft, feathery flakes. They descended slowly, idly, yet with a gentle implacable force, settling on people's heads and shoulders, coming to rest on sooty window ledges, drifting into the corners of doorways. People looked up and some of them smiled: it was snowing, the first snow of the year! Emotion overcame me, a kind of tragic nostalgia oceanic in scope, and I loved everyone in sight – office boys scurrying past, a gent in a homburg carrying a briefcase, a woman loaded with shopping, a couple of girls giggling as they slip-staggered on the snowy pavement. The world! The human world! I felt myself expand spiritually to encompass everyone and everything in life. The snow caressed my upturned face with its frail, vanishing hands. I was alive! I was here and now, and would never be here again; I was tremblingly alive, a unique individual with his future rising before him, a bright mist.

When I got home I went to my room, found some paper and tried to describe what I had felt as the snow descended, the wonder and poignancy of that moment and the sensation of being uniquely myself, yet also capable of loving the world. I didn't get much beyond a description of the snow idly twirling down upon the city like manna or a blessing, but afterwards I sat marvelling at what I had written, feeling as though I had committed an irrevocable act. Yet I did not then go on to write anything else, and in time the self-glorying moment faded from my mind.

It contributed, nonetheless, to a restlessness that now began to affect me, a fear that I was becoming immured in my clerkly role, that what I considered no more than an ironic façade of respectability was in danger of becoming my reality. Office routine became stale and I found the attitude of the clerks to their clients objectionable, especially as I was supposed, in the interests of departmental loyalty, to emulate it. I mentioned something of this to Dad on his next visit home when, as usual, we were prowling the streets in search of a shop and cigarettes. When he heard I no longer wanted to be a clerk, he suggested that I came and worked with him in the hotel kitchen as an apprentice or commis chef. Apparently there was a vacancy, the latest commis having been called up for National Service. It seemed a good idea: it would get me away from the mouse hole of a basement flat and those dreary evenings of fags and detective stories, and it would fulfil my growing desire to experience the world beyond the Housing Department. Mother was not pleased; she had hoped I would become boss of the department in time, if not Town Clerk; but I pointed out that I would have to leave anyway in little more than a year, when I would be collared for National Service.

'It's a good trade,' Dad assured her. 'Plenny of money to be made these days as a chef.'

She sighed and shrugged and let me go.

The hotel was in the centre of the city, close to Deansgate, a huge sooty pile of commercial Gothic. I had rarely visited Manchester and I found it bewildering at first, an amorphous city lacking specific limits. In Liverpool, the city centre slides irrevocably downhill towards the river, slithering to a halt at the great buildings on the waterfront. The river prohibits further development. But Manchester seemed to ramble on indefinitely, sprawling in every direction, threatening smaller towns in its vicinity: Salford and Bury and Oldham. It was rooted in Lancashire, in cotton and brass, whereas Liverpool had a unique identity created by Irish and Welsh immigrants and sundry other nationalities; it had a brawling, savage and adventurous history and there was something both feckless and valiant about its inhabitants. To my mind, Manchester, though a wealthier city and swollen with the portentousness of business, lacked the wit and vitality of Liverpool. And these immediate impressions, exaggerated by homesickness, were perhaps the first stirrings of the epic novel I would eventually begin to write.

The living-in staff had squalid bedrooms in the hotel basement, three or four often sharing the same room, waiters with porters, waitresses with chambermaids. But Dad and I had a room to ourselves, an envied privilege despite the fact that it held little more than two narrow beds. A lightless corridor piled with broken furniture and boxes of provisions ran from the bedrooms to the kitchens. The main kitchen was a huge clattering place often writhing with an emergency, for it seemed impossible to create a meal without floundering into a panic. There were hotel residents to cater for, as well as patrons of the restaurant, perhaps as many as three hundred diners at one sitting. Cooks rushed about, banging pans on to the stove, yanking open oven doors and slamming them shut again. They cried out to one another, 'Where's the fucken lamb? There's never going to be enough béchamel,' and snapped orders at the commis chefs, 'Stick it in the bain-marie. Haven't you chopped that parsley yet? Where's the hors d'oeuvres?' Steam gushed from the steamers, smoke rose from the stove where something had begun to burn.

Had the head chef been less of a martinet, the work would have gone more smoothly and efficiently. He was a big, fat man, with a large, lardy face and pale, cold eyes, who reminded me of Desmond Flood, one of the most feared skitters at the seminary. The chef was not above skitting – 'Get a move on, dopey! I'll bet you move faster when your misses drops her drawers' – but he preferred bawling. The kitchen resounded with his voice every mealtime, causing the cooks acute anguish, Dad as much as anyone. As a result, food was often blunderingly prepared, with less care and skill than would otherwise have been the case, which again raised the chef to shrieks of anger. Fortunately, he wasn't in the kitchen all the time, and some days he hardly appeared.

'He has fits of depression,' Dan Teacher, the chef's deputy and chief sycophant, told me. 'Days when he can hardly get out of bed. You've got to feel sorry for him.'

There were four chefs in all. Dad was in charge of breakfasts and also helped prepare lunch, Fred (Dopey) Argyle was the patissier responsible for cakes and desserts, and the head chef and his deputy saw to the main meals, assisted by whoever was on duty. There were two commis chefs, and two kitchen porters who washed up and prepared vegetables. I looked good in my natty check trousers and tight white jacket, an apron bound about my waist, a cocky white hat on my head – dapper, adroit, ready for anything; and most of the time I enjoyed the work. There was a skill to be learned – how to chop vegetables without chopping your fingers, how to prepare hors d'oeuvres, how to make simple dishes. In my spare time I sometimes went out with the other commis, a lad of my own age. We went to the cinema and once to a dance although I couldn't dance, both hungry for girls.

Dad was eager to impress me; he flourished his culinary skills, slicing meat dramatically, stirring a roux, standing at the range like a captain on his bridge surveying an array of pots and pans. At the hotplate serving luncheon he was lean and wiry, hopping from one foot to another while shovelling food on to the silver dishes the waitresses took to the tables. He sang and laughed, spoke in comic accents and fooled about. He harangued the waitresses in a comic French accent – 'Now, ladies, please! Leetle ladies, please, you stop zis giggling, yes?' They were fond of him.

One day I was making crêpes, juggling two iron pans at once in the usual non-stop method: pour the batter into one pan and while it's sizzling pour batter into the other and while that's sizzling turn over the crêpe in the first pan and while that's cooking turn over the crêpe in the second pan and while that's cooking remove the crêpe from the first pan and add a dab of fat and while that's sizzling remove the crêpe from the second pan and add a dab of fat and while that's sizzling pour batter into the first pan ... As each crêpe was removed from the pan, it was piled on a plate. The plate was put near the top of the stockpot to keep warm. One day I happened to jog it with my elbow and half the crêpes slithered into the stock, Jesus fuck! Dabbing with a slotted spoon, I fished for the crêpes in the odorous, greasy stock where bones and anything edible was thrown; but before I'd rescued more than four, the head chef pounced on me, grabbed me and hurled me away, bawling curses. 'Stupid fucking idiot! You're as useless as your daft old dad!'

Furious and humiliated, quite forgetting that I was supposed to be a cowardly weakling, I cursed him in turn – 'It was an accident, you fat oaf, you fucking great bully!' – and he gave me the sack on the spot.

Dad was horrified; he did not attempt to defend me. The head chef was a volcanic mountain of a man and he was scared of him. He blamed me: 'Do you wanna get me the sack? You wanna keep that temper of yours under control!'

And now that my temper had cooled, I too was appalled at my behaviour. Returning home, I went on the dole. Mother and Maggie were shocked.

'What in heaven's name have you done? I just don't understand you,' Mother cried, close to tears. 'You're so – ! You can't stick at anything. You left the seminary; you left that good office job – '

'I left the seminary because I'd lost my vocation – '

'Oh, get out of my sight!'

'You made her cry,' Maggie informed me later.

'No wonder. She's been left with the wrong son.'

Racked with shame and fear, I applied to the local labour exchange, a large gloomy building, hard and bare, walls tacky with green government paint, windows opaque with dust. The light was yellowish, the composition floor was studded with trodden-out fag ends. The place was crowded with men drawing the dole and looking for work, or dodging it. They lounged against the wall and queued at the counter, eyeing me indifferently. I was fearful and flung back a few years, a child once more; I was a tender child peeping among the tree-trunk legs of grown men. They were smoking and spitting, fucking and blinding; a sense of failure and resentment clung to them – 'NEXT!'

I found myself facing a large man with a loud voice – 'NAME?' – an ageing clerk with a pachydermatous face, whose round spectacles held tiny images of the electric lights suspended from the ceiling.

'I want to …'

'SPEAK UP, CAN'T YOU?'

I cringed at the wailing-wall of the counter, which was scarred as though frustrated applicants had torn at it with their fingernails. I was afraid everyone would learn my private business.

'WELL? CAT GOT YOUR TONGUE?'

I confessed to having been 'sa … sa …'

'SACKED, WERE YOU?' The clerk winked at the men in the queue behind me. 'HOW OLD DID YOU SAY YOU WERE? … SEVENTEEN, AND ALREADY YOU'VE BEEN SACKED!' His voice, pretending shock, soared about the place, bouncing off the walls. 'AND HOW COME YOU WERE SACKED, LADDIE?'

I was hot and flustered, writhing with shame, taking back the spuds, taking back the boots all over again. I was convinced that everyone in the hall had stopped what they were doing and were now listening, with raised heads and cruel smiles, to the interrogation. I began a halting explanation, the crepes, the stockpot, but the clerk didn't understand, unless he was dissimulating to prolong my embarrassment.

'NOW LET'S GET THIS STRAIGHT. YOU SAY YOU WERE COOKING…WHAT WERE THEY: CREPES? LIKE IN CREPE SOLES, YOU MEAN?'

Behind me, a couple of men were sniggering. And the clerk's jeering bellow, the nasty spectacles branding his fat face … Suddenly it all became too much. This wasn't Father Prefect or the shopwalker in Boots and Shoes, this was just a penny-ha'penny dole clerk, for Chrissake! And I simply couldn't, wouldn't take any more. Even as the clerk was bawling, '… AND ALL THESE CREPES FELL IN THE SOUP?' it came to me with the force of a mystical revelation that I didn't have to take any more, I had a right to be treated decently and fairly. Something in my head said as much, something shoved my voice out at my enemy – though it wasn't really my voice; it belonged to the Willards and the BBC.

'If you'd just listen to me for a minute instead of shouting all the time, not giving me a chance!' Yes, that was the way. Like putting on an act – 'I've come here for help, not to be shouted at as though I was a fool!' That was it. You simply showed you weren't afraid and you were no longer afraid. It was the voice that did it; I could hide behind the voice and not be afraid.

The clerk tried to swell himself huge, roaring, 'NOW JUST YOU LISSEN TO ME!' But I was on my way now and would not be stopped. I demanded to see whoever was in charge.

'Where's the manager, the supervisor? I've a complaint to make!' I made my voice curt, I strained myself guards-officer tall, my bearing erect and affronted.

'Now just a minute,' the clerk said, with a wheedling smile. 'There's no need to get aeriated.'

I had triumphed; I had discovered how to handle the situation. You didn't have to shout and threaten to "go higher up", to "write to the press"; style and language were what mattered, having the words and knowing how to use the voice, the middle-class voice, the accent of authority. At that time, there was hardly a clerk in the land who wouldn't whimper and jump at the sound of the boss voice of England.

It wasn't difficult to get another job and I soon found one, becoming an assistant projectionist in a local cinema. In the projection box I learnt how to tend the machines, thread the film through intricate sprockets and ignite the carbon pencils; in a back room I rewound the reels by hand, letting the film pass between finger and thumb so that I could register any tears; cutting and mending the film with a touch of cement when necessary. Easy, peaceful work. There were two senior projectionists, young men recently released from the forces, and a jolly girl who let me practise kisses on her, although she was too common to take seriously as a girlfriend. There were free films every day, three or four times a day, and rather better wages than I'd been getting as either a clerk or a commis. I hoped this would mollify Mother, but she feared for my character and mourned the loss of my glibly respectable clerk's facade. I had been sacked, gone on the dole and taken a job without prospects (for all that I protested I was practically an engineer). She wondered if I was not taking after my slipshod grandfather and would flounder from one job to another, all my youthful promise squandered.

I worked most evenings at the cinema. In my free time I read detective stories, the brief learning I had acquired at the seminary was steadily smothered beneath a weight of bloodied corpses. Of a Sunday I went to Mass, a habit I couldn't yet bring myself to break. We still attended our old parish church in the district I had known as a child and I preferred to go on my own – that way I could daydream my way through the service without being jogged awake with an elbow in my ribs. And one Sunday at Mass, with spring round the corner, I fell in love. It was a girl in the pew in front, across the aisle. I could see part of her face, the delicate curve of her cheek. She had a slender figure and might still have been at school. She wore a jacket and skirt, a headscarf knotted beneath her chin; quite ordinary garments I swiftly invested with sentimental significance. I couldn't stop looking at her, the strands of fair hair that escaped her headscarf, the slope of her back and the delightful way it curved out at the-the – buttocks seemed too vulgar a word; she was too pure and virginal to have buttocks or a bottom, a bum or an arse, hideous concepts I rejected violently.

When the Mass was over, the congregation rose and filed into the aisle, but I stayed where I was until the girl left her pew, genuflected – how sweetly she did that, how modestly! – then turned to leave. I stared up at her yearningly and our eyes met; nor did she seem indifferent, I felt sure there was a flicker of interest in her eyes; her lips may even have moved in the faintest of smiles. Then she went by. I scrambled out of the pew, made the Blessed Sacrament the briefest of genuflections and followed her, staring at her legs, the exquisite bones of her ankles. But others joined the crowd in the aisle and we became separated. By the time I reached the exit, she was nowhere to be seen.

I did not catch a tram home at once but wandered through dingy, familiar streets that might have offered nostalgia could I have thought of anything but the girl. Was this love I felt? Was it love at first sight? Whatever it was, it was surely closer to sacred than to profane love. Like Dante and Beatrice, whoever they were.

I thought of her constantly in the week that followed and spent many of my free hours mooning about the streets in the vicinity of the church, in the hope of meeting her. It was April, the weather was fine and towards evening a poignant glow in the west seemed the raised banner of love. I was nervous going to church the following Sunday, but the girl was there, I need not have feared disappointment. Absently thanking God, I entered the pew immediately behind her. Had she attended that particular Mass in the hope of seeing me again? I stared oafishly at her slight sweet figure, the golden lights in her hair. She half-turned and gazed about as though expecting to see someone. She gave me an indifferent glance, and its possible significance – was she truly indifferent or disguising her real feelings? – preoccupied me for the duration of the service. Again, when the Mass was concluded, I waited for her to leave first and followed her out of the church, making sure this time that I kept her in sight.

She walked home alone. I followed, lurking, ready to take evasive action should she happen to look back. She walked with a straight back, head in air, and I imagined her smiling. Was she conscious of being followed and was she pleased? She lived in the main road along which I had once flown in my Supermarine Spitfire, clutching a bag of rotten spuds. She stopped at a door next to an undistinguished café, closed of course, unlocked the door and went inside. As she did so, she glanced to one side and saw me. Hot with shame, I crossed to the other side of the road, my head bent, eyes fixed on the ground, hurrying away. But perhaps she was smiling after me tenderly …?

I was alarmed the next Sunday when Maggie insisted on accompanying me to church. She suspected I was not attending Mass and was thus recklessly accumulating mortal sins. I insisted she was mistaken. In that case, she concluded triumphantly, I should have no objection to her company. 'Unless you're afraid of being seen in the street with your big sister.'

She thought that was why I went alone, because I was ashamed of being seen with her. At least Mother wasn't with us, and I was thus spared a familial prisoner's escort; she had a few little jobs to do for Mrs Willard and would attend a later Mass. When we got to the church I made sure I led the way down the aisle. The girl was there, occupying the same pew as before – it might have been a street corner where she waited for a date with me – and I slipped into the pew behind, obliging Maggie to follow. The girl looked round and smiled happily. I was astonished, flooded with gratitude: but it was Maggie she was smiling at. They knew each other.

'It's Ingrid Johannsen,' Maggie whispered. 'I know her poor sister.'

As so often in those days, I felt that Fate was in charge, maybe even God: everything was planned and meant to happen this way. I couldn't wait for the Mass to end. When the dawdling priest finally left the altar, we joined Ingrid in the aisle and left the church together. Maggie introduced me: 'This is my baby brother, Ingrid.'

The girl smiled, enjoying the female put-down. When Maggie asked how her sister was, she shrugged wryly: Olga was pretty much the same as always. Then, eyeing me curiously, she asked if we would like to visit her. We walked home with her. She was actually at my side, I was practically intimate with her, marvelling over the fact that her head reached only to my chin, staring at her wonderfully small feet in neat shoes. I could not believe my luck. Ingrid Johannsen. I had always wanted to meet a foreign tart. Already I had her down as a wartime refugee who had escaped with her family from a country brutally invaded by the Wehrmacht.

She stopped at the same door as before and from something Maggie said, I realised that her family owned the café next to it. They lived above the café, up some dark narrow stairs. Her sister lay in a small front room, a woman of about thirty, bedridden for years. Although it was a single bed, it took up half the space in the room; its head was behind the door as you entered and there was less than a yard between its foot and the window, out of which Olga gazed day after day, intensely interested in whatever went on in the street below. The furniture was old and undistinguished; the walls were covered with pictures of saints and the Holy Family.

My first impression was that Olga was made of wood; her body lay like a plank in the bed and her face had the glistening patina of lightly hued oak. But though stricken with a terrible disease, she did not seem depressed. Although she could move little more than her forearms and her head without pain, and even then with difficulty, her smile and the brightness of her eyes sprang at you as soon as you approached. Her hair lay about her on the pillow, falling away from her emaciated, radiant face. Her voice sounded as though her throat was parched. Her purple lips wrenched back in a painful smile when she saw Maggie – apparently a regular visitor – and she seemed delighted to make my acquaintance. One of her long bony hands was bandaged at the wrist, the other she held out to me, its skin shiny red, the joints swollen. After I had shaken it, she left it on my arm caressingly for a moment. I pitied the poor creature. But she had no use for pity. What she wanted above all, especially with strangers, was to drain you of all the information you could give her. Maggie had already told her something of me, and she thus knew that I had failed to become a priest. 'Well, never mind, never mind!' she cried in her rasping voice. 'I'm sure Our Blessed Lord has some other task in mind for you, just as important.'

She wanted to know all about my job in the cinema, whether I enjoyed working there, how the film was projected, how many hours I worked and whether I got on with my boss. The slightest detail interested her and you felt she would have nodded enthusiastically, repeatedly, had she been able to bend her head that much.

'It's not much of a job,' Maggie intervened. 'He could have done better. He was a junior clerk with the Corporation.' Then she asked Olga how she was, whether she was feeling any better.

'Oh, pretty much the same!' Olga cried, stretching her smile and showing her teeth.

She turned to me once more, making conversation like the hostess of some grisly salon. She wanted to know whether I had a girlfriend, which I denied loudly for Ingrid's sake, and asked which was my favourite saint. My favourite saint? I hadn't one; saints had never interested me much, they never seemed real. I chose Joan of Arc at random, chiefly for her youthful militant sex, and Olga cried, 'Oh, yes, she's a wonderful saint! Do you know that when they burnt her, her heart wouldn't burn? The heart that loved God so much. It would not burn!'

Given the amount of blood in a heart, this wasn't as miraculous as it seemed. But one didn't argue with Olga, pity forbade it; and this gave her power. She was the centre of the home, enthroned in her suffering, and must not be contradicted.

'The Little Flower,' Maggie was saying, having been asked to name her favourite saint.

'Oh, St Anthony, I suppose,' Ingrid said in her turn. 'Of Padua.'

'Yes, I like him,' I told her. 'He's good for finding lost things.'

She laughed and got up from her stool in the corner, saying she would make some tea.

'Can I help?' I begged, rising, astonished at my boldness.

'If you like.' She rolled her eyes at her sister.

I followed her along a gloomy lobby to the kitchen at the back. It overlooked a desolate yard and was small and crowded, with a stained sink and an old gas cooker. 'We have a bigger kitchen downstairs,' she said. 'That's where Mum does most of the cooking.'

'For the café?'

'Yes. Rock buns, mostly. The pies and sausage rolls we buy in, and I make the sandwiches.'

It was the first time I had been alone with her, and the smallness of the kitchen enabled me to draw close, furtively sniffing her. 'Is your mother ...?'

'She went to the eleven o'clock,' she answered, referring to the Mass. 'She'll be back soon.'

'So there's just you and ...?'

She changed the subject and assumed a proprietary air, telling me where to find a tray and some crockery. 'The sugar's in that cupboard,' she directed, and I loved being ordered about by her. She was seventeen, three months older than me, and had left school without any qualifications. 'I could've gone to grammar school, I'd have loved to; but Mum needs me in the café.' I watched her make the tea; it was a moving performance, the charmingly practical way in which she poured boiling water into the teapot... 'You must be educated; you went to that seminary place. Why did you leave that good job you had with the Corporation?'

'I got fed up with the way they treated people; members of the public, I mean, people who were often desperate for accommodation. They treated them like dirt.'

How true was that? Being in love meant tampering with the truth, all to get an approving smile from a girl. They had such power – !

'If you'll just take the tray,' she said, preparing to leave.

'You'll be at Mass next Sunday, will you? You'll be there? The same Mass?'

'I'll be there,' she laughed softly.

I carried the tray into the front room and she followed with the teapot. Olga, unable to lift her head from the pillow, drank hers from a cup with a spout that Ingrid held to her lips. She sat on the side of the bed to do this and I admired the swell of her hip. Her skirt was hitched beyond her knee, revealing a little of her thigh. While we were drinking tea and nibbling an arrowroot biscuit, her mother returned. She paused on the threshold, a small sturdy unsmiling woman.

Ingrid began to introduce us: 'You remember Maggie Leape, Mum.' But her mother had already turned to Olga. As she did so, her face softened with tenderness.

'Her husband ran off, some years ago,' Maggie told me when we left the house; 'and she's never seen him from that day to this. He was a sailor, a Norwegian. Then he left the sea and started that café. But when it looked like there was gonna be a war, he scuttled off back to Norway. A lot of good that did him! He was killed when the Germans invaded.'

'So there's just Ingrid,' – I loved saying the name – 'she and Ingrid, running the cafe?'

'That's right. Poor Olga can't do anything, obviously. What did you think of her? Isn't she marvellous?'

'What's the matter with her?'

'Rheumatoid arthritis.'

'Isn't that what you had?'

'Yes, but I was lucky; it never got as bad as Olga's. Hers is incurable, they say, and she's been like that for years. It just shows you the value of religion. I mean, how could she ever have borne it without her Catholic faith, her belief in God? And knowing that though she may be suffering now, it will all be made up to her some day.'

I couldn't wait until Sunday. I called at the café during the week, late one morning, not having to be at the cinema until the matinee at two. It was called The Rest Awhile Café and held no more than six tables, at each of which four people might have sat with some crowding. In the windows either side of the door a large potted plant squatted before a flimsy net curtain. Inside, at the far end, was a counter and a cash desk. The counter was topped with a glass case, which displayed Mrs Johannsen's rock buns and scones, a few meat pies and a couple of sausage rolls. There were about half a dozen customers, mostly middle-aged women with hats, gossiping happily over a pot of tea. Mrs Johannsen was not present. Ingrid was serving at one of the tables; she wore a practical apron over a blouse and skirt, her arms were mostly bare and her fair hair was drawn up on her head in a faulty arrangement that allowed tendrils to escape about her ears. I had never seen anything as femininely charming as those blonde tendrils hanging about her pearly ears.

She looked up and saw me and grimaced with annoyance, shaking her head. I sat at one of the tables and studied the menu. A pot of tea was sixpence, rock buns fourpence each, meat pies ninepence. Ingrid approached my table, an order pad in one hand, pencil in the other.

She found it difficult not to smile, though with a hint of reproach. 'What are you doing here?'

'I'd like a cuppa tea and a rock bun, please.'

'You'll catch it, if Mum sees you. Or I will.'

'I had to see you again.'

She sighed and rolled her eyes heavenwards. A slight flush showed she was pleased. 'Well, I can't talk to you now, I'm busy. And it's embarrassing,' she added. 'I'd rather you didn't come. I'll see you on Sunday.'

She went off, returning a moment later with my order. There was too much milk in the tea and the rock bun was hard. But she had served me with her own hands! I was hopelessly in love. Life was nothing but Ingrid Johannsen.

On Sunday I wondered whether Maggie would insist on accompanying me to Mass again. I put it to her on Saturday night, making it seem as though it was a matter of indifference whether she accompanied me or not; but she was not fooled. Her weathered face lit up with a knowing smile. 'She's a nice girl, isn't she?'

Now that I was smitten by Ingrid, there was no fear that I would miss Mass, and she probably assumed Divine Providence had arranged it that way, my love for the girl (an unwitting agent in God's Plan) ensuring that I would remain a Catholic. 'Well, I was talking to Mother,' she went on. 'I thought it was time we gave the local church a try, support local industry! So that's where we'll be going.'

I slept poorly that night, obsessed by the thought of Ingrid: whether she liked me, whether I stood a chance with her. She was already kneeling in the pew when I entered the church; I knelt beside her, waiting for the Mass to begin. She was pleased to see me. Was she relieved? Had she spent an anxious night wondering if I would turn up? I doubted it, I could not believe I meant that much to her. I wanted to talk to her, but couldn't think what to say. She wore a different headscarf, one with a bolder pattern, and had chosen a pretty frock to wear beneath her jacket.

'You look nice,' I managed, grimacing at the banal compliment.

She did not respond; her attention was taken by the priest, who had appeared at the altar. Throughout the Mass she scarcely seemed aware of me. She was totally absorbed in the service and I loved the pale rapture of her face uplifted to the altar. I knew her prayers must be for her sister and I loved her goodness as though it was itself an aspect of beauty.

The Mass over, we left the pew together. I was tinglingly aware of her presence; but when we reached the rear of the church she was accosted by someone who seemed to know her well – a man who might have succeeded Frank as a scoutmaster, for he had the shiny, virtuous look of one who spent time with his chums in the open. He was very tall and thin, you could see him galloping across the country in shorts and running shoes, and he smiled down upon Ingrid, ignoring me.

'Hello, Tom,' she said faintly.

He must have been at least twenty-five, far too old for her. He somehow got himself between us as we left the church and I wondered how we were to get rid of him. But did she want to be rid of him? His voice swarmed over her, gurgling compassion for poor Olga and narrating his adventures as a patrol leader and a schoolteacher. I was frustrated and feared I would lose the girl. But then she bent across him, staring at me wildly. 'Weren't you going to show me that place?' she asked.

'The place? Oh, yes, the place!' I fumbled my Ingersoll out of my top pocket and glanced at the time. 'Yes, it's getting late, we'd better …'

'Yes, we'd better …' She grinned falsely at Tom. 'Have to go and see this place!'

'Oh, well …' He was taken aback, halted halfway through an account of a dinner his mother had given a visiting bishop.

'Remember me to your mother,' Ingrid called as we hurried off together, giggling furtively.

Somehow her hand was in mine. My heart bounded with happiness. Her cool, soft hand. But Tom's familiarity worried me. 'Who is he? Is he one of your boyfriends?'

'I don't have that many!' she laughed. 'I've been out with him a few times. My mum likes him.'

'Do you like him?'

'He's all right.' He had taken her out, kissed her no doubt … 'I think I might get to like you better,' she added.

'Why? What have I done to deserve it?'

'You're not like everyone else. You sort of go your own way, don't you? Tom would never have left a good job with the Corporation. His mother wouldn't have let him.'

'Is he fond of his mother?'

'He calls her his best girl.'

We were now close to the road where I had once lived and I took her there, pointing out the window of what had been my attic room, where I had lain in the dark listening to the clank of a shunting train and thinking of God in Eternity. The air raid shelter had been demolished, but you could still trace its faint outline in the road. We spoke of the bombing, I told her of Benny's death and she murmured comfortingly. We went into the park opposite, found a bench near the duck pond and sat down. The day was overcast but it was unlikely to rain. Some kids were playing at the pond, shouting boisterously. A man came by with a dog on a string.

'I can't stay long, I'm afraid. Olga will be wondering where I am.'

'You do a lot for your sister?'

She washed her, treated her bed sores. 'She suffers a lot of pain. I read to her, to take her mind off it.'

They had gone through much of Dickens, Thackeray and Walter Scott; she had read more nineteenth-century novels than I had – 'And we listen to the wireless a lot. She loves comedy shows. She loves to laugh. She used to be ... before the illness she was such a bouncy, happy girl. And think of it, Peter; I mean all the life she must have thought she had, years and years ahead of her to enjoy! I couldn't bear what she has to go through, day after day.'

I was absorbed for a moment in Olga's suffering, wondering how one would put it in writing.

'If we make enough money – maybe not this year, but hopefully next – I'm going to take her on the pilgrimage to Lourdes.'

'Do you think Our Lady will cure her?'

'Well, it'll be a holiday for her, if nothing else. And God knows she needs a change from that room and that bed! It'll be quite an adventure. We've neither of us ever been abroad before, even though we're half Norwegian.' Then, as though it was something shameful: 'You know my dad left us, don't you? It was before the war. I was only eight at the time.'

'Why did he leave?'

'For one thing, he wanted Mum to live in Norway and she never would. For another, he wasn't a Catholic, it was a mixed marriage, he would never convert.'

'Were they divorced?'

'Oh no!' Her face became plain and prim. 'Catholics don't get divorced.'

'Do you miss him?'

'It was sad when we heard he'd been killed,' she sighed, smiling reflectively. 'He was a big man, with a big sandy moustache. Couldn't speak English very well. Used to laugh a lot. And get drunk! What I remember best was when he opened the café and we were all excited and working like mad to get it started. I was only a little girl but I can remember the excitement of it all. It seemed then as though everything was going to be wonderful.'

'Do you enjoy working in the café?'

'It's all right. Cashing up at the end of the day can be a bit nerve-racking, Mum gets annoyed if I'm sixpence short, but it's nice meeting people. I don't want to do it forever, though.'

She glanced at me speculatively. What did she see sitting beside her? A youth with a body that had been reasonably put together, with a sombre face and chestnut hair, a pose of assumed confidence. I stared at her folded hands in her lap, conscious of her thighs, the gentle rise of her breast. How was it I could worship her as an unsullied virgin and at the same time take an acute sexual interest in her young body?

'Do you like being a projectionist?'

'What? Well, I get to see a lot of pictures! And it's not stuffy, like working in an office. I'm really only filling in time, though, before I'm called up for National Service.'

'Oh, yes, when you're eighteen.'

'After I've got that out of the way, things will be very different. I shall start to make my own life then; and I think, you know ... I don't want to sound boastful, but I think I'm going to be something rather special.'

'In what way?' Her head was bowed, she was gazing at the scuffed, clayey earth beneath her feet.

'I haven't decided yet. There are a number of possibilities.'

She raised her head and looked at me. Her lips were curved with a tender scepticism that suggested she had heard this sort of thing before, and I wished I had not spoken. Yet I was quite sure I had something, some quality however undefined, that made me superior to Tom and any other boyfriend she may have had. Not superior in every sense, of course; I couldn't run as fast as Tom, and my mother would never be my best girl. But superior in some way he could never have attained.

'I have to go,' she said, getting up. 'Have to get back, so that Mum can get to Mass.'

'Your mother doesn't like me, does she?'

'Why do you say that?'

'Mothers never do, for some reason.'

'What matters is whether Olga likes you, and she does. She's taken a fancy to you, for some strange reason! She asked me to bring you back with me. Do you mind seeing her?'

'Of course not.'

We left the park, no longer holding hands for our relationship was no longer that simple. When we reached the high street I asked her to come out with me on my day off. I held my breath in painful anticipation, but this was unnecessary, she had assumed I would ask her for a date and was quite happy to consent. I felt a surge of joy, life was so wonderful!

Her mother was waiting to go to Mass, dressed in hat and coat, when we arrived. She chided Ingrid for keeping her waiting and I feared her displeasure, but her heavy face greeted me with a strained smile. I wondered if Olga had been talking to her, perhaps pleading the case of the young lovers. Nevertheless, I was sure she would have preferred a settled suitor with impeccable credentials like Tom, to a callow youth with seemingly slender prospects.

She hurried off to Mass, hunched up and clutched together like a woman soured with frustration. We entered the sickroom and I went to Olga. She gripped me with her shiny red hand. 'You can kiss me if you like!' she laughed. 'Don't be shy.'

I bent and touched her flushed cheek with my lips. She called to her sister, 'You're not jealous, are you, Ingrid?'

We began to see each other regularly. There was something bland and settled about it, a respectable suppression of passion. We went to the pictures – 'A busman's holiday for you, poor thing' – and walked all over the city, kissing while sitting on benches in its various parks. We went to New Brighton and I took her to the Chamber of Horrors, showed her the water torture. At Formby among the sand dunes, she changed into a bathing costume and presented herself to me, smiling shyly, hands hovering about her genitals. I saw her bare feet for the first time, her lovely legs, her bare shoulders, and tried to hide a hard-on. I was in bathing trunks and she scanned my body with interest, glancing at the swell of my erection with a furtive smile.

I rarely saw her more than twice a week – on Sundays and on my day off. But I visited the café sometimes in the morning when her mother was busy in the kitchen at the back. I loved to watch her working, her slim figure weaving among the tables, her girlish smile as she showed newcomers to a table and her barely controlled impatience when a dawdling customer couldn't decide between a rock bun and a buttered scone; the way she would stand then and gaze about idly, catching my eye and widening her eyes in a way that perfectly conveyed her exasperation. The café had lapsed into the doldrums of middle-aged ladies and buttered scones. It made little money.

I wanted to be with her all the time and was instantly jealous if I found her smiling at another man. I held her tight and kissed her repeatedly in a kind of delirium: her lips, her eyelids, her throat. 'Give her a Frenchie,' my fellow projectionists would have advised, but I would not go so far. In fact, I had never given a girl a Frenchie. To thrust my tongue into Ingrid's innocent mouth would have been an unpardonable violation, and I was sure she would have rejected it with horror. As for touching her breasts, her bottom … Out of the question. So for six months I confined myself to chaste if copious kisses, whether or not she privately wanted and expected more.

I told her I loved her. She was flattered, but did not at once respond as I had hoped. Female intuition would have warned her that when a young man tells a girl that he loves her, it's often a slot-machine gambit with the object of arousing her and being rewarded with a more passionate response. Was that my game? There was no such ambiguity in Ingrid's case: once she told you she loved you, she meant it for life.

I told her of my difficulty in loving my mother: 'I'd begun to think I couldn't really love anyone, until I met you. I was always afraid to show my feelings, afraid of being laughed at and repulsed. But now I feel so free! I want … I just want … I don't know! I worship you, Ingrid. I want to give myself wholly to you.'

But again, could I be sure, could I be absolutely sure that, even unknown to myself, this was not a crafty contrivance to arouse her love? How could you ever know when you were being totally sincere?

Nevertheless, it did the trick. She held me and kissed me. 'I really do love you, Peter, and that's something I've never told any boy before.'

I swelled with a joyous gratitude. This was succeeded by a blissful sensation of peace and security. I was loved! Ingrid loved me the way no one had ever loved me before.

I took her home and introduced her to Mother, who had once met her as a schoolgirl in a siren suit, all dressed up for an air raid. Ingrid was apprehensive but Mother welcomed her and treated her kindly. She was glad I had found such a decent girl. Ingrid would settle me down. Once I had finished National Service, she would make sure I got a good steady job and stuck to it; then we would be married, rent a snug little house and produce children ... I guessed all this from the speculative look she gave us.

Ingrid was intrigued and impressed by the basement flat. She did not share my opinion of my home. 'It's a really lovely district. All the trees, and these big houses. You're very lucky.'

'But we don't belong here. We're only here on sufferance.'

'Where do you belong?'

'I don't feel I belong anywhere, except with you.'

At a later point, Dad met her and made a loving, fatherly fuss of her. 'You're far too good for him!' he told her. And to me, in private: 'You look after her, do you hear? If you break her heart, I'll break your neck.'

At the conclusion of every date I was expected to take Ingrid home and spend a little time at Olga's bedside. We always had to give her a detailed account of where we had been, what we had seen and done. She listened avidly, with a flushed feverish glitter. 'And then you went there, did you? And then what did you do?' I felt wrung-out whenever I left the sickroom and was unhappy with the thought that, after I left, Olga would cross-examine Ingrid, wanting to know all the doting things I had said to her, how often we had kissed and whether we had gone further than kissing. She would not let Ingrid go until she had gleaned everything she could of our affair: 'He said he loved you, did he? And what do you feel about him? He's a nice lad, isn't he? Do you feel romantic about him?' – I could imagine how it might go, and Ingrid would cooperate in the interrogation. The horizon of her life was dominated by Olga, and she felt guilty; it wasn't fair that she should have all the fun, being loved and kissed by an attractive boy while her poor sister lay crippled, barely able to move. After a while I found myself coldly calculating the odds on my happiness. How long was Olga going to take to die? And even when she did die, would Ingrid be free of her? Would she ever feel free to enjoy life wholly and without guilt? If we were to be married and Olga was still alive, what would happen to her and her mother? Were we all to live together? Was I to take over the management of the café?

I began to feel constricted at times. Ingrid was a devout Catholic, her family was as rabidly Catholic as mine, whereas I was starting at last to feel my way out of the metaphysical murk. I once asked her if she ever doubted her religion, and confessed my own doubts. If God was wholly good and all-knowing, why did he allow Olga to suffer? If he was wholly just, why would he cast my atheist but essentially virtuous brother into Hell?

She was troubled by my questions, they made her feel stupid; a cloud came over the sunny simplicity of her love. 'You shouldn't think like that. There must be a reason for it. God knows what He's doing, Peter! I don't like it when you have these doubts.'

'Will you pray for me?'

She did not register my sardonic tone. 'I always pray for you. I pray that you won't get knocked down crossing the road, or fall sick of some terrible disease. I'm terrified sometimes that you'll die.'

The thought of this pure, innocent girl praying for me was very pleasing. Yet I could not keep my growing doubts to myself. They had lain at the back of my mind since Frank's death, since leaving the seminary and even before that, since Benny's harrowing death; and now, probably because I had begun to read seriously, they had elbowed their way into my consciousness. There was the age-old question of the Trinity, for instance: 'How can the Godhead be both Three and One at the same time, Ingrid? Tertullian – ' Tertullian? I had found the quote somewhere. 'Tertullian said he believed precisely because it was absurd.'

She wrinkled her brow at that.

'It's a wonderful thing to say, crazy and wonderful, completely defying reason. *Credo quia absurdum est.* And I can see why the church insists on it. Three is One and One is Three – not in the world we live in, of course, but in the realm of the supernatural, which isn't bound by everyday logic and where everything is possible. It's almost quantum physics' – *Quantum physics?* I enjoyed books of popular science and the ecstasy of incomprehension they induced – 'The Church grandly and defiantly insists on the impossible, the incomprehensible; it insists that believers commit themselves beyond the bounds of reason and logic.'

'With God nothing is impossible,' she wavered.

'But some things are bloody difficult to accept, don't you agree?'

She frowned at my use of "bloody".

But she loved me, she accepted me with all my faults, the doubts perilous to the soul, my ranging intelligence and the dangerous authors I read: Bertrand Russell, David Hume, Friedrich Nietzsche. And I loved her, I wanted to be with her and look after her always. Consequently, when the time came to leave her for National Service, our parting was tearful and passionate. She kissed me wildly. 'And you'll write to me, won't you, darling?'

'Whenever I can. And of course I'll see you every time I get some leave.'

'And it's only for eighteen months, it will soon be over. Then we can think about getting married!' She gazed at me solemnly. 'You won't go with any dirty women while you're away, will you? Promise!'

I promised.

Maggie thought I should follow in Frank's footsteps and try for the air force, but indifference led to my being shoved into the army. I said goodbye to Mother, we were constantly saying goodbye – evacuation, the seminary – and it was about the only time we kissed with any fervour. 'Now cheer up,' she said tenderly.

I was miserable because I was leaving Ingrid behind. But it was also the hateful business of going to a new place, meeting a horde of strangers, taking back the spuds. 'I don't want to go,' I confessed.

She gave her slighting laugh. 'You've got to do your duty, lad. Your father did his duty in two world wars; and as for Frank – '

'That was different. This is peacetime. Where is the enemy threatening England?'

'Russia,' she said at once. 'Russia would invade us like a shot, if we let them.'

'Why should Russia invade us?'

'Russia is communist, and the communists envy all we've got.'

'All we've got?'

'Our traditions! The Royal Family. Our empire – until this Labour government gives it all away!'

'Look at what they're doing in Berlin,' Maggie said.

It was 1948 and there was a crisis, the Russians had blockaded Berlin. 'You might be fighting them in Berlin yet!' Mother cackled grimly. 'If they invaded us, we'd all be slaves of communism. That's why we need an army.'

'And the atom bomb,' Maggie added.

'The atom bomb is supposed to be the deterrent that makes armies superfluous.'

'You're always trying to make out you know better than us.'

Joining the army was like being born again, I was once more an intruder and they were all piled on top of me: corporals and sergeants, second-lieutenants, captains and majors. The army was a going concern of massive tradition and it did not welcome temporary, unenthusiastic additions to its ranks. Like the rest of my intake, I found myself thrust into an incomprehensible organisation that, in the time it had existed without me, had created a rigidly hierarchical system of interrelated units, each cherishing its own traditions, its battle honours, whether gained in a good cause or not. It was also predominantly male; I was in a vast secular seminary with rules and customs that were often unknown until one transgressed and was punished.

'We're in the army,' I told my mates, another Rennet, 'not to serve our country or to fight the Russians, but simply to be punished by superiors who hate us.'

'You're always grousing, you.'

Encased in rough khaki uniforms or nondescript denims, we were bullied and marched about, burdened with meaningless tasks and duties. Once again I lived in fear, harried by a malignant tribe of Father Prefects. I was a private soldier whose sole function was to conform, to obey unthinkingly and to kill if necessary. '*They've given me a rifle to kill with,*' I wrote to Ingrid. It shifted about awkwardly on my shoulder and I had to drill with it, slinging it up and down to barked orders. Many of the intake were charmed by their rifles and cleaned them assiduously; I loathed mine and it made me stupid, I could barely tell the bolt from the magazine (was it the magazine?).

Then I had to fire the thing. We were taken to the firing range and made to lie down with hips and legs swung to the side in an unnatural position. What was the point of that? Although I held the rifle as instructed, both elbows digging into the ground, butt firmly into my shoulder, the noise when the weapon went off astonished me and the recoil hammered into my shoulder.

'That's because you're not holding it firmly enough, laddie!' the sergeant major said, idly swiping my legs with his cane. 'And next time, try and hit the target. Imagine it's a Russian coming at you.'

Once again I was in a chain gang of male company, sleeping with them in a snoring smelly barrack room, eating with them in a huge bare canteen, working and cursing with them day after day, longing for the leave that would allow me to rest my weary head against Ingrid's chaste bosom. I tried to fit in, be one of the lads, but it wasn't easy when I knew I was superior to them, despite the fact that I lagged behind them in military skills, invariably lost at cards and could never manage more than a pint of ale. Most of my fellow squaddies depressed and sickened me. I confused them with the louts who had once debagged me, and despised their low intelligence, their foul language and boorish manners, their ignorance and lack of aspiration, their indifference to beauty and tender feelings, their cynicism and bigotry, their conviction that as part of the great British nation they were superior to all inferior races: yids and niggers and wogs.

They did not despise me, but were mildly curious about the difference between us. I was uneasy lest they discovered I had been to a seminary; it was shameful to have wanted to be a priest. They were incredulous when learning that I came from Liverpool. 'You don't sound like a Scouser,' they asserted.

Mother had always insisted on her children being well spoken and my time in the seminary and as a clerk had reinforced this, not to mention my linguistic adventure in the dole queue. There was also the fact that when I read books by middle-class authors, I heard their voices in my head and it affected my own voice. In any case, I was fascinated with the resources of the English language and felt it should be spoken with respect. But at first, reluctant to attract attention, I roughened my voice and added a few chunky obscenities in case they suspected I was that most loathed of creatures, a nancy boy.

Initially I was too distracted by the army to think much of Ingrid; but once I began writing to her and got her letters in return, I missed her greatly. I longed for her physical presence, her voice, her smell, her soft warm body in my arms. Each day I awoke with the hope of a letter, and there were usually two or three a week. They were never as long or quite as exciting as I could have wished: '*I wish I was clever like you, then I could write you a wonderful letter full of interesting things; a letter that would really explain just how much I miss you and love you.*'

After initial training we were given a week's leave. I returned home in my uniform, because she wanted to see it. 'I'm so proud of my soldier boy!' she said, kissing me and stroking the khaki.

I could not tell her how alienated I felt in the uniform; it might as well have been a convict's tunic. I had grown up since the war and was no longer consciously patriotic. Nations and states, flags and uniforms seemed wholly artificial constructions. I could not look at a bit of soil and connect it with the word "England"; there was no real connection. I was becoming something of a nominalist, which the church viewed as heretical.

We had been apart for eight weeks and Ingrid was gratifyingly passionate when we met again. Of her own accord she brought my hand to her breast, pressed her loins against my hard-on and was not in the least bit repulsed when I slipped my tongue into her mouth. But no sooner had we unclasped than I was taken in to see Olga, who insisted on learning every detail of army life, her bright eyes staring at me fixedly.

Because I had once been a clerk I had been put in the Service Corps, and when I returned from leave I was assigned to the stores in the huge camp at Catterick, a posting I shared with three National Servicemen as supinely indifferent to duty as I was. We were supervised by an NCO, a skiving regular soldier who visited the stores as little as possible, so we often had the place to ourselves. When necessary, sighing as we doused cigarettes, put aside whatever we had been reading or abandoned a game of pontoon, we would issue items of kit from the stock piled on shelves and in bays throughout the length of the great chilly shed where we spent our days. 'Got your chitty, have you?'...'Snot signed by your section leader.'...'Blankets, two, for the use of '...'Havven got any of them. Are they supposed to be in the stores?'

I thought it was time I fucked a woman. I use the term deliberately; it would be a mere biological necessity having nothing in common with making love. With Victorian sophistry I reasoned that by expending my lust on some whore, I would be safeguarding Ingrid's virginity. My mates in the stores had both fucked a woman recently and had favoured me with a relishing account of the experience. The woman was to be found in a certain pub in Richmond frequented by soldiers from the camp. One of my mates took me there and introduced me to her. She was a fairly large woman, with dark hair and a ripe lipstick smile: Bella. In her late thirties, I supposed. I bought her a drink – 'Make it a double,pet' – then she took me to a small house she rented in one of the town's backstreets. She showed me into a front room with a single bed, then left me while she thumped upstairs and ordered some noisy children to keep quiet. There were a couple of easy chairs in the room and I sat in one, waiting for her. There were no bedclothes on the bed apart from a greyish bottom sheet and a pillow. I was anxious, wondering how I was supposed to behave, terrified of making a fool of myself or being laughed at by the woman.

She returned and locked the door behind her. 'We don't want to be disturbed, do we, darling?' Then she explained her terms; it was rather like a game, Strip Bella Naked. For half a crown she would take off her blouse – 'All right?' I nodded and she took off her blouse, revealing big breasts in a soiled pink brassiere. Another half-crown and she would take off her skirt. I nodded: five bob so far. Knickers and a suspender belt; meaty white thighs in nylons. She heeled off her shoes. That cost me nothing, but it was five shillings before she would remove her suspender belt and stockings.

'How far do you want to go?' she asked with a glinting smile, motioning me to sit beside her on the bed.

My army pay was meagre, but I had saved up for this event and I was ready to go all the way. Ten shillings got rid of her brassiere, then she lay back and let me fondle her breasts, sprawled half across her big pink body like Ahab on the white whale. She was now naked but for her knickers; it cost another ten shillings to have them removed. Her belly was large and white and there were stretch marks, pink weals from the pressure of her underwear. But what mattered was that at last, a few inches from my nose ... I stared furtively: there was the thing itself, somewhere, buried in coarse brown hair. I felt faint.

'Don't you want to get inside?' she murmured. 'Cost you a quid.'

I nodded and shoved my dick inside her roomy cunt, thinking of how many had been there before me. Just two pound ten altogether, not counting the double whisky I had bought her beforehand. Worth it?

I felt the usual cliché, that some rite of passage had been undergone, an experience involving momentary ecstasy and a large helping of disgust. In my case it was largely an ideological act, a matter of sinning in order to eradicate my sense of sin, and it was marginally successful in that respect; but it had nothing in common with the tender act of love, the sacramental encounter of flesh upon flesh, that I expected eventually to enjoy with Ingrid. At the same time I was ashamed of having yielded to lust (a wank would have cost me nothing), of acting just like any other raw recruit, and of having succumbed to the greater licence of the times. Shortly afterwards, I visited Bella again.

I spent some time with Mother and Maggie whenever I was on leave, but there was little pleasure in it, it was essentially an obligation. How lovely if I could have returned home with happy anticipation, greeting them with joy and being received with loving warmth … On one occasion I learned that Dad had left the Manchester hotel. 'Was he sacked?' I asked, thinking of the maniacal chef who had sacked me.

'Of course not.'

He was working in the kitchen of a hotel in Southport now and he wanted me to visit him, having seen little of me recently. 'You're privileged,' Mother said, in her huffy way. 'He's never invited me.'

The hotel was on the seafront, although the sea is scarcely visible at Southport. It was a handsome building in a Georgian style, one of the biggest in town. Lunch was being prepared and I hung about in the kitchen, sampling trifles of food and keeping out of the way of the head chef, a morose Scotsman named Fergie, who mumbled and grumbled but hadn't the energy to be tyrannical. Dad was his sous chef. When lunch was over Fergie grumbled away to his room, and the rest of the staff, a porter and a commis, went off duty. Dad stayed behind and served me a meal in the deserted kitchen. He sat opposite me while I ate, pouring me another glass of beer, getting up to fetch me a dollop of ice cream. He moved with his old sprightliness, humming a tune and cocking his head before driving an imaginary football into the goal. He looked much better than when he had first left the sea; his face had filled out, making him appear younger, and he had put on some weight.

'Aye, I'm happy here. Should see the room they've given me; every bit as good as any of the guest rooms. The money's good, too; and I get a fair amount of time off.'

'Then why don't you come home more often?'

'There's nothen for me there, now. Jessie's gone off to Yankeeland, you're in the army and I've never really got on with Maggie. As for your mother ... She's getten on all right without me.'

'Are you sure?'

'She duzzen need me any longer.'

I finished my meal and he cleared the table. As he did so, a woman entered the kitchen. 'Peter?'

We both looked up. Dad smiled. The woman returned his smile warmly. 'Has Fergie gone off already?'

'In his room. Can I be of assistance?'

'You always are!' And again the smile slipping between them.

He introduced her as Mrs Callum, the manageress. 'Don't get up,' she begged, extending her ringed fingers.

She was in her forties, yet still a good-looking woman with a tidy figure, a pleasant face, rich black hair set in swirls and curls. I would have rather had her than Bella ... 'So this is your big son!' she cooed.

'Aye. The owney one I got left.'

'Of course, yes ... Oh dear,' she sighed; then reverted to business. 'I wanted to see Fergie about tomorrow's menu, but I'm sure you can help me.'

She had a piece paper in her hand and they bent over it together, their bodies close, laughter breaking through their discussion of the menu.

'She's a really nice lady,' he said when she had gone. 'She's got her eye on me!' he laughed. 'I mean for Fergie's job.'

'She wants you to be head chef?'

'Oh aye. He's not up to it, y'know; he's all at sea when it comes to haute cuisine.'

I was surprised he even knew the term.

I returned to Liverpool later that evening. The next day was Sunday and I went to Mass with Ingrid, although I no longer went to Mass when alone. The priest performed at the altar; at the Communion he knelt and raised the host. Ingrid bent her head but I gazed insolently at the wafer, rejecting the miracle. She had begun to sense my indifference and it worried her, wrinkling her brow in a manner that was quite unattractive. I had changed in some way she did not understand; I was no longer the innocent lad I had been before joining the army. There was something anarchic, iconoclastic in my manner, though she would not have used either term. My mauling passion when we kissed alarmed her and she pulled away, disturbed and confused.

'What's got into you? You're like an animal!'

I could not confide in her and we were both upset. Our affair was no longer blithe and simple. I regretted this, yet knew there was no going back, things would never be the same again. What would they be in the future?

'Is anything the matter?' she asked. 'You're not going off me, are you? Do you still love me?'

'Of course.'

'You'll tell me, won't you, if you ever stop loving me? I wouldn't want you to pretend, just so as not to hurt my feelings.'

'I love you!' I exclaimed, irritated.

I was quite glad to get back to Catterick. I had been in the army for a year now and I had given up trying to be one of the lads. I no longer munched obscenities with every other word, nor could I agree that the Jews had all the money, that niggers' dicks were an abnormal length, that the Royal Family and the flag were to be reverenced, or that England was the greatest of all countries. I had decided simply to be myself, whatever that was, and no longer cared what the others thought. I forewent friendship, became hard and proud, indifferent to loneliness. Let the lads go their way and I would go mine. I spent most of my spare time in the camp library, which was reasonably well stocked and usually empty. I read a great deal; and at length, recalling the excitement with which I had once written about a snowfall in the city, I began to write a few simple things – poems and stories. But I did this furtively, not simply because I did not want anyone to see them, but as though I did not want to know, myself, what I was doing.

Catterick wasn't far from Richmond and thus but a few miles from the seminary. I was often in the town and sometimes walked along the riverside track to the abbey ruins, the Drummer Boy stumbling along in the dark beneath me. I kept meaning to visit the seminary, but it was towards the end of my National Service before I dared do so, and even then my resolve weakened as I approached the castle. I had imagined it would be amusing to present myself in butch battledress to whoever remembered me, but I was still afraid of Father Prefect. Yet what could he possibly do to me: give me No Tea, swing me round by my ear?

Nevertheless, his image, the congested red face nutcrackered between the black of his biretta and the white of his collar, was still fearsome.

I did not approach the castle from the front, but in keeping with my military status encircled it from the rear, along a lane that bordered the playing fields and the high wall that enclosed the grounds. There was a gate in the wall, which we were only allowed to use when being marched to the playing fields on those twice-weekly occasions when sports were permitted. I passed through the gate afflicted by fear and excitement, an intruder once more. I was besieged by memories – the clang of Father Prefect's handbell, the tedium of services in the chapel, the endless petty conflicts with other boys; but also the kindness of some of the priests and the companionship of fellow victims I had found here. Here was the great lawn on which one must not walk, encircled by the drive, which one must only walk along in a clockwise direction. But – I frowned, amazed, for there were a couple of boys strolling along the drive in the wrong direction. In the distance, another boy ran across a corner of the lawn, taking a short cut. Making sure I was in the right place, I stared at the rear of the castle – the Palladian terrace (out of bounds), the tall windows of the classrooms, the pinched windows of the third-floor dormitories – and shook my head, bewildered.

When the kids drew near I spoke to them. They were first years, but they looked so insouciant I wondered if the seminary had vacated the castle and some private school had taken it over. The boys assured me it was still a seminary and that they meant to become priests some day, serving God in the missionary field – though they did not put it quite like that; in fact, there was little to distinguish them from cheery, pragmatic boys elsewhere. I could not see them as images of my pale subdued earlier self. I told them I had once been a seminarist here, that I knew the Rules, and pointed out that they were walking along the drive in the wrong direction. What if Father Prefect or one of his Gestapo caught them? Weren't they afraid of being given No Tea?

They gazed at each other, puzzled; then they recalled that, yes, there had once been some rule about walking only one way round the drive. But it was no longer in force, nor were the boys prevented from walking on the lawn, though you weren't expected to play footer on it,obviously.

'What about No Tea?' I demanded. 'What about Father Prefect? Doesn't he scare you stiff?'

Father Langen was Father Prefect now, they said, and he was all right. He never tore up your bed and No Tea was no longer a punishment; they were given lines instead. 'In Latin!' one of them groaned. The previous Father Prefect – 'Old Crippen!' I interjected – the previous Father Prefect, together with a number of priests, had returned to Germany after the war, their places being taken by some Irish and American priests.

I asked what they knew of my erstwhile friends, Jim Kapowski and Simon Parker. What of Paul Chisholm, whom I had once admired: surely he was a novice now? But the only name they recognised was Simon Parker, who was indeed a novice. The others had left.

I let the boys go and sat on a nearby bench, gazing at the castle resting blandly in the afternoon. Should I not have been pleased that the rules had been relaxed and that the boys were presumably happier? Perversely, I lamented the lost regime: no ravaged beds, no No Tea. The place had gone soft.

I realised I was sitting on the same bench I had shared with Frank, the time he had visited me. How priggishly disapproving I had been of his swearing and smoking! In the bright silence of the afternoon I was aware of him, he was closer to me than he had been for years, his heavy figure in his crumpled uniform, his strained eyes half-closed against the smoke of a cigarette. I seemed to hear him speaking again of a bombing raid and what he hoped to do when the war was over, his very voice! He had wanted to work for the union, rouse the workers to their rights – Oh my poor brother! I wept. I could mourn him now as never before, his goodness and innocence, the bitter injustice of his death.

I was not due any more leave for some time and this enabled me to concentrate on my reading and writing, which gave me continual pleasure. I was growing in intelligence and cultural experience. I read some existentialist philosophy and Tolstoy's greatest works, I discovered James Joyce and Henry James. There was a gramophone in the library and some records of classical music; I heard Beethoven's *Eroica* for the first time, and Brahms' Double Concerto. There were volumes of reproductions on the shelves and I discovered the works of Botticelli, Poussin, Manet and Cezanne. Such creativity, such beauty! It made me want to write something. But what?

These preoccupations often took Ingrid's place in my thoughts. She was relegated to the back of my mind, a tiny forlorn figure wrinkling her brow piteously. It was easy, a slick instinct, to convert her into a character in a story. The immersion in culture gave existence a vaster dimension and I anticipated an exciting future after I left the army. When I went on leave and called on Ingrid, the faded failing café and the rooms above seemed shabby and sterile as though life had expired there. Olga herself, for all her cheery courage, seemed to extend her paralysis throughout the home. I knew I was changing irrevocably, for better or worse. I might have halted the process, I suppose, closed the books, destroyed the scraps I had written, turned my back on Beethoven and Cezanne and all the others; but I had no intention of doing so. There was an engrossing novelty in my life, something great and durable, and I could not let it go.

In September, leaving her mother to look after the café, Ingrid took her sister on the pilgrimage to Lourdes in the hope of a cure. I saw her soon after they returned and she was bright with excitement. 'Oh, Peter, I wish you'd been there! That was the only thing missing, really.' She spoke of the crowds of pilgrims: 'There were these little old ladies in their black dresses, peasants from Italy. Oh, and it was so moving to see them, all humble and pious! You got such a wonderful impression of people's faith, and – oh, you know, the greatness of the church. There were hundreds of sick people, many on stretchers and all of them hoping to be cured.'

'And were they all cured?'

'Well, of course not. You know it doesn't happen that way.'

She hurried into an account of the street theatre of Lourdes, candlelit processions and the singing of hymns, the blessing of the sick at the grotto and the marvel of the great Basilica. And France itself, of course, the excitement of being abroad, the strange food and heady wine, the strong sunlight of the Pyrenees, the colour and vivacity of a French town.

'You would have loved it, Peter,' Olga added. She swore she had never felt better in her life. 'It did me so much good, because it was so uplifting. You felt the whole place was wrapped up in Our Lady's mantel!'

I examined her carefully, wondering if indeed she did look better. She had not got up from her stretcher at Lourdes and walked for the first time in years, a living miracle, yet she seemed stronger and it was possible she could move a little more than before.

Ingrid had a present for me. 'I didn't know what to get you.' It was a half-bottle of brandy, which I would share with my mates in the stores. She had a number of trinkets she had brought back with her – some postcards, a string of rosary beads, a statue of Saint Bernadette for her mother, a gramophone record of the pilgrims singing hymns. The trip to wonderland had made her more Catholic than ever.

'What's this?' I asked.

It was a small statuette of the Virgin, made of glass.

'Oh, that's ...' Ingrid smiled with pleasure. 'You see, it's a bottle, really.'

It was filled with Lourdes water from the sacred spring at the grotto, where the Virgin had appeared to the peasant Bernadette. Pilgrims were allowed to sample it, taking it from taps at the side wall of the grotto.

'It's a bottle? How do you open it?'

'Oh, well, you see – ' Smiling with pleasure at the novelty, she opened the bottle by screwing off Our Lady's head. I laughed helplessly. She grew pale with mortification, her eyes glittered hatred. 'You shouldn't make fun of holy things!'

On my next leave, I examined Olga closely. Had her condition really improved as a result of the pilgrimage? If by any chance she was cured, it would severely challenge my loss of faith. But although she held me and kissed me with her usual strained animation, it was clear she was no better; if anything, she had suffered something of a relapse after the excitement of Lourdes. I could not help feeling relieved, as though my apostasy was of greater importance than the poor woman's recovery. There was an element of corruption in my relationship with the Johannsens.

After the café closed for the day, I took Ingrid out. It was a broad golden August evening and we went to Formby; we lay among the sand dunes where she had once appeared to me in her bathing costume, lovely and shy. I would probably never see her fully naked, never get between her thighs and loot that feathery blond nest. We held each other and kissed, and she told me how much she loved me. I lit a cigarette and smoked reflectively, gazing out across the estuary, the ships at the Mersey Bar. There were other couples in the sand dunes, and some in the woods behind us. Although it was warm, the sky was covered with thin skeins of cloud which obscured the sun.

'Well, Lourdes doesn't seem to have helped poor Olga much.'

Ingrid was alert and defensive at once. 'All the same, it was a wonderful experience for her, for us both, one we'll never forget. And she may still get better, you know; cures don't always happen straight away.'

'But what if she doesn't?'

'Well, we must just accept that it's God's will, I suppose. Anyway, I'll keep on praying for her.'

I despised her stupidity. 'What is the point in praying for her? I mean, have you examined what you're saying? If God has permitted her condition, he's not going to change his mind and cure her just because you're praying to him. He cannot change his mind, don't you see? If he is perfect, and I assume you believe that He is, then He's not subject to change.'

She could not understand this and it hurt her. She sat slumped against the curve of the sand dune, her face lowered and brooding. I lay opposite her, leaning on my elbow, hopelessly sorry for her. Yet if I could just get her to understand ...! She was so lovely in her maidenly vulnerability, and I felt that I still loved her. I wanted her – yes, even to be my wife eventually. But could I accept her as she was, made dull and stupid by superstition?

'How can you believe in a God who is blandly prepared to let Olga suffer? Because he must know about her, if he's omniscient. And if he knows, yet won't do anything to relieve her suffering – to say nothing of the immense amount of suffering in the rest of the world – how can he possibly be the good and omnipotent God you worship?'

'Oh, stop it!' she moaned. 'Stop it!' She raised her head and gazed at me, her face anguished. 'You've changed so much. It's all those books you've been reading!'

She sounded like my mother.

'I just wish we could talk about these things without getting into a row. If I could only explain ... I've been learning so much about the church recently, its history I mean. For instance, I'd always assumed that a doctrine like Original Sin was a fundamental part of faith, as though Christ himself had announced it. But that's not so! Original Sin was invented by Augustine in the fifth century. And then there's

Transubstantiation, changing the host into the body of Christ,' I went on, overriding the protest she was about to make. 'That was invented by someone called Radbertus as late as the ninth century. And when some abbot denied Transubstantiation and claimed, like the earliest Christians, that Communion was just something you did in memory of Christ, his monks murdered him! The point is, these were both human inventions, neither was established by God.'

'So you say!' She sat up, her arms about her knees, her hair slightly lifted by a breeze that came off the river as the sky began to fade into night. 'What matters, Peter, is that these holy men were inspired by God; but you're just too arrogant to accept that!'

I remained where I was, leaning on my elbow, staring into the glossy sand and the tough grass sprouting from it. 'By encouraging people to believe this stuff, getting them to accept the impossible, the church is really keeping people stupid.'

'Oh, so now I'm stupid!' she cried, inevitably. 'Everybody knows there are doctors and professors and all sorts of clever people – much cleverer than you! – who are devout Catholics. You ought to try arguing with them about it!'

I thought of her in her life, dominated by the guilt and compassion she felt for her sister, tending Olga day after day and never ceasing to pray for her. If it came to a decision, she would probably choose Olga and Catholicism over me. Did it not, after all, give her life more structure and meaning than mine possessed ...? But that wasn't true: I had my writing, my future. Then I wondered if we were not both enmeshed in a myth we could not do without.

'I should have told you before, but you've probably guessed it anyway.'

'What?'

'I am no longer a Catholic; I've left the church.'

'Oh, I guessed that much!' she said bitterly. She switched around and faced me. 'What you're trying to say is that we're not going to be married. Isn't that what you're saying?'

CHAPTER FIVE

When I left the army I was determined to live in London, which I had begun to visit when my leaves were no longer taken up with Ingrid. The capital's showy promise of success excited me and I was convinced I would become something remarkable there.

Nothing had changed at the garden flat; we still lived with our noses on a level with the Willards' sparkling lawn and Mother still contentedly charred for them. She seemed glad to have me home and was almost shy, even deferential, full of soft smiles. Deferential? It was disconcerting, for I believed I no longer wanted her love, I had learned to get on without it. It was going to be difficult to tell her of my plans; she would be disappointed if she assumed I meant to stay at home.

I confided in Maggie – 'You want to go and live in London?' She bent her spectacles over the proposal. 'I wanted to live there once, like our Jessie.'

'You?'

'Yes, even me! I think I'm as entitled to my dreams as anyone, even if they come to nothing.'

'The problem is Mother.'

'Your mother's a problem?' She laughed briefly. 'Well, you can't go haring off again when you've just come home, Peter. She's seen nothing of you. Anyway, I've persuaded her to turn over a new leaf. I had a good talk to her. I told her you were the only son she's got left and she should make the best of it. We all know you'll never take Frank's place and sometimes you're a disappointment, but I told her she must put all that behind her and make a new start, maybe show you a bit more affection.'

'She's never really loved me, Maggie.'

'Oh, don't be such a whinger! How much have you ever loved her? Me mam's had a hard life, God help her; and you've never tried to make it any easier. Think of all the years she's given you. She gave you your life!'

'Well, yes. But not with any great enthusiasm, I think.'

'Oh, you know nothing about it! I'll tell you something you don't know, something she'd never dream of telling you.'

'And what is that?'

'When she was carrying you, there were complications, you were lying on her liver … or was it her kidney? Anyway, it was considered dangerous enough for the doctor to suggest an abortion. You know what that is, don't you? But she wouldn't dream of it; she struggled through and it must have cost her God knows how much pain, but she made sure you were born.'

'I never knew that.'

'It's what mothers do. A baby's the biggest thing in their lives and they'll go through hellfire to produce it. So just think of that the next time you feel like criticising her.'

And if she had died before giving birth? It was astonishing to reflect that I might never have existed.

Maggie asked why I wanted to go to London and I stutteringly confessed that I, that the fact was I … hoped to become a writer. 'Don't tell Mother, will you?'

'Why? Are you ashamed of it?'

'She might not understand. Anyway, what do you think?'

'About you being a writer?' She smiled a little. 'Well, are you clever enough, that's the first thing? And you need a good education. I know you got taught at the seminary, but you didn't get any qualifications. You need qualifications. You should have gone to university.'

I pointed out that Shakespeare had not gone to a university, nor had Jane Austen or George Eliot, Charles Dickens or Bernard Shaw, or John Steinbeck or … many first-rate writers.

'Yes, but you don't compare yourself to them, do you?'

No, of course not, by no means. And yet … But I dared not, even to myself, admit the wild conviction of greatness growing within me.

'You want to go to London to be a writer,' Maggie resumed. 'But you don't know anyone there; think how lonely you'd be. And what sort of job would you get? Where would you live? I don't see why you can't write just as well here.'

'What is there to write about in Liverpool?'

'There are loads of things … The poor. Poor people. People who've never had a chance. There's plenty in Liverpool. Anyway, you've all the time in the world. I wouldn't mind being you, twenty years old and the world at your feet! But you've got to think of me mam. She needs you, Peter. God knows what's happening with her and me dad. You know he's been made the head chef?'

'He wrote and told me. Do you think he'll be a success? He's rather old, and scarcely au fait with the old haute cuisine.'

'Oh, stop skitting at him! You've never had much respect for him.'

'I just hope he hasn't taken on too much, that's all. What about him and Mother?'

'Well, because he's got all these extra responsibilities, he gets home even less than before, even though Southport is nearer than Manchester.'

I thought of Mrs Callum – *'She's got her eye on me!'*

'That's why I'm sure me mam would like to have you around; though, of course, she's not gonna beg you to stay. She's got her pride. But you owe her something, surely? At least ... a year. Suppose you give her a year; then, if after that you still want to go to London, you can go with a clear conscience.'

Feeling virtuous, conscious of the great sacrifice I was making, I stayed home and looked for a job. There were a fair number to choose from in 1950, provided your aspirations were modest, and I became a receptionist at the Adelphi Hotel. My background in the council office was an advantage, so was my army service in the quartermaster's stores, my neat appearance – the new suit Mother bought me, my hair carefully combed – and the accent I had filched from the middle class.

Mother was quite pleased and probably relieved: 'It's the best hotel in Liverpool. Your dad would have loved to work there.'

She assumed I would be promoted to manager eventually and saw me off to work every day with a good breakfast. Maggie was at the table as well, but I got the bigger and better helpings. My mother was cosseting me. Was this how Frank had felt? But I didn't want to be Frank, nor did I want to be a hotel receptionist. I am a writer, a writer! I kept telling myself, whenever my dream of London fame, of a resplendent artistic destiny, wilted beneath the routine of daily work.

Nevertheless, the job was interesting. I may have lost out on London splendour, but it arrived at the hotel's reception desk every day in the form of business magnates and millionaires, popular writers and broadcasters, aristocrats and statesmen, film stars and famous entertainers. Every week a new batch would appear. During Grand National week the place was crowded with wealth and celebrity; the spacious foyer with its plush carpeting and glittering chandeliers, its page boys and mounds of expensive luggage, resounded with talk of horses and racing, who'd won or lost a fortune. I was surrounded by characters ripe for fiction – the hook-nosed earl with a frothy tart on his arm, that beautiful woman who seemed lost and forlorn, the heavyweight boxer with his scrunched-up face, the pestering horde of spoilt children getting up to mischief, feared and loathed by the staff. What need had I of education when I was learning so much from observing a rich, corrupt, egregious and moving, pitiful and comic representation of humanity? Experience was what a writer needed, the University of Life, not the talent-stifling straitjacket of formal education.

Some of the guests were courteous and friendly, some were indifferent and some were rude, flaying me with humiliation – 'Take that smirk off your face! If you can't find me a better room, I shall leave at once' – but it was all grist to the mill. That was the best of it. Painful experiences could be transmuted into material to be written about, sometimes as a form of revenge. In any case, I wasn't really a humble hotel receptionist any more than I had been a respectable clerk, a commis, a cinema projectionist or a storeman soldier.

I was particularly attentive to the female guests, helping them with their registration, answering queries with my best smile, imperiously summoning a porter to carry their luggage. With beautiful girls, dazzling blondes, sultry brunettes, wrapped in furs, in light summer dresses that clung to their bodies, I was deferential and kept my distance, intimidated by the radiance of their beauty. I was more at my ease with mature women, anyone beyond thirty-five provided she was good-looking and approachable. These ladies sometimes favoured me with intimate smiles, their eyes gazed into mine with amused speculation; and eventually one of them, warmer and more intimate, lonelier or more desperate than the rest, invited me to her room and into her bed.

It was not, I learned later, an uncommon experience for a young receptionist who was personable and obliging. 'These randy old tarts'll take anything they can get,' Jason the hall porter explained.

My tart was rather old, perhaps forty, but once she had put off her silken underwear and offered me her female nakedness, all that mattered was making the most of her; and indeed – laughing, caressing, abandoned, inventive – she was a royal fuck. I wanted her again the following day, but she had left. Jason thought she probably went from one luxury hotel to another, seeking one-night stands, embarking on a heroic saga of sexual satiation. I thought of her fondly, but never saw her again.

I no longer had anything to do with Ingrid; the affair had expired once it became clear that neither of us was prepared to change our views on religion. But it was more than that. I had begun to find her limited intellectually; she had come to realise that my capacity for love was not unlimited. Mother and Maggie were unhappy with the outcome and I was far less indifferent than I appeared. I missed her at times, her sweet face and figure; I longed to hold her and kiss her, and simply be with her, witnessing her quiet goodness, her honesty and steadfastness. I sometimes found myself hovering in the vicinity of the café, walking swiftly past its windows for a glimpse of her as she served at table. I wished also that I could visit Olga, for I was fond of her and unhappy with the opinion she must now hold of me. The only person to welcome the break would be Ingrid's mother, who had never liked me, and I could imagine her consoling her tearful daughter with an I-told-you-so embrace. I wished I could have done something to amend the situation, making Ingrid happy without me. What I missed was the power of prayer; I would have liked to say a novena for Ingrid and Olga in the belief that God would heed my prayer. It would have relieved the guilt.

Dad rarely visited home and I told myself I must be kind to Mother to make up for his absence. Had to tell myself this. My filial acts were never spontaneous. I haven't that free, springing gift of love and gratitude, pity and tenderness, I have observed in others.

'Of course he's made up now he's a head chef,' she sniffed sceptically. 'I only hope he can make a go of it.'

But she did not seem to mind his being away – 'She duzzen need me,' he'd said. Some interests, which she'd abandoned with Frank's death, as though enjoying them would offend his memory, she had now resumed: church activities, whist drives, visiting friends and relatives. Best of all was working for Mrs Willard, pausing over the hoovering to exchange genteel gossip with the lady.

I was now twenty-one and still without anything substantial written. There was a cold war with Russia and a hot one in Korea; General MacArthur wanted to drop atom bombs on China; the Rosenbergs were sentenced to death and the Festival of Britain opened. But none of it meant a great deal to me and I ignored world affairs once I discovered the major theme of the epic novel I would write. In the meantime, a junior receptionist, I worked under the supervision of Kate Langford the senior receptionist, who liked me and teased me playfully. Above Kate was the reception manager, then the duty manager and finally the general manager. The actual owners of the hotel were somewhere in the far distance and we never came across them. There was no tyrannical Father Prefect, no bullying NCOs; the hotel was a happy place in which to work and I soon felt part of a family in the sense that an event that befell any one of us – a chambermaid was having a baby; the chef's son was getting married; an irate guest had insulted the duty manager; a waiter was sacked – was felt by all.

It was boring living at home. I should have been writing, but my room would not accommodate the smallest of desks and I was never away from work long enough to sustain concentration. I took to wandering about the city in my free time, especially during the long summer evenings after work. There were particular streets, buildings, city scenes and the light at certain times of day, that made me linger as though listening for what they had to say. I gradually became familiar with the character of the city and the people who lived in it. Often I went down to the waterfront, the docks where Dad had taken me aboard his ship, and the broad river flowing out to the Atlantic. I visited the district where we had once lived; there were still bomb sites in the backstreet; our house was patched up and another family lived there, another boy would be running along the backyard wall. I tried to find the stinking court where Mother had once lived with her hapless parents, but it had been pulled down years ago. The memory remained, however, and I began to find in the city other memories that were not my own – the memory of slaves carried to America in Liverpool ships; memories of Irish immigrants, of the poor of the Victorian city crammed into verminous cellars and courts, diseased and dying with never the chance to live. Scenes began to form in my head; characters began to speak lines of dialogue.

One day a man entered the hotel and strolled up to the desk, a middle-aged man with a dark narrow lively face. He wore a blue suit and the sort of snap-brim trilby a Yankee gangster would not have despised. 'Gimme the best bridal suite you've got,' he said; 'money no object!'

It was Dad. I hoped he would say nothing that would disclose our relationship. He had arrived from Southport that afternoon and Mother must have told him what time I would be finishing work. 'I'll see you then. We must have a talk.'

He found a seat in the lounge, pulled the Daily Express from his pocket and soon became absorbed in the racing page.

'Who's that odd cove?' Joe Peake asked. 'Is he staying here or what?'

'That one? He's a millionaire, travelling incognito.'

When I finished work, I dragged him out of the place. Town was crowded; people had finished work for the day and were heading home; they strode along smartly, lighting cigarettes, chatting happily; they stood in queues for trams and buses. 'Let's get summat to eat,' Dad said.

He took me to the Lyons snack bar on Lime Street and ordered beans on toast, tea for two. I asked how he was – 'In the pink! Never felt better in me life! Well, except for a bit of a hernia and that.'

And how was he making out as head chef? – 'Piece of cake! There's nothen to it. We've got a new cook in my place and I let him do the donkey work, keeping the more sophisticated stuff for myself. Mrs Callum, Shirley – you met her, didden you? – she has great faith in me. It's what I've always wanted, to be in charge, be a bit of a boss at last. I feel a different person. Feel I can really get somewhere at last.'

When we had finished eating and were drinking a second cup of tea, smoking a cigarette, he said, 'By the way, it might, you know, some day ... if things turn out right ...'

'What?'

'Well, the way things are moving, in the end it might come to me leaving your mother.'

'Have you mentioned it to her?' I asked at length.

'Not yet. It might never happen. It's just a possibility at the moment.'

'But if it did happen, you would be leaving her for Mrs Callum?'

'Shirley. I've never met a woman like her. I don't know what she sees in me ...!' he smiled, shaking his head modestly. 'Suddenly, it's like a whole new life is opening out before me.'

'Dad, you're – what? Fifty-seven?'

'What's that got to do with it? It's what you feel inside that counts. Inside, I know I'm still in the prime of life, I got years ahead of me.'

'And what about Shirley? Does she feel the same way?'

'I think so. Yes!' He raised his head defiantly. 'I've only to say the word, make the right move ...'

'She's not married then?'

'She was once; got divorced about ten years ago. No kids. Husband left her and she's had to make her own way ever since, an uphill struggle by all accounts. But she's intelligent and ambitious. The owners are very impressed with the way she runs our place.'

'And what about Mother?'

'She won't miss me. Probably be glad to see the back of me.'

'You're making excuses.'

'Don't tell me what I'm doing! I know very well, if Shirley and me did happen to get together and make a go of it, your mother wouldn't like it; but you've got to realise that sometimes a man and a woman find each other and – and realise they can give each other a life with some meaning to it. And happiness. Know what I mean? It's been so long since I've been really happy, son. I'd forgotten what it felt like.' He leant forward urgently. 'This may be the greatest chance of my life; probably my last chance for a new start; and if it's there, if the chance is there, then I'm not gonna let it slip through my fingers.'

'Don't you think Mother loves you?'

He lit another cigarette – Senior Service, now that he was a head chef. 'We're too old and too used to each other – or we've never got to know each other at all, and now it's too late. Your mother's been living her own life for some time now, living it inside herself, miles away from me. And it's got worse since poor Frank died. It worked all right while I was at sea, the marriage; but once I come home for good, we found that we really hadden that much in common. We'd grown apart.' He flicked cigarette ash pensively. 'Besides, there's other things. Moving to that house, for instance, the "garden flat"! Pretenden we're up there with the upper classes, even if it's only cleanen for them. I want summat more than that, summat different out of life before it's too late.'

He appeared to be asking my permission to proceed. As I was no longer bound by the church's concept of adultery, why should I not encourage him? Take your chance of love while you can, Dad, and good luck to you! ... But I couldn't see her hurt.

'Dad, you're infatuated with this woman and it's blinded you to the shame and misery it would cause Mother, should anything come of it.'

I was gentle but firm, an elder brother refusing to condone the folly of a spineless younger brother. 'You have a duty to stick by the woman you married.'

'Well, that's just your opinion,' he muttered mulishly. 'It duzzen happen to be mine. I've been frank with you, hoping for a bit of understanding and sympathy. Some hope! You're too much of a young prude, just like Frank was.'

As we got up and left the place, he grabbed my arm: 'You won't say nothen to your mother, will you?'

I promised I wouldn't.

He was going home; I did not accompany him. I thought I might go to the pictures. I wanted to see Billy Wilder's *Sunset Boulevard* but there were long queues at the cinema. I turned away, rambling down through the seething city towards the river, the lives of strangers coming at me in waves. It was an April evening with a bright, lingering sky and I felt on the brink of all the goodness of the year. On one of my days off I must go into Wales and look for lambs and flowers. I could take a girl with me. The thought of lying in lush grass beneath a tree with the soft body of one of the chambermaids beside me ... I should have been concerned about Dad's foolishness, the anguish it might cause Mother if he went off with Shirley; but there were too many distractions, especially the distraction of myself.

People approached and flowed past me – a gaggle of office girls happy at leaving work; an anxious, elderly clerk who had given his life to the office and probably regretted it; a pale young man, tense with ambition or fear of the sack. I understood and pitied them all. I was full of a loving compassion for suffering humanity – shabby elderly women on their way to clean office premises; successful businessmen getting into their cars or hailing a taxi; skinny office boys sucking on a Woodbine; a workman in overalls who reminded me of Frank; and a Chinaman, a Negro, a couple of Lascars from a ship in dock ... Everyone! Everyone!

By the time I had reached the Pier Head and the river, somnolent beneath a darkling sky, I had the plan, the vision, of the epic novel I would write. I had it, I had it! There were tears in my eyes. How perverse to imagine I would have found myself in London. Clearly, I was meant to stay in Liverpool, the World Soul had arranged it that way, rewarding me with the inspiration of a great novel that would record the city's myriad voices telling their stories amidst cries of joy and anguish – a novel that would make me famous and loved.

The World Soul?...This gaseous entity had taken the place of God. It was composed of all the hopes and aspirations of suffering mankind, a spiritual force field animated by a desire for the moral progress of the race. The project was carried out by directing certain chosen individuals along a life track that ensured their fame and influence as great artists and thinkers, or spiritual and political leaders. Mahatma Ghandi was a Directed Individual, moulded and driven by the World Soul, as were Mozart, Beethoven, Tolstoy and any other genius you could think of. Major features of my own life – the lack of a mother's love, the failure of a father, being deprived of the moral support of an elder brother, my spiritual awakening in the seminary, my struggles with sex and God, my growing intelligence, my lost love, my oceanic love for mankind – seemed deliberately designed by the World Soul in its creation of another Directed Individual.

Mrs Willard – Tamsin; she let me call her Tamsin – began taking an interest in her charlady's son. She would stop and chat when our paths crossed. She took pleasure in telling me the names of the plants in the front garden; in return, I volunteered to mow the lawn. She gave me a grateful smile. 'Frederick finds it hurts his back.'

She wasn't a bad-looking woman, and her tall slim figure seemed to protest against the dull conventional clothes she wore – a plain skirt falling below her knees, sturdy rayon stockings and a draggling cardigan she pulled out of shape by jamming her hands in its pockets. Her hair was sandy, short and thick, sprouting at the sides; she had a weathered, freckled face and gentle eyes. Although she was in her forties, she grew younger the more I saw of her.

I mowed the back lawn as well as the front and it became a regular task, yards and yards of grass over which I pushed a scrubby little mower with blunt blades. 'I'm glad you're doing these little jobs for her,' Mother said.

While mowing, I could hear her playing the piano in the front room. Once, catching sight of me, she called me inside. She was alone in the room; the professor was in his study, grunting and sighing as he marked student assignments. I complimented her on her playing. 'Is it Chopin?'

'Schubert.'

She played the piece again, skilfully so far as I could judge. Seated at the piano, her face intent upon the music, she seemed young and feminine. Tamsin. I thought of her as a gawky, vulnerable schoolgirl in her vicarage home; then as an ardent undergraduate among her books, securing a First with ease. Why had she married Frederick, a man of desiccated temperament? She would surely find little excitement in the marriage; one could imagine him pausing in the act of love-making to castigate the bumptious advocates of quantum physics.

We talked and I impressed her with the smattering of high culture I had acquired. Thereafter she often played the piano for me, and the professor was never present to spoil the talk that arose from the music, the reverent tones in which she spoke of great composers, which gave her the appearance of an artless girl. She was whimsical sometimes and enjoyed embarrassing me with my ignorance of the further reaches of literature. This cruel teasing was sexual sublimation, of course, and I began to dream of making love to her. Despite teasing, she respected my intelligence and it was not long before she declared that I should go to university. 'You could study for it at night school. I could give you some extra tuition, if you like.'

But I shook my head; I already had my life's work mapped out, I told her; I was going to be a writer.

She said nothing for a moment, gazing at me absently. Then she murmured, as though faintly puzzled, 'A writer?' She gave a dubious smile. 'But what have you written?'

'Well, nothing much so far, haven't really had the time; but it's the only thing I want to do. I've done some short stories. Would you like to read them?'

I had written two while in the army, three since. She asked me whether they had been published. None were, of course, though I had offered them, beautifully handwritten, to all the best magazines.

'It's rather a grand ambition!' she said, with a droll moue. 'How exactly do you mean to go about it?'

Well, obviously I would ... I would write more stories, get them published; then a novel, get that published – 'I want to write a novel about Liverpool.'

'About Liverpool?' she echoed, faintly incredulous.

'It's never been done before. I mean, a sort of panoramic view of the city and its people.'

'Liverpool ...' she mused. 'How much have you written?'

'Well, actually, I've not started it yet.'

'I really think, you know, Peter, you're better sticking with what you've got. I mean, you have quite a good job at the Adelphi; you could make that your career. I'm sure there are some quite splendid opportunities ... It's rather dangerous, don't you think, to nurse what might well prove to be an ambition far beyond your reach.'

I spent the next few days talking to myself and gesturing plaintively. Then I left home. I needed somewhere I could call my own, a room with pictures on the walls that I had chosen myself (not the Sacred Heart or the Virgin and Child, images that followed me everywhere in the basement flat). I needed my favourite books on a shelf and a desk at which I could write, a desk that would generate inspiration every time I sat down to it.

I shook my head in advance when informing Mother of my decision, forestalling any objection she might make. She was upset and wanted me to stay – 'I thought we were getting on really well at last!' – perhaps rueing times past when she would have demolished my decision with a blow to the head. But I do her an injustice; I think she was genuinely concerned about me and perhaps even conscience-stricken. However, I was free of her now; I was no longer afraid of her and was too intent on my purpose to be seduced by pity. I had done my duty, stayed with her longer than the year Maggie had initially suggested, and now I had to leave. I assured her she would still see me at least once a week (the Sunday roast would be a welcome change from my own cack-handed cooking), and I would continue to support her financially. But she insisted, a tearful martyr, that I must keep all my wages for myself.

'You won't find it easy, living on your own. There'll be all sorts of expenses you've not thought of.'

I knew where I wanted to live. There were some tall old houses near the Anglican cathedral, abandoned by the respectable middle class and long past their best. They were divided up into bed-sitting rooms occupied by single tenants, students in the main. They did not usually possess a resident landlord, merely a caretaker in the basement who did a bit of cleaning, and this promoted freedom and independence. I found a room in one of these houses. It was at the front, on the top floor, like the attic where I had spent my boyhood. The view from the window was blocked by the gigantic chocolate tombstone of the cathedral tower. Worn linoleum on the floor and damp patches on the wallpaper, which I would hide with reproductions of Impressionist masterpieces cut from an art magazine. There was a creaky bed, a table and a couple of chairs, to which Mother added an easy chair and a chest of drawers from the abundance in the flat. I put up a couple of shelves for my books and made the plain wooden table my desk. It was June and the weather was warm, which was just as well, for the room did not possess heating unless I lit a fire in the grate. But this relative austerity, this promise of rough, impromptu living, was what I wanted after the confining comfort of home. It was the first time I had lived alone and the room gave me an identity, a sense of what I assumed to be my true self.

And rioting in my head, my epic novel of Liverpool. It would tell of a young man who meets a girl at a party, falls in love with her and then loses her; she disappears and no one seems to know where she might be. Following the faintest of clues, the young man searches for her throughout Liverpool, allowing me to include features of the city both present and past. The girl is never found. Did she ever, indeed, exist? Or was she no more than a vision created in a drunken stupor at the party? In searching for her, however, the young man discovers Liverpool and – what? Does he abandon his search eventually, having discovered in the city the theme for a great novel? Does he find a real girl in place of the vision? The conclusion was undecided, but that didn't matter, it would all develop of its own accord once the novel got under way.

On a chosen day I got up early, stared at the cathedral tower for some time, then sat down at the table and began to write, the World Soul hovering at my shoulder. There followed one of the sunniest periods of my life; I had never been so happily fulfilled. It helped me get over Ingrid, a compensation for lost love. My happiness now depended solely on myself, on the characters and ideas that arose in my head, and the choice words and billowing sentences with which I gave them life, inscribing line after line like carving some great monument. I had no doubt that I was writing a great novel, and it would be far more than the mere story I supplied as a concession to common taste. Together with the vivid panorama of Liverpool life, I had the moral aim that D. H. Lawrence thought essential to a novel. Like Christ or Henry Thoreau (*Walden* had impressed me greatly), I wanted to tell people they were living the wrong sort of life, burdening themselves with needless possessions, worshipping the false gods of capitalist acquisitiveness. I wanted to reach the fallen and, with the power of my words, raise them up out of their degenerate lives like Frank once in the backyard. I might just as well have been striding across a missionary field preaching the word of God.

The house contained three bed-sitting rooms on each floor, together with the usual offices. Two student teachers, pretty and lively girls, shared two large rooms on the ground floor; a veterinary student had a smaller room at the back. A dark, uncarpeted staircase led to the first floor. Two students of architecture shared the front rooms, Alan and Geoffrey; the room at the back, next to the kitchen used by everyone, was occupied by a postgraduate student immersed in a thesis. Two rooms adjoined mine on the top floor. Sylvia, an art student, lived in one; Greg, the only non-student apart from myself, had the other. He worked in a shipping office and he and Sylvia were friends. Often I would pass them talking on the threshold of one or the other's room. They smiled at me and we exchanged an occasional word, but I did not attempt to develop the acquaintance. I kept to myself, not only from shyness but also because I felt inferior to the predominance of students. This annoyed me – in what way was I inferior? Merely because I was a hotel receptionist without academic qualifications? But that was a misleading facade, for I was really a writer embarked on a great novel, the darling of the World Soul. Yet I could not shake off the feeling of inferiority; I was ashamed of my job and told no one of it.

It was a noisy, lively house; there was always something going on, someone rushing up or down the stairs, people talking and laughing on the landing. There were impromptu parties, usually in the large rooms shared by Alan and Geoffrey, although in the course of the evening, when the number of revellers might have risen to thirty or forty, the party would migrate to most of the other rooms on the first two floors, creating a riot of laughter and drunkenness, arguments and muffled love making.

Most of the tenants got on well with each other; they were like a family, sometimes quarrelling, sometimes backbiting, but generally enjoying each other's company. I observed them wistfully from outside; I did not feel entitled to join the family. One of the student teachers gazed at me meaningfully when she passed, but I did nothing about it. She would have made a pleasant companion; but after Ingrid – and I still often thought of her – I wasn't ready for another involvement. I feared for my concentration on the novel, which was difficult enough to maintain as it was. At night, after work, I was often too tired to write and most of the weekend was spent struggling to develop what I had written the weekend before while trying to hold off the reproach of the World Soul.

The students led more colourful lives than I did; they were enjoying their youth more than I was, for all the secret pleasure I found in writing. They had friends, parties, lovers, and the security of a promising career. They seemed to have plenty of time to themselves whereas I was tied to a daily routine. I had liked my job at first, the procedures that had to be followed, the variety of guests one dealt with, the friendly staff; but I was dissatisfied now.

One Sunday as I was writing a page, Maggie called on me. The front door of the house was never closed during the day; visitors merely walked in and found the room they wanted. Burglars were unknown; they probably assumed that students would have little to steal.

Maggie had never visited me before and she gazed about curiously. 'Well, it's not as bad as it might be,' she pronounced, concluding her inspection. 'Pity you've got that Protestant cathedral stuck outside.'

'Would you like a cup of tea?'

I wanted to be rid of her, anxious to get back to work, fearful of wasting the precious hours of a free day. But she remained standing in the centre of the room. 'Dad's come home. He's left his job.'

'Left the Southport job? Why?'

'I don't know! You don't think he's gonna tell me anything, do you? But it's upset him, you can see that.'

'Do you think he got the sack?'

'God knows. I just thought I'd let you know – as we don't see much of you at home now. I think he'd like to see you.'

I called at the garden flat that evening. There was a fire in the fireplace. Although it was summer, the flat got little sunshine and was somewhat damp. Dad sat at the fireside looking shrivelled and bent. When he saw me, he smiled faintly. Mother made me a cup of tea and cut me a slice of one of her disappointing Madeira cakes. Dad asked how I was, how was the job, how was my room? But he wasn't interested in the answers. He stared into the fire, hunched and miserable. Mother was about to attend church for the evening service, and Maggie went with her. When they had gone, he became slightly more animated, lit a cigarette and told me why he had left the job, speaking urgently to convince me.

'Your mother thinks it was too much for me, but that's not what it was. That manageress was really difficult to work for.'

'Do you mean Shirley?'

'Shirley, aye,' he confirmed bitterly. 'She certainly took me in! Buttering me up, letting me believe we were the best of pals; but when the gloves were off, she was a slave driver, wanted everything done at once, expected me to work all the hours God sends, and kept me short-staffed to save money!'

'So you left?'

'I mean, no one, I don't care if he's the best chef that ever lived – bloody Escoffier himself couldn't have satisfied that woman!'

'But what will you do now?'

He threw his fag end into the fire. 'What can I do? I'm fifty-seven years old, son. Who's gonna give me a job now?' He stared into the fire, his face worn and grieving. He sighed heavily. 'I thought I was on to a good thing there. What's left for me now?'

On my next day off I went to Southport, though I'd little idea what I meant by it. I was acting without thought and without apprehension, taking the rotten spuds and the rotten boots back to the shop. I may have lost my innocence, but I had gained a certain impatience and indifference that served me for courage. The loss of Frank may have had something to do with it. And that time at the dole.

Shirley was in her office in the hotel. Luncheon was over; it was a slack time of day. She greeted me amicably: Was I in need of a room? Had I not seen the receptionist? Her face, carefully made up, was smooth with the desire to be of service. Then she looked more closely and recognised me. She stopped smiling and asked what I wanted. I told her Dad was most upset at leaving the hotel. 'He enjoyed working here. He liked you. He was proud of your faith in him. But now it's as though he's lost all will to live. It's hit him very hard, undermined his confidence, and I was wondering – you'll probably think it a bit of a cheek, but I was wondering if you couldn't maybe, you know, give him another chance.'

She gazed at me steadily, seated behind her desk, a compact middle-aged woman with a formidable air of authority. 'You want me to take him back?'

'He left of his own accord, didn't he? In the heat of the moment? I know he regrets it now. I'm sure if you gave him another chance – '

'It's out of the question. I'm sorry to have to say it, but your father simply wasn't up to the job. I had every hope in him when I made him chef, but he let me down.'

Apparently it had not been long before Dad had discovered that being in charge of a kitchen was more difficult than he had imagined. 'A piece of cake!' he had assured me; but when problems arose, he had failed to handle them satisfactorily. 'For instance, we had this wholesaler; a good man, I'd had him for years. But your father, who was already having trouble keeping within the kitchen budget, got it into his head that he was overcharging. Instead of using some common sense and approaching the matter tactfully, he tried to bully Herbert, flew into a rage and insulted him – someone I'd dealt with for years, who I considered a friend! Naturally, he took his business elsewhere and your father had to find someone else – who proved to be just as expensive and was far less reliable, his stuff not nearly as good.'

I could imagine Dad flaring up at the man, blundering and failing, panic-stricken. For the first time in his life, he was a boss and he couldn't handle it, he lacked the comprehensive grasp of a situation all successful bosses must possess. In the past a boss, however reviled, had protected him from ultimate responsibility. When that protection was removed, he was exposed and there was nowhere to hide. It led to trouble with his assistants, whom he treated in an overbearing manner, confusing them with an order that might be immediately contradicted by another.

'I've always had good relations with my staff, and he was spoiling it. Then the cooking began to suffer. The kitchen was chaotic, no one could tell what he wanted, he kept changing his mind; food was wasted or burnt, and guests began to complain. They began to send back dishes they claimed were uneatable, something which had never happened before. Of course, I couldn't let it go on, and so ...'

'You sacked him?'

'We agreed it would be best if he gave in his notice.' She smiled compassionately. 'I'm sorry, Peter. You can't find any of this very pleasant, but I feel I must be frank with you, and I'm sure you understand my position. There's nothing I would have liked better than for your father to have made a success of the job. I'm sure I gave him every encouragement. But ...' Her bosom rose in a sigh. 'He just wasn't up to it.'

The visit to Shirley and the news of Dad's failure disturbed and distracted me. I found that I could not continue with my novel. Suddenly there was a blankness in my mind, paralysis of the imagination, and I couldn't produce a word. I was unable to think, couldn't summon to mind any of the characters I had been living among. Where had I gone wrong? It reduced me to howling frustration and I cursed my stupidity, stabbing the desk with my pen and ruining it. I charged through the streets wild-eyed, seeking inspiration or at least some sort of clarity, hoping for the stimulation of words, passages of dialogue and description that had previously occurred to me unbidden. But the city scenes that were once ripe with tales of love and lamentation were now quite meaningless, nor was there anything in the faces of the passing crowd to excite the imagination. I returned to my room, flung myself on the bed and, seething with a blind sobbing rage, cursed myself for ever having assumed I could write, wrathfully rejecting the fantasy I had blithely wanked up in myself. I read and reread the last page I had written and could find nothing wrong with it. I reviewed the structure of the novel and it seemed quite sound. Then why ...?

It must be a Writer's Block, I decided. I was proud of it, in a sense, as I had once been proud of being bombed. I was suffering a well-known professional hazard, an honourable neurosis. It put me up there among the martyred fellowship of great writers. But when the infernal blankness lasted beyond a week and threatened to persist indefinitely, I panicked; my precious novel was sinking irrecoverably out of sight and there was nothing I could do to save it. I felt ashamed of being unable to write: what would Tamsin and my family think, if they knew? Oh, Mother's vindicated smirk; Tamsin's refined shrug! I felt guilty, as though it was a sin. I sought distraction, as though the block was an enemy I might fool by feigning indifference; I went to the pictures, read lightweight novels, got drunk and was sick. But nothing helped. I lay awake at night, struggling futilely to recapture the vision that had once possessed me, fretting into wearisome dreams when finally I slept. Inevitably insomnia, together with my unrelieved anguish, affected my work at the Adelphi. I was moody and preoccupied.

'What's the matter, love?' Kate enquired.

'Cheer up!' the duty manager said. 'It might never happen.'

I smouldered with anger and misery. Oh, the banality, the stupidity of ordinary, ignorant people! None of them could have any idea what I was suffering.

The situation gathered momentum and slid from bad to worse, especially when Kate, my teasing boss, my tender protectress, went on holiday. The hotel became a great burdensome bore, a pretentious and decadent monument to luxury, and I hated it, hated my job, hated everything and everybody, snuffling weary hot tears inside myself. I committed the receptionist's unforgivable sin and was rude to the guests, brusquely dismissing their enquiries, treating their problems with an insulting indifference. I neglected my appearance, failed to shave, sometimes failed to wash, and was no longer the spruce, obliging young man the Adelphi had hired. I failed to carry out certain duties and made mistakes for which I did not apologise. If I did not like someone's manner, I was capable of telling them there wasn't a room available. I overslept, when I finally got to sleep, and arrived late for work, oppressed by the fact that I was still unable to write and might never write again, fearing the loss of all my glittering dreams.

'Buck up, lad,' the duty manager said. 'This is the second time you've been late this week, and it's still only Wednesday.'

'Oh fuck off,' I said.

We agreed it would be best if I handed in my notice.

I stood on the pavement outside the Adelphi, abruptly shaken into sanity. I was without a job, expelled from the family that had welcomed me: the friendly porters, the cheery chambermaids. Until the damned novel had taken over my life and destroyed my peace of mind I had enjoyed the job, and I regretted losing it. I felt like going back inside and begging to be reinstated. Instead, I went on the dole. It was no longer a fearful experience; indifference enabled me to give the clerk a deadpan account of what had happened, and I nodded like a veteran when I learned that I would begin to receive unemployment benefit within a short while.

I went back to my room and smoked a cigarette, staring at the tower of the cathedral. Then something occurred to me, there was a sudden glowing lift to my spirits. I realised that if I could remain on the dole indefinitely, drawing a weekly pittance and somehow living on it, I would have every day free in which to write. How wonderful ...! I felt once more under the benign direction of the World Soul. I was filled with hope and a joyous sense of freedom. My head cleared, the block lifted and I was able to write again. There was a funfair in my head, swings and roundabouts; the days stretching ahead were entirely my own, provided I could avoid taking any of the jobs the dole sent me after. But it wasn't difficult to convince prospective employers that I was not the person they wanted. A scowl, a lounging indifference, were sufficient.

I called on Mother and was apprehensive, tensing my jaw the way I always did when I had something embarrassing to confess. It was during the afternoon and she was alone; Maggie was at work, Dad was out somewhere. She seemed pleased to see me, though obliged to conceal it beneath a wry resentment. 'You're a stranger! I'm surprised you remembered where we lived. Oh, you shouldn't have bothered,' she added, accepting the bunch of flowers I had brought. 'Mrs Willard lets me have all the flowers I want from the garden.'

She offered me a cup of tea; I asked how she was – 'Oh, I manage. I'm getting along all right.' She moved between the kitchen and the scullery, making the tea, hobbling somewhat from the rheumatism in her joints. Her narrow figure was bony with age, her face was drawn and lined, but she was as neatly turned out as ever, her grey-streaked hair was drawn back smoothly and she wore a clean pinny of a sprightly floral pattern. The thought that I had descended from her loins was very strange; the fact that she had suffered in bearing me, created a troubling obligation. But she was made for suffering; it confirmed her pessimistic view of life and gave meaning to existence.

She brought the tea to the table. When I asked after Dad, her manner suggested that she had forgiven him for previous neglect. 'Your poor dad! They treated him really badly at that place and it's taken a lot out of him, could have ruined his health. And of course, he feels bad about having had to leave; you'd think it was his fault. They wanted him to stay, they knew they wouldn't get anyone else who'd slave for them the way he did. But he'd had enough.'

'And now he's on the dole?'

'Well, he can't help that,' she cried, bristling up resentfully as she was wont to do when provoked. 'It's not his fault. There's nothing he'd like better than another job, but who's going to give him one at his age?'

While working, he had always sent money home. Now they were reduced to his dole pittance and Maggie's wages.

'I'd like to help,' I sighed. 'But as it happens, I'm on the dole myself.'

Her mouth fell open with shock. I gave an account of what had happened, largely truthful. I could have claimed it wasn't my fault, I was the victim of exploiting, insensitive bosses, but I did not feel the need to; when it came to the point, I was no longer apprehensive and it was remarkable how calmly and relentlessly I could shove my words into her aghast face. 'I never meant to make a career of being a receptionist; I'm not cut out for it. There's only one thing I want to do in life – has Mrs Willard told you I mean to be a writer?'

'She has.' Having absorbed the shock, she was grim-faced now, gathering the outraged energy to blast me. 'She thought it was unwise, those were her very words.'

'That's too bad.' Now I was fluttering a little, my coldly cruel equanimity deserting me. 'I'm sure she'll change her mind when my book is published and I'm famous.'

'When will that be?' she laughed harshly. 'When Nelson gets his eye back?'

I stood up. You were always better on your feet; you could dodge round the ring and duck under the ropes if necessary. 'The fact is, I left the job and went on the dole on purpose, because I needed the time. It takes time to write a novel, especially one as big and important as the one I'm engaged on.'

'You're dreaming, lad!' she snorted. 'How can you write a book? You haven't been to university. You couldn't even finish your education at the seminary. You're on the road to ruining your life, that's all you're doing!'

'I know what I'm doing!' I was blabbing now, racked with misery and self-pity. 'Why in God's name can you never understand and – and sympathise and support me? I've got intelligence and talent, but you've never given me credit for it! You've always underestimated me, you could never bloody see me for your beloved Frank.'

'Don't you dare speak of your brother like that!'

'I just wish you'd understand,' I wailed, exhausted. 'I need the time. I must write this book. The fact is, I don't think I've very long to live, I'm pretty certain I shall die young.'

This was a conviction I'd acquired recently. I would die when I was about thirty-five, physically and mentally exhausted by the immense task I had accomplished, the great works I had created.

'Oh, son, let's not quarrel.' She gazed at me with a kind of remorse. 'Come and sit down and drink your tea.'

I returned to the table, opened my tobacco tin and rolled a cigarette. She sat down beside me and looked as though she would like to touch me. 'I know what all this is really about,' she sighed.

'What do you mean?'

'You've been missing Mass, haven't you? You've started losing your faith. Ingrid told Maggie all about it.'

'Ingrid?'

'I don't know what's got into you. You used to be such a good little boy!'

She seemed helpless, faced with my reckless behaviour. A career choice beckoned. If I worked at it, I could become a scallywag whom she would pray for and love desperately, the more my conduct broke her heart.

'Is it because of Frank dying?' she asked, gazing at me with her black Irish brows, her eyes full of ... love? Was that a mourning love in her eyes? 'Did you lose your faith because God didn't answer our prayers and look after Frank?'

But the tears in her eyes were for Frank, not for her scallywag son. Nevertheless, she took my hand and pressed it urgently. 'Well, do you think I didn't have the same doubts? It was a terrible time for me, the worst in my life, and it was a big struggle to get to the point of believing that it was all for the best, that God knew what He was doing. Then I realised we're all in the hands of a merciful God and that I should be thankful, really, because I'd had all those years with your brother, who made me so happy and proud; and it was more, much more, than many a poor mother gets. I'm sure he's in Heaven now, looking down on us, and that's the great consolation of religion, Peter, don't you see? This life is nothing; it's a Vale of Tears, that's all it is. It's what comes after that matters. Eternity! What's going to happen to your soul after you die, if you carry on like this?'

'How is Ingrid?' I asked. 'And Olga. How is Olga?'

Mother gave one of her grim smirks. 'Ingrid is engaged to Tom Butterfield. They're getting married soon. You lost a lovely little wife there, I'm afraid.'

The other tenants were more aware of me now that I spent most of each day in the house; I often met them on my way out for a walk in search of inspiration or beef dripping to spread on bread, and their curiosity was aroused. Eventually Paula, the student teacher who had gazed at me invitingly, asked what I did: was I a student, a postgraduate perhaps? I confessed to being a writer and this soon spread through the house, gathering admiration as it went. I took my place in the family: I was The Writer, the gallantly impoverished chap in the garret who might well be creating a masterpiece – a novel to rival James Joyce or Thomas Wolfe – Thomas Who? But at the time, believing the American to be a great writer, I aspired to emulate the vast egocentricity of his novels, the romance of a heroic writer struggling with a Laocoon of words and images, memory and desire. Everyone admired my dedication, my integrity; they were impressed by my poverty, never suspecting how I revelled in it. They often invited me to eat with them in the communal kitchen, meals flowing with wine and beer when the students had money. At parties I was a centre of attention, talking airily of my writing, the problems of character and structure, the torments of the artist.

I became particularly friendly with Alan and Geoffrey, and spent much time in their room. They had a gramophone with a powerful speaker and plenty of classical records. We would lounge about, sipping wine and listening to Beethoven, Bartók and Stravinsky, the *Rite of Spring* crashing through the house. On Sundays we read *The Observer* and commented on the news, the Korean War floundering bloodily to a truce, the defeat of the Labour government – 'The only decent government we've ever had, and the stupid mob gets rid of them!' We mourned the deaths of Andre Gide and Wittgenstein, neither of whom we had read; we read *The Catcher in the Rye* and praised it temperately; we discussed the hydrogen bomb and concluded that the end of the world was probably nigh. We were convinced we would all die young, burnt out, and agreed it was better to die at the peak of a full life than linger on into the futility of old age. Neither Alan nor Geoffrey was especially keen on becoming an architect; Geoffrey would rather be an artist and Alan longed to be a poet. Geoffrey's paintings were scattered about his room, rather gloomy abstracts, but I said I found them most interesting. I read Alan's poems and said the same. I let them read selected passages from my novel and they said the same. We got on splendidly together. Alan had a slim, elegant figure and a saturnine expression of which he was proud; Geoffrey's frame was more robust and he had a beard, a fairly unusual accoutrement in those days. We gossiped about the other tenants, who was sleeping with whom – I was amazed and appalled. Could it be true that some of the girls were having carnal relations with some of the men?

'Oh yes,' Geoffrey yawned. 'Greg and Sylvia.'

'Greg and Sylvia?' They lived next door to me and I had never suspected it for a moment.

'Paula and Steven,' Alan added.

'Paula and Steven?'

She had given me the eye and all the time she was being fucked by Steven, the veterinary student! The revelation was staggering. These young people were living in sin. I had never known anyone who was living in sin. Although I pretended amused tolerance, inwardly I was hot and confused, my Catholic morality shuddering with shock. In time I came to tolerate the practice, even to applaud it as courageous defiance of conventional morality, but in the deepest recesses of myself where Catholicism still lurked, never to be eradicated, I always had to severely remind myself that extramarital love-making was perfectly all right, no sin was involved. Had I spoken of my perturbation to Alan and Geoffrey they would rightly have assumed I was jealous. It never occurred to me that they, too, were probably living in sin.

One day, Dad paid me a visit. It was odd to find him in my room in this jolly, ramshackle house full of middle-class undergraduates on a bohemian spree. In his blocky, ill-fitting suit he looked decidedly out of place; he could have been applying for a job as a humble handyman. While I made him a cup of tea, he rebuked me embarrassedly – he had never been a dominant father – for not visiting home more often.

'Your mother misses you, y'know. Well, at least she always wants to know what you're getten up to. She's sorry about the row you had; I've an idea she feels it was partly her fault. Well, that's to be expected. For as long as I've known her, she's been blamen herself for one thing or another, when it wazzen really her fault. It's her background. Wudden surprise me if she thought she was to blame for all her mother's misery – for getting born, I mean.'

'That's interesting.'

I was surprised he had worked it out, and reproached myself for not having suspected it. After all, I was supposed to be the novelist, replete with steady-eyed psychological penetration.

'But what you've got to understand is that it's all very puzzlen for her. I mean, that you're writing a book. That's right, izzen it?' He gazed about the room, the books on the shelf, writing materials on the table, the slim manuscript of my novel. 'You're writing a book?'

'A novel, yes.'

'A novel.' He smiled and shook his head wonderingly. 'She thinks you'll never do it, coz you haven't the education, but I told her it's talent that matters.'

'You stuck up for me?'

'I've always felt there was summat different about you.' He sipped his tea. 'You might be famous some day, make piles of money!'

'I don't care about the money.'

It was art that mattered, a rarefied aspiration quite beyond the squalid accumulation of cash. Whilst I wanted to be published, I knew instinctively that my work would never appeal to more than a discerning few. I told myself I did not want the life of a best-selling author, which I thought of in terms of Savile Row suits and luxury hotels, a mad sports car and a villa in the South of France ... My ideal was life as part of an intellectual elite. There would be enough money to live on, of course, for my novels would be translated into the better European languages and the editors of prestigious journals would offer me reviewing work. I would have a charmingly lovely artistic wife (a musician, a sculptress – Ingrid would never have fitted in, after all), and we would live in Chelsea, where we would entertain a few like-minded souls; there would be select dinner parties bristling with brilliant conversation.

'Not like me,' Dad was saying. 'I never did nothink out of the ordinary.'

He had lost much of his former ebullience, no longer jerked about jokily, heading a football or attempting a tap-dance. He had never been fat and was now quite stringy. His face was sallow with an unhealthy pallor, the flesh hanging dispiritedly about his mouth and chin. His eyes were dull and hooded. There was no chance of his getting another job and I asked what he did all day.

'Oh, I find lots to do!' he insisted. 'I've been doing a bit of gardening for the Willards. She's got me mowing the lawn. She asked after you, by the way.' He claimed he read a lot; he enjoyed the slick novels of Thorne Smith and John Paddy Carstairs. He went to Goodison for Everton's matches – 'Maggie bought me a season ticket for me birthday' – had a bet on the gee-gees now and again, and often wandered down to the Pier Head, 'To watch the boats.' He sighed and shook his head. 'I usta hate goen to sea, yet I miss it now. That's life, izzen it? My bloody life, anyhow. I go to the landing stage and watch the ships heading out to the Mersey Bar, the lucky sods sailing on them. All those places I went to – Bona Zers and Valparaiso, New York, Montevideo – and I never made the most of it. That's the story of my life, son. Go thou and don't do likewise.'

'But you're all right, are you, apart from that? I mean, you're not sick or anything?'

He said he was as well as could be expected at his age – 'Though I've gorra hernia the size of a football.'

'A hernia? Well, go and see the doctor.'

'I have done. They're hauling me into hospital for an operation, next month.'

'Does that worry you?'

'I doan like the thought of being cut open.'

'It's a minor operation, nothing to worry about, a piece of cake. And you'll feel much better after it, I'm sure. You'll be your old self again.'

'I'll never be my old self again.' He drank his tea, smoked a cigarette, then got up to go. 'I'd love to read what you've written,' he said, eyeing the manuscript. 'What's it about?'

'You'll find out when it's published. I'll dedicate it to you, if you like.'

'Would you really?' He shook his head with pleased amazement.

'But of course, it may never be published.'

I returned to my novel with a worried sigh, for I was struggling with a problem that threatened to assume frightful proportions. It wasn't Writer's Block this time, it was simply a lack of nerve arising from the magnitude of the task I had undertaken: a novel that would attempt to dramatically summarise the multitudinous life of a city. I had begun to fear that I might not be able to do it. And I was alone, unaided, struggling up a Himalayan track into a rocky, mist-swirling wilderness, hardly daring to look at the immense cliff of material I still had to climb – the story of my young man searching for a fabulous girl, a briefly glimpsed vision of beauty; the story of my poor grandmother, which I meant to stand as an indictment of Victorian poverty in Liverpool; and then the slave trade and the adventures of privateers (I assumed there were privateers; anyway, I liked the name and connotations) ranging out over the Atlantic from the windjammer port of Liverpool; and then, switching back in time (for I had the hazy notion, influenced by John Dos Passos, that the novel should be structured like a patchwork quilt), bringing all my emotional forces to bear on the city in the war, braving the bombing. And Benny's death, and Frank's death. There was even more that would have to be included if my novel was to be truly panoramic: an episode based in Chinatown, another about West Indians, another sobbing over a poor, betrayed virgin in a slum, and one about a jolly crew of undergraduates ...

I longed to discuss my problem with someone. I had felt this during Dad's visit, but his admiration was so pleasing I had not wanted to disillusion him. In any case, what advice could he have given me? Alan and Geoffrey would have understood my anxiety and would doubtless have encouraged me, citing similar problems suffered by other writers and assuring me that I was, indeed, as talented as I believed. But it was precisely this that prevented me from confiding in them. I had begun to suspect that the three of us formed a tight, mutually supportive circle that shunned outside influence. It was as though we were squatting around a campfire of mutual admiration, warming ourselves with a conspiracy in which we knew the answers to any questions that might arise. It was another backstreet gang and had begun to cause me some unease.

My friends became aware of a change in my demeanour. I was no longer as amusing as I had once been; I sulked and was snappish, and would then heave a great sigh, confessing that writing a novel was damned hard work – 'The fact is, I live in a week what another person might manage in a year. And it's exhausting; takes an immense, emotional toll. It's little wonder that I fear I'm marked down for an early death ...'

But Greg and Sylvia, Paul and Steven, were unmoved; worse, they were perhaps sniggering behind my back, or at least smiling pityingly and shaking their heads. They were growing tired of me; they suspected pretentiousness and were bored with the torments of the artist. Although I might still consider myself part of the family, I was now undoubtedly a poor relation. And I envied them. They were smugly ensconced in a conventional course of education that would carry them smoothly to a secure and esteemed career, to a spouse and a home and children, a successful life. And what had I to set against this? I was nobody and nothing; a deluded fool fondling impossible dreams of greatness in his barebones attic.

Poverty was another problem. I got little money from the dole and rarely managed it as well as I might. I spent more than I should on paper and pens, for I was finicky about such things. I could only write on pads of an expensive paper, with a fountain pen with an italic nib; and because of my habit of madly driving a pen into my desk whenever writing proved frustrating, I was regularly put to the expense of buying a new one. I sought the cheapest food on the stalls of St John's Market and it sometimes made me sick. I was often hungry and constantly craved a smoke. I searched the gutter for dog-ends as I had once searched them for shrapnel. The ones I found I hastily snaffled up and thrust into a tin, and it was while I was engaged in this activity that I met Tamsin Willard.

She was smiling down at me. Rising swiftly and faltering a laugh, I explained that I thought I had seen a shilling in the gutter. She was glad to see me. 'How are you?' she asked, as we walked together. She surveyed me sympathetically. 'Living on the dole can't be much fun. Do you get enough to eat?'

'That's the least of my problems.'

'You have problems? Would you like to talk about them? If I can be of any help ... I miss the talks we used to have.' She stopped and held my arm to prevent me walking on. 'Now I'm going to offend you horribly, I dare say, but what I would like to do is take you in here' – we were outside a Chinese restaurant – 'and give you a good feed.' She smiled appealingly. 'Would you object terribly to that? ... You wouldn't? Good!'

We entered the restaurant. It was lunchtime and the place was fairly full, but we found a table. Tamsin commandeered the menu.

'Now, what would you like? Chow mein, sweet and sour pork? I think I'll have chicken with cashew nuts.'

I was overwhelmed by her kindness and felt like crying. I had never seen her away from her home and she seemed different, or perhaps it was the effect of our unexpected meeting. I had forgotten her face and it was a pleasure to see it again, her broad mouth and prominent cheekbones, her bashful blue eyes and the way her sandy hair stood out from her head. It was autumn and quite cold. Beneath her tweed topcoat she wore a two-piece costume of sturdy wool. The restaurant was warm and when she unbuttoned her jacket I was aware of the shape of her breasts in her modest blouse. And beneath the table her long legs, her woman's feet. It was more than a year since, a gigolo receptionist, I had made love to a woman.

'I feel somewhat embarrassed,' she confessed, smiling. 'Not about being here with you,' she added at once. 'No, it's jolly nice to see you again, Peter. But the last time we talked I fear I was less than encouraging about your writing. Now your mother tells me you've embarked on a novel.'

'She thinks I'm a deluded fool and wasting my life.'

'Really? The way she put it to me was, well, as though she sought my opinion in, you know, the hope of feeling proud of you. It was something so very strange for her, you see, especially the fact that you hadn't a job, and – '

'What did you tell her?'

A beaming Chinaman brought our order and hoped we would enjoy the meal. When he had gone, she said, 'I told her you might have talent and it was quite possible you could write a novel.'

'But you've never read anything I've written!'

'I know. I lied to please her.' She shrugged. 'I don't know whether you're talented. You're intelligent, sensitive, and I think quite courageous, because you must be aware of the ... ' – she dug into her chicken with cashew nuts – 'the penalty of failure.' Then she hurried on, raising her eyes from her plate and gazing into mine. 'But what about the novel? Is this the one you told me about? How is it going? How much have you written?'

I plunged into a frank account of my problem, my loss of nerve in face of the seemingly endless ramifications of my novel. I spoke all through my chow mein, barely tasting it despite my hunger, and she attended closely. I spoke freely, confident that she would not treat my outpouring insensitively. Her steady gaze and her receptive silence assured me of that. I had wondered, inevitably, if she might be game for a fuck; but the longer we were together, the less that seemed likely, nor did it seem to matter. What did matter was that I felt I had found a friend in whom I could confide. And it was different from Alan and Geoffrey; there was no mutually supportive conspiracy involved. It was better than Ingrid, for Tamsin was older and more experienced, more intelligent and better educated. I had never been friends with a woman where sex was not an issue and I soon began to value its advantages.

I stopped talking about myself and gazed at her hopefully. Her response was hesitant and I was afraid she considered my problems absurd, but that wasn't the case. She declared herself impressed with the panoramic sweep of my novel: 'It's so grand and, oh, I don't know – young!' But as I was clearly having difficulties with it, she suggested that I put it aside for the present, in fact for a few years while I got myself some education. 'You see, if you went to university, if you read literature, it would give you ... a perspective, and I think that's what you need. You're still so very young,' she mused tenderly. 'Oh, you have years and years ahead of you! You can do so much in that time.'

I refrained from pointing out that I would probably die in a few years. Instead, I argued that going to university, getting a conventional education, would ruin my creativity, my originality.

'You're not afraid, are you?' she asked, tempering the challenge with a smile. 'In my view, a university course would prove whether you have talent or not. If you do have talent, then it should be robust enough to survive education. Indeed, it should thrive on it.'

I scowled morosely, unconvinced, and probably disappointed that she had not at once proclaimed me a genius. She ducked her head a little to look into my face, smiling pleadingly. 'Let's not quarrel. Shall we be friends?'

'Yes, if you can bear it.'

'Oh, I've had to put up with sulkier characters than you, my lad!' She glanced at the rather mannish watch she wore. 'I must go.'

She paid the bill and got up; I held her coat while she got into it. 'It's been lovely seeing you again, Peter. I'm glad you felt you could talk to me. It was most interesting. I don't have all that many people I can have a really good talk with. Let's do it again, shall we? Keep in touch; let me know how you're getting on.'

'What do you mean? I don't understand.'

'Well, that's what they say at the hospital, anyway: he's dangerously ill.'

Maggie stood at the window, looking out at the cathedral tower. I was bewildered and resentful, didn't want this distraction. 'But what happened? It's just a hernia, isn't it? There's nothing dangerous about a hernia operation.'

'Well, there is in me dad's case. Complications have set in. The surgeon said it's the sort of complication you've always got to be prepared for, a thousand-to-one chance. That's all me eye, if you ask me. Obviously, there's a cover-up going on. They've done summat wrong and ... Since when has a hernia been a dangerous operation? Anyway, are you coming with me, or not?'

'To the hospital? You mean now?'

'They've put him on the Danger List, so we can visit him any time.'

'Yes, well, all right.'

I got my coat and we left. It was about nine o'clock, a windy night. Among the trees that fringed the cathedral an owl screeched once. We walked to the main road and caught a tram to the hospital.

'We thought it would all be over and he'd be out in a couple of days,' Maggie said. 'That's what he thought himself, even though he was a bit anxious about going under the knife. Now he's on the bloody Danger List! God knows what's going to happen. I've written to our Jessie; I think she should come over and see him.'

She sat beside me in the tram, her face drawn with anxiety: my sister, whom no one ever addressed by her full name, a wiry spinster in her thirties, accepting her fate with sardonic fortitude. It had given her a tough jaw and a mothballed smell that would safeguard her virginity forever.

'How is Mother taking it?'

'Well, she's upset, of course, as you might expect. It's like a thunderbolt out of the blue. And it's such a shame, just when they were getting along together.'

'And you really think ...?'

'Oh, they're doing all they can for him, I suppose. The surgeon himself – that's the wonderful Mr Montague Price! – told us he was fighting hard. I mean, Dad was fighting hard. And if he could just hang on for a few more days, he would pull through.'

'That's good.'

'And, of course, we're all praying for him like mad. You'll say a prayer for him, won't you?'

We left the tram. The hospital loomed above us, darker than the night. Part of it had once been a workhouse and there was a cemetery adjacent. 'That's handy,' I said, and we laughed. I was still new to the game and surprised by how much levity was allowed in a tragic situation.

As close relatives of a patient on the Danger List, we enjoyed certain privileges. 'We've got this special pass that lets us in to see him any time – when they're not doing things to him, I mean.'

We walked, bent against the wind. There was a kind of sentry box you had to pass, manned by a uniformed porter. Maggie showed her pass with a prim flourish and we entered the building, crossed a forlorn waiting room where shabby people waited to hear the worst, and walked along a corridor permeated by a threatening antiseptic smell. Parked against the wall, ready to carry desperate cases to the operating theatre and thence perhaps to the mortuary, were some clumsy trolleys of solid metal, the paint worn away in places, a sheet of clammy grey material suspended across the frame. It was the sort of contraption you'd expect to find in a concentration camp.

'It's all right,' Maggie said, squeezing my hand. Outside the ward, she stood me up against the wall. 'Now, just wait here a sec while I see if it's all right.' She went off through heavy swing doors that shushed to a close behind her. I leaned against the wall feeling sick, my life piled up suddenly against this blunt emergency like a calamitous traffic accident. There was subdued activity all about me; nurses in starched uniforms swished past; somewhere, nameless liquids were being flushed away. I caught the mutter of a hurried consultation, the squeak of rubber wheels as a screen was drawn about a bed. It was all taking place close at hand but in secret, it seemed, in some dreadful region of pain and despair. 'You can go in now,' Maggie said, appearing suddenly beside me.

'Aren't you coming?'

'Oh, he doesn't want to see me.'

I groped my way into the ward. Most of the lights were out, windows showed merely the dim haze of a city night and I could scarcely distinguish the beds jutting out from the wall. Each bed was occupied by someone seriously ill, maybe dying. Christ! What was this dying, this death thing, that had suddenly thrust itself, foul and black, into my life? I had been cheered by the talk with Tamsin and had begun tentatively writing again. Now I was suddenly plunged into this shit-heap. I could hear someone snoring. Someone muttered in his sleep, someone sighed and groaned. As I faltered over the polished linoleum, a voice said, 'I'm here, son.'

It wasn't Dad's voice. Peering in the gloom, I stammered, 'No, I'm looking for …'

'It's me,' Dad chuckled grotesquely. 'What's left of me.'

I could see him now. He lay in – no, he lay on the bed, though under stiff hospital bedclothes. The bed was cranked up in the middle, leaving the patient with his belly higher than his head. (The Chamber of Horrors, the water torture.)

'Is that you, Dad?'

I approached the racked shape. Thin red rubber catheters were attached to his body at either end.

'Whadda ya think of … this then?' He grasped my hand, wheezing a laugh. 'God knows what they've done to me. I'm gonna … complain … to the authorities, when I get out.'

I bent over him and kissed him, wildly eyeing the thin red tube snaking out of his nose. He didn't smell good and I couldn't get over the change in his voice. It was like being in a seance when the medium goes into a trance and speaks in a voice from the grave; or when people talk in their sleep in a voice that is shockingly different, the coarse and blurred utterance of the primeval id. Partly it was because his false teeth had been removed, leaving his mouth a slack, rubbery aperture. He asked how I was and thanked me for coming. He kept hold of my hand to reassure me, sensing my fear. I didn't know what to say. It seemed offensive to offer the usual nostrums – offensive to me, I mean; to my nice linguistic discrimination – yet I found myself doing so. 'Never mind about me; you're the one that matters. And you're going to be all right, Dad! You'll pull through. Mr Montague Price thinks you're bearing up very well.'

'That so? Is that what he says?' He paused, as though making a rapid check throughout his body. The snorting sounds he made when breathing were like a miniature lawnmower at work, surging forth then travelling back in a long recovering sigh. 'I'm … not in much pain, y'know. All … numb down there.'

'That's good. That's a good sign.'

'Must be, mustn't it ... not feel ... much pain.'

'Pipe down!' someone shouted from one of the beds.

'Nurse!' someone else cried. 'Where's the fucken nurse?'

I didn't stay long at his bedside, although it seemed long. He became drowsy and there were stretches of silence in which I became distracted and absent-minded. At one point, I found myself trying to remember what Freud had said about the effect on a man of the death of his father. Eventually, I got up. 'I'll come and see you again tomorrow, all right?'

'Thanks for coming, son. Gunnight. God bless.'

I crept away, exhaling the enormous breath I'd been holding, and rejoined Maggie. We left the hospital and waited at the stop for a tram. She took it for granted that I would come home with her to see Mother. 'She'll be coming here later, herself. She stays the night at his bedside.'

A tram arrived and we boarded it, mounting to the upper deck for a smoke. 'Did you see the tubes?' she asked, as we found a seat. 'Oh, they're marvellous things! It's marvellous what they can do nowadays. He's not allowed any solid food, y'see, so they feed him on glucose, down a tube and through his foot!'

'And the other?'

I stared out of the black window. The tram stopped beside some small shops huddled in the night. No one got off. The conductor rang the bell and the tram lurched on.

'The other tube runs from inside his stomach, I think; out through his nose and into a bottle under the bed. It's emptying all the ... stuff from his stomach.'

'I see.'

'How did you think he looked?'

'Terrible.'

'Don't let on to Mam though, eh?'

I had journeyed with him on this tram years ago. The pet shop still stood on the corner, and as we passed it I recalled a story he had told me. Perhaps he'd made it up, a yarn to amuse the little feller: 'See that shop? That pet shop with the rabbits and mice in the window? Guess what. They usta have a parrot on a perch in the doorway, a wicked old sod he was, holding his scraggy head on one side and scratchen it with his claw, as though he was thumbing his nose at you. Well, I was standen in the doorway one day, keeping outta the rain, and while I'm standen there, I can feel like a tugging at me jacket, and when I look down there's no buttons left! The ruddy parrot's reached over and eaten all the buttons off me jacket!'

'That's right,' Maggie said. 'Have a good cry.'

We left the tram and walked along the sedate, tree-lined avenue to the Willards' house and the garden flat. Trees raved in the wind. Clouds raced across the face of a large round silver moon. Mother was in the living room that we still called the kitchen. The electric light was on, but it was weak and dim. All her life she had lived in a dim light: candlelight as a child, gaslight as a young wife and mother, and now, in her late fifties, the cheerless radiance of a sixty-watt bulb. She sat in a rocking chair beside the fire, hands clasped tightly in her lap. There were rosary beads on the table beside her and a novel of Ethel M. Dell's. I had called a couple of times since our quarrel and a reconciliation had been achieved. I wanted to go to her, fling my arms round her, but – was it the fear of being repulsed? Or simply coldness of heart? She was glad to see me, however; when I went to her and kissed her cheek, she held my hand hard. She glanced up at Maggie, her lips set to hear the worst.

'Much better,' Maggie said emphatically. 'Wasn't he, Peter? You ask Peter.'

'Much better,' I confirmed.

Mother squeezed my hand. 'Thanks for going to see him, love.'

I was embarrassed both by her expression of gratitude and by her use of an endearment. 'What we must do is keep his spirits up,' I declared, and rambled on at some length concerning the superiority of morale over matter.

'There was a cable from Jessie,' Mother told Maggie.

'She's coming over?'

'I hope she'll get here before it's too late.'

'Too late for what?' I asked.

'Oh, she's convinced he's going to pop off any minute!' Maggie said. She spoke loudly to Mother, stooped over her, her tone withering: 'I've told you over and over, they'll see to it, they'll put it right, he'll get better!'

'Mr Montague Price will get him better,' I said.

'He said your dad was fighting hard,' Mother said.

I was dismayed by her apparent frailty. She seemed old and weak, helplessly dependent on others for support. We sat beside her to comfort her, all crouched together beneath the sickly light bulb, and for a brief moment I was one of them, one of the unfortunates at the bottom of the social heap, bossed by employers, bamboozled by priests and fucked up by bungling surgeons. You had to emerge from them if you were not to be kicked around and cheated of your right to a fulfilled life.

I visited the hospital again the next morning. It looked better in daylight, a benevolent and reassuring establishment busy with health care and cures, banishing fear and death with robust common sense. Nurses smiled as they passed me, strong healthy girls in country-maid uniforms, their bare arms clean and rosy. Porters strode past, whistling, laughing, flirting with the nurses. The place was filled with life, the ward was drenched in sunlight; there were vases of flowers here and there, glass jugs of water sparkled merrily. Nurses moved from one bed to another tending the patients, chatting and laughing. Mother sat in the chair she had occupied during the night; she looked up with a weary smile as I approached. Dad was awake. He lay as before, belly uppermost, a sacrificial offering to intrepid medical science. He stared at the ceiling and I could see more clearly now his physical deterioration, his sunken cheeks, the grey waxy texture of his flesh.

Mother got up, stiffly cranking herself upright in the manner of elderly people. She patted my shoulder. 'Well, he's had a good night.' She looked at Dad. 'Got some good sleep, didn't you?'

He turned his face towards us and scowled, then resumed his inspection of the ceiling, his nose thin and sharp.

'They're going to try another operation,' Mother went on. 'That will do the trick, I'm sure.'

'That's what they said ... last time,' he told me, when she had gone.

'Yes, but this time they're sure to get it right.'

'Must know ... what they're doen,' he said resignedly.

'Of course they do! It's just a matter of ... ' What was it just a matter of?

'Just ... like I'm ... bloody 'speriment! They keep trying ... new things. Yesterday, they give me ... four injections! Me arm's all swollen up.'

There were tears in his eyes. The little lawnmower surged out in a breath, drew back in a long rattling sigh. There was a trace of green slime on the bright red tube that emerged from his nostril. When he moved his head, the tube dragged his nostril up in a snarl, quite as though he was a fish hooked and landed.

Patients in dressing gowns of a faded plaid strolled about the ward, blinking in the sunshine. They reclined in dingy armchairs and chatted with one another or lay in bed, smoking and reading the paper. Some were playing cards. None looked especially ill, the sunlight saw to that. One of them, in passing, paused and grinned at Dad: 'All right, are you? You'll be all right.'

'Who the fuck does he … think he is?' Dad grunted. 'Montague bloody … Price?'

'I suppose, actually,' I rambled chattily, 'the patients do almost as much as the medical staff in effecting a cure. It's obviously very important to keep up morale.'

'They told me … minor operation. Piece of cake! Said I'd be … out in a few days.' He slewed his eyes at me frantically. 'Now look at me!'

I put myself in his place and tried to feel my way past myself, put myself on the jacked-up bed with my guts mangled from surgery, two operations within ten days and now the prospect of a third. 'They'll have to open him up all over again,' Mother had said. One of those concentration-camp trolleys carried me to the theatre to be opened up all over again. Then I was brought back to the ward and my body was once more invaded by loathsome catheters that would feed me and drain me whether I was alive or not – 'You hear me?' Dad rasped.

'Sorry!' I hung over him in startled contrition. 'Is there something you want?'

'Lift me … up a bit.'

I looked round, not sure if it was allowed. There wasn't a nurse in sight.

'Carn do it … on me own!' he cried.

I got my arms round him and, holding my face away from the smell, hauled tremblingly at his inert body, anxious lest I wrenched him out of his tubes.

'Carn move myself,' he wailed, lying exhausted on the pillow. 'I'm trapped, son, fucken … helpless. They can do anything they like to me …'

'I won't let them.' (Let them what? What?) 'Not if it seems wrong, I won't.'

'Never goen … get outta here!'

'Of course you will. Listen, I've some good news. Jessie is coming to see you, all the way from Seattle; we're expecting her any day. Isn't that good?'

'Jessie …' he sighed. 'Give us … a Woodie.'

His Senior Service days were over; he was back on Woodbines. There was a packet on the bedside locker. I grabbed it and burst it open, hooked out a fag and stuck it between the dried slime on his parched lips. When it was lit, he made a mighty effort and sucked painfully, but after one or two drags he shook his head, wincing as a heave of phlegmy coughing coursed through his chest and tore at his belly. I removed the Woodbine and crushed it out. Ahr-HAARR! he coughed, Ahr-HAARR! With a sighing groan, he subsided on the pillow.

'Goen to … die, aren't I?'

'Well, of course not!' I dared robustly. 'Stop feeling so sorry for yourself. There are patients here far worse off than you are.'

'Why are they … walken about then? Why aren't they … strung up like me?'

'You'll be up and about in a few days, I'm sure.' I was getting the hang of it now. Just keep feeding them happy lies.

There was a commotion at the far end of the ward and an authoritative briskness entered the place with the arrival of a surgeon, accompanied by the ward sister and a couple of housemen in flying white coats. It was Mr Montague Price.

'You'll have to be on your merry way,' a nurse told me.

'Cumen to … see me,' Dad whispered fearfully.

I kissed his bristly cheek and left the ward, but waited in the corridor outside. Its walls were painted a dull, utilitarian green; a grimy window looked on to a back area where there were bins and wheeled containers, a wisp of steam escaping from some outlet. I paced up and down, hands clenched behind my back. Mr Montague Price was joking with the sister as he left the ward, a deferential houseman holding open the door. I stepped forward and they all frowned; a houseman motioned me aside but I held my ground. Addressing the surgeon, I gave Dad's name and requested an explanation of his plight. I strove to appear coolly confident, faintly ironic, one eyebrow raised, standing as tall as I could, quavering the best accent I could muster.

'What has gone wrong? I thought it was merely a simple hernia operation?'

I fretted over "merely" and "simple", should not have used both. The surgeon brushed past me irritably, white coats swirling to shield him. 'We are doing everything we can.' The ward sister glanced back over her shoulder, frowning indignantly, as the group retreated down the corridor.

The Willards would not have allowed them to get away with it. They would have known someone in the hierarchy; they would have used their contacts, their Cambridge credentials, their cultured voices and accomplished style. They would have obtained a full and courteous explanation, even an apology. Montague Price would have realised at once that they were not to be brushed aside.

I went home. There was no one about. Mother was in bed, Maggie was at work. I made a pot of tea and sat with it at the table, smoking a cigarette. There was a knock at the door and I went to open it. Tamsin stood there, her tall figure stooped apologetically. 'I saw you come in. Have you been to the hospital? How is he?'

In the kitchen, I poured her a cup of tea. 'Fraid it's not the ... the Darjeeling you're probably used to.'

'Oh, Peter!' she protested. Then we both laughed. At that moment, there was no one's company I would rather have had. I told her the terrible state Dad was in.

'And he needn't have had the operation, that's the worst of it; he was quite healthy, he's barely sixty and might have lived many more years with the hernia held in place by his faithful old truss! It's all so unnecessary, that's what I can't get over. You go into hospital for a routine operation, expecting to be out in a few days, and you're plunged into a nightmare of pain, trapped in a hospital bed at the mercy of blunderers who don't know what to do with you. And a few days later, you're dead!'

The idea excited me; I felt I must write about it some day, I would make a great tragic work of it.

'But the worst of it is, if he does die, he'll have died without ever having realised his potential. Fulfilling himself, I mean. He's more intelligent than you'd think; he could have been more than a second-rate cook. I mean, he could have been successful in another field. But he was born poor and tied down by poverty, he never discovered the world that lay beyond the crummy existence to which he was condemned. And you can repeat his experience over and over again in the working classes.'

She reached out and touched my hand. 'You love him.'

'Yes, but maybe not in the way you're supposed to love a father. He's more like a ... a younger brother, a bit of a scamp! I've never been able to take him seriously.'

Jessie arrived home glowing with the refulgence of the United States, the freedom and confidence of the swaggering country to which she now gave her allegiance. We had not seen her for some years. She was nearly thirty and had put on weight. Her clothes were expensive, her hair was dressed elaborately, her manner was buoyantly patronising. She greeted everyone loudly and effusively, in an accent closer to America than Liverpool; she lavished kisses, distributed presents. Mother cherished and admired her.

'Well, how is he?' she demanded. She wanted a full report on Dad's condition. Maggie offered it mumblingly. Now that Jessie was back, she felt herself disappearing into the background. 'It's your free health service,' Jessie decided. 'Doctors are smothered with patients; they don't have time to give anyone the attention they need. Back in the States, he would have been diagnosed sooner and everything would have been all right. You can't get better medical care anywhere.'

'You'd have to pay for it.'

'You get nothing in this world, my lad, without paying for it. Ain't no such thing as a free lunch!'

I went with her to the hospital. She breezed into the ward trailing perfume, swinging her hips, raising happy smiles among the patients. Dad was pleased to see her, grateful that she had travelled thousands of miles to be at his side.

'Well, Chuck drove me to the airport and I got a flight to New York ...' She told him all about her journey home, the passengers in the Boeing, an impertinent air hostess, the grubbiness of London and the filthy train to Liverpool. That's the way to do it, I thought, admiring her flow of words. Take his mind off it. Indeed, so taken up was she with her own affairs – the dancing school and the flourishing business Chuck had taken over from his father; her lovely home and sweetie-pie daughter – she scarcely seemed to notice Dad's condition. He gazed up at her open-mouthed, the little lawnmower racing to keep up with his admiration and love.

When she had finished regaling him with her news, she bent over him to say goodbye. 'Now look here, I don't want any more of this nonsense, do you hear? You get well, my lad, and be quick about it, or I'll wanna know why!'

Dad grinned like a corpse.

'I suppose there's no hope for him,' she said, as we left the hospital.

They carted him off for the third operation and I did not see him again until the following day. At first I couldn't find him, they had moved him to an alcove in the ward. It contained only two beds, the other bed empty. He had been shunted out of the way, so as not to disturb the other patients with his dying. The ward glowed with a passionate sunset unexpected in November, but the alcove was in shadow and there was a large black shape beside Dad's bed. It was Father Doonan, the priest who had helped march me into the seminary. He gave me a deep confiding smile, his eyes glowing genial scorn for my apostasy (of which Mother would have given him a tearful account). He gestured at the suffering figure on the bed. 'He's very low. Be careful what you say. His soul is on the brink.'

'Of what?'

'Ah, if we only knew!' He clutched my arm. 'Pay close attention to what your poor da's going through. Let us pray it will be the means to bring you back to Mother Church.'

'There's always a silver lining.'

He held my gaze hard, staring into my face. 'This is death, young man. Death. Don't you understand? How can we hope to be saved from the terror of death, if we don't believe in an all-merciful God?'

'That's what it's all about, religion, isn't it?'

He released me. 'I'll pray for you,' he threatened.

He left, acknowledging the half-curtsey of a nurse, who now entered the alcove. She took Dad's temperature and did something with his tubes. He gazed up at her from the pillow, infinitely weary. The nurse laughed down at him. 'You didn't want to go, did you?' She turned to me. 'We had such a job getting him to theatre!' And again to Dad: 'You were a naughty boy! Struggling and swearing, calling Mr Montague Price for everything!'

Dad gazed at me, trying to recognise me, floundering in a drugged stupor. He seemed to have slipped a little further down into that dark, suffocating region from which rescue was no longer possible. Had the latest operation been any more successful than the others? And what were the operations for, what were they trying to repair or prevent? Montague Price had spoken to Mother, but had not given her an explanation. Something had clearly gone wrong during the first operation – an ill-judged incision, a mislaid swab, a misplaced epidural – but we were never to learn what it was. Peritonitis, the death certificate blandly concluded.

'*They bury their mistakes*,' Maggie said.

The nurse left and I sat by his bedside. I began to say the usual things: How are you; you'll soon be better. He did not seem to be listening. But then suddenly, staring at me desperately, he said, 'I've had … a … lousy life, son.'

I had never heard anything more appalling.

'All them years goen sea, I never … enjoyed it … Fucken crew … always complaining! Always … some boss … Then come home … kids don't know you … wife never understood. A bloody lousy life!'

He began to cry, floundering in that last stage when the mind sloppily unravels itself, spilling secrets over which one has brooded for years, rarely daring to face them openly.

'You don't really mean this,' I said. 'I've always thought of you as a happy man, a good, brave, happy man. You were always … joking,' I finished lamely.

'Me own … fault. I was … never … much good at anythink. Chance I had … hotel chef … lovely woman … cudden do the … fucken job.'

He drifted off into a suffering doze, holding on to my hand. I was alone with him in the dark alcove, looking out into the sunset-rosy ward with its rows of tidy beds. My arm was cramped awkwardly across the bed and it soon began to ache. I tried to inch my hand out of his grasp, working stealthily; but it was difficult, he held on tight. It took me a while to free myself and I became absorbed in the task. Eventually, after I had carefully prised open two of his fingers, he relaxed his grip. I recovered my hand and massaged it tenderly, a bloated lump seething with pins and needles.

The ward doors slammed open and a troupe of nurses entered. The place was suddenly filled with movement, the clatter of utensils, the aroma of cooked food and the authoritarian voices of young women. They pushed trolleys fitted with metal containers from which they served the evening meal to those patients well enough to eat 'Wakey-wakey, Mr Fletcher! Sit up now and get this down you!' They moved from bed to bed, shaking patients awake and yelling at them boisterously. 'Mr Wilson? Come on now, Willy, let's be having you!'

It was a diversion for the patients and they wrenched themselves up in bed, grinning at each other. They joked with the nurses, cackling wisecracks slurred with feeble sexual connotations; elderly men for the most part, with dry hair and leathery faces, grey stubble on their chops. Scrawny and dissolute in dishevelled pyjamas, they sat up in bed munching their grub, sly-grinning and disreputable, scraping away at their plates, famished vagabonds. The sight gave me pleasure, I felt something like love.

Two nurses trundled a trolley past the alcove. 'Nothing needed here,' one said.

The other smiled at me: 'Would you like some?' She dolloped stew on to a plate. 'Here. Don't let Sister see!'

I ate hurriedly, crouched on the chair, hoping Sister wouldn't see; I shovelled up the stew, embarrassed to be eating heartily while my poor father was dying. He opened his eyes and looked about fearfully. 'Where ... am I?'

I swallowed a mouthful, put the plate aside and bent over him. 'It's all right.'

He stared at me. 'It's not ... all right!' His gaze travelled about the alcove, its windowless walls, the empty bed. 'I know ... this place!' He grabbed me, suddenly alert and coherent. 'It's where ... where they put you when there's ... no hope of recovery!'

'Oh, I'm sure that's – '

'Got to ... get outta here!' He held on to me with desperate strength, straining to heave himself up in bed, his face tense and quivering, eyes large in their dark caves.

'No, you mustn't!' I bleated. 'You'll tire yourself. You have to lie still; it's for your own good.' I was afraid he would jerk himself free of the tubes, the nasal tube writhing out of his stomach, slimy and bloodstained; the other tube torn from his foot, leaking glucose.

'Get a knife!' he ordered, glaring at me. 'Cut these ... bloody ... tubes!' He was in the death house, trapped and dying, and they would finish him off if he did not escape. 'Cut the ... tubes!' He held me fast and I was dragged down into his flushed, hoarsely breathing face, his stink, his death. 'Get a knife! ... Good boy!'

I shook my head frantically. 'You've got to lie still! You'll kill yourself!' He was dragging me down, and, to save myself, I grasped his bony shoulders, pressing down on him, holding my face away.

'Knife! Cut the ... tubes! We can ... go home!' he sobbed.

But I held him fiercely like holding someone under water, preventing him from rising. 'You'll get me in trouble!'

He gave up, turning his face aside and lying still.

'I'm sorry! Oh, Dad, I'm so sorry!' I peered at him in the half-light. 'Are you all right?'

He lay still. Was he asleep, in a coma, dead? I daren't touch him, but leaned close enough to confirm that he was still breathing.

Some time later, Mother came to take my place. 'How is he?'

'He wants to go home, Mam. Can't we get him home?'

'I don't know.' She was fearful of authority. One had to do what one was told. 'They won't let him go, in this state.'

'They've no right to keep him if he wants to go home. Christ – !'

'Don't swear, son.'

I left the hospital feeling morally disorientated, as though both past and future had been scraped away. It was another windy evening. I pulled my dingy overcoat closer and walked the streets, it didn't matter where, resenting Dad's fatal illness. Because it had happened to him, or because it was happening to me? But surely I felt love and pity, and – sorrow, was it? I walked, head bent, not looking where I was going, down off one kerb, up on to another, passing buildings and people without looking up. Oh God! I thought, suddenly overwhelmed with anguish. What had I been about to say? Oh, God, help me? For the first time in years I felt the lack of a personal God, the inner Jesus implanted by the Catholic Church; I felt a need for God, not for my salvation but to assuage my helplessness. If only I could have prayed for him, shifting the burden on to God's broad shoulders! ...Well, that's what comes of losing your religion, I told myself in my mother's voice. You're sorry now, aren't you? Yes, I'm sorry! I wailed, making a sick joke of it. 'Oh God! Oh God!' I cried, stumbling on, unable to shake myself out of myself, unable to break from a habit of vilely intricate rationalisation, achieving pure and simple sincerity.

I caught a tram, climbing to the upper deck. It was full of people with jobs and homes, children and spouses, settled in their lives and seemingly content. They were bent on a night out at the pictures, the dancehall, the pub, and were talking to each other, laughing, smoking, reading the paper. The sound of their gravelly voices moved me. The working class. I thought of them in their lives, in the workplace and at home, in the pub, on the terrace at a football match, playing with their kids in the park: their friendliness and their tolerance, their fundamental decency, their noisy companionable lives. They have each other, I thought. It was better than God.

I reached the house where I lived and said hello to someone I passed on the stairs without recognising who it was. I opened my door and stood at the threshold, looking at my room with dismay: the grubby linoleum, the faded wallpaper with its damp patches, the doleful furniture, the sordid unmade bed and the black window with its flimsy curtains. Beyond the window, beyond the cathedral and the centre of town, was the river that swept out towards the ocean. The thought of its bounding freedom made me yearn to be out and away, everywhere else in the world at once, escaping a frustrated nausea at my limitations, my shabby faults. It made the room seem even more repulsive; a lonely, impoverished, isolated dump.

I went to the table, sat down and reached for the manuscript of my novel: thirty-six pages, eighteen thousand three hundred and twenty-two words. I turned to the first page and began to read what I had written. By the time I reached the last page, it was late at night and I was cold. The room was cold and it closed about me, chilly and damp. I pushed the manuscript aside and put my head in my hands.

We gathered about his bed in the alcove, Father Doonan presiding. It was the first death I'd witnessed and I didn't want to miss a thing, anxious to record it in my notebook. But after such a lousy life, Dad merited no more than a nondescript death; there was no anguished cry at the last, no raising himself to shake a fist at fate. He was in a coma and it was as though he was stealthily floating away from us on a dark, subterranean journey towards death.

Mother sat upright on a chair at his bedside, her hands clasped tightly, face brooding. Jessie crouched close to her; Maggie snuffled noisily in a corner. Father Doonan bent over the dying man, muttering and sighing, performing the Last Rites. Towards the end, Dad had been encouraged to remember his sins and make an Act of Contrition. So much for his bold rejection of religion! But when I, in my turn, was faced with the agony and terror of death, and the idiotic World Soul no longer sustained me, might I not be tempted to seek such reassurance, however illusory?

The coffin remained at the undertakers until the funeral; it would never have made it down the steps to the garden flat. 'Go and pay your respects,' Mother said.

I found it perched on trestles in a room decked out like a chapel; it was open and there were two tall candles at the head. The candles and wreaths created an atmosphere like church on a Sunday, an admonitory odour. The coffin was narrower than I had expected and smelt of varnish. Dad was inside, his face discreetly covered by a cloth. I lifted the cloth and there he was, shrunken and dead. His nostrils were plugged with cotton wool, his false teeth had been replaced and the upper set rested on his lower lip, giving him something of a rabbity grin. I thought of that day in the backyard when he had mounted a box to look at Carol over the wall – 'Oh, dem big, big eyes!' – jigging his hands and elbows, giving his Al Jolson smile.

Back at the garden flat, Maggie made some tea. We spoke solemnly of the dead man – what a good husband and father. I remember this and I remember that. When he used to come home with the presents. His jokes, his tap-dance. Then Mother got to her feet and went to see if the Willards needed anything. Maggie took the dishes into the scullery.

'Let's get out of here,' Jessie said.

We left the flat and strolled along the avenue beneath its bared trees, talking of Dad and his lousy life. It was a pale grey afternoon and the wind had dropped. Jessie wore a lush fur coat over a powder-blue costume, its skirt reaching to her knees, revealing her sturdy dancer's legs. 'I'll have to get something black for the funeral. Oh, God, it's so ... I know!' she exclaimed suddenly. 'Let's go over the water.'

She hailed a taxi and we were driven to the Pier Head, the first time I had been in a taxi. We caught the ferry to Seacombe on the opposite shore. It was crowded with office workers on their way home, clerks and typists from the shipping offices, maybe even the municipal offices where I had once worked. At Seacombe, we left the ferry and made for the promenade. Jessie said: 'Frank and me and our Maggie used to walk from here to New Brighton. That was before you were born. We couldn't afford to get the ferry all the way. All we had was a bottle of water and some jam butties wrapped up in the *Echo.* God, they were lovely times! I've always loved this promenade.'

It ran directly from Seacombe to New Brighton, pausing briefly at Egremont, once a hamlet frequented by smugglers, or so it was said. There were stout railings all the way to prevent you falling into the river, which lapped against the sea wall at high tide. We walked into a weak sunset forming in the west; freighters rode at anchor, waiting for the tide.

Jessie began to speak of my future; perhaps that was the reason she had got me out here. Sisters never lose their penchant for taking you in hand. 'Mam thinks you're wasting your life with all this writing. Maggie, funnily enough, is on your side. She thinks you might be a famous writer some day.'

'That's sweet of her.'

'Well, she's always been one for lost causes. There was no one more devoted to me dad. But what are you going to do with yourself? You can't stay on the dole forever. You could come and stay with us in the States,' she added. 'Make a new life there.'

But I no longer admired America, I was now left wing and sympathetic to the Soviet Union, views I flourished among the students but which I did not share with my family.

'And what about this book you're supposed to be writing?' Jessie went on.

'I'm no longer writing it. I've given it up. I'm not a writer, I ... I don't feel enough, I don't love my characters the way you're supposed to. I'm glad I found out before it was too late. I could have gone on and on and wasted my life in trying to write, hopelessly deluded!'

But even in saying this I could not resist seeing it in terms of a novel, the story of a man who wastes his life in the crazy belief that he is a great writer ...

Jessie commended my good sense in destroying the novel. 'It's just like me when I thought I was going to be a great star. You'll probably feel a bit miserable for a while, but you'll get over it. What will you do then? I think you should get some sort of an education; you could go to night school, get to university, you're clever enough. You could maybe even become a teacher.'

But I was thinking of the climax of another novel, a scene in which an old man who has led a blameless life as a teacher meets a one-time sweetheart who laments the fact that he renounced writing when he was a young man, for he was truly talented and could have become a great writer …

By the time we reached Egremont, Jessie had had enough; high-heeled shoes made walking difficult and she decided to abandon the project of walking all the way to New Brighton in memory of her childhood. 'I'm going back. But you go on, if you like.'

'Yes, I wouldn't mind, if you don't mind.'

We parted. She headed back to Seacombe, I continued along the promenade. New Brighton tower rose in the distance, the fairground and the Chamber of Horrors.

Reviews for Tony Sullivans' earlier novels:

In The Palm House

... a fine debut. Mr Sullivan is a novelist to watch

Daily Telegraph

This humane, thoughtful, densely packed book makes a most accomplished debut

The Listener

An astonishingly assured first novel: tender, funny, unshowy but brilliantly sustained

Time Out

Mad Hannah Rafferty

There is a prize for that most difficult of arts, the second novel, and Mad Hannah Rafferty should win it ... It is as fine as it could be about what could never become true.

The Times

Redolent with indigenous Scouse humour and resilience ... Hannah Rafferty's deftly written story will remain in the mind long after gaudier and more celebrated fiction has been forgotten.

The Sunday Times

Chiefly About Hooke

Sullivan views the amateur writer's sublime capacity for perpetual self-delusion with a large measure of knowing irony. Yet he is not without sympathy for those who diligently add to the notorious slush pile ... Certainly all would-be writers should read this funny, insightful and assured novel.

The Sunday Times